HELP THE ANIMALS

I have always been an animal lover. Now, I'm in a position to do good for the animals I love. That's why I've decided to donate 5% of my net proceeds to the Best Friends Animal Society. They do wonderful work saving the lives of dogs, cats, and other animals in need. Best Friends is a widespread organization, with multiple locations. A donation to them would go toward their goal of making all shelters into no-kill shelters.

Thank you everyone for purchasing Morgan's Mount. May you enjoy every twist and turn of the spiral staircase on your way up the east tower.

If you want to learn more, follow me on RobertJFosterWrites.wordpress.com

MORGAN'S MOUNT

Robert Foster

Morgan's Mount

Dedication

I want to thank my brother, author John C. Foster. I got my love of reading from John and he's my proof that a Foster can publish a book.

Next, I want to thank Heather and Eddie Owens for being the best family members a guy could hope for.

Vincent Casset was generous enough to offer his musical ability to help me with marketing the novel. It's nice to have talented friends.

All of my favorite authors sing their editors' praises and now I understand why. Without my editor/guide, Elizabeth Suggs, I would have gotten lost in the self-publishing jungle long ago.

Contents

Chapter One

Philadelphia, U.S.A.

The guy in the blue hat was dealing. His name was Stuart Robinson, and he was no problem. Robinson came in a couple of times a week, played for a while, and always went home with his head hung low. His mediocre playing, paired with a hell of a lot of bad luck, left him in perpetual debt.

Five cards lay face down on the table. Marco flipped them over and had to stifle a laugh. A Jack, a two, four, seven, and a nine. This hand was as bad as any he'd gotten that night, which fit his plan perfectly. The worse he played, the more the guys would want him to stick around. Things had been going well, for the most part. They'd been playing for a little more than two hours, and Frankie didn't seem to have a clue of the trouble he was in. He viewed his opponents as a couple of suckers off the street, which is exactly what Robinson was. The only complication was the guy in the corner. The big bald mother who looked like

Michael Chiklis all jacked up on 'roids. He wore one of those sleeveless white tops that showed what a shit he was. His name was Chet or Chevy, something like that. The guy wasn't even joining in the game. He just sat there the whole time, with a look on his face that begged someone to give him a chance to kick some ass. This guy was not part of the plan. Marco didn't have any information about him, and that had been looming over him all night. He didn't like complications.

"You?" asked Frankie.

Marco drew his mind back into the game long enough to say, "Fold."

Frankie, that scarecrow-looking scumbag, started laughing. He was thin as a rail with a black goatee so long that it tried to compensate for his lack of chin. It was no suprise that somebody wanted him out of the picture. The file hadn't explained the reason for the contract, but it didn't matter anyway. Marco knew a lowlife when he saw one. He was looking at a man every parent would instinctively pull a child away from.

"You sure as hell know how to fold 'em, don't you buddy? I'm starting to think that's the only word you know how to say."

If he only knew. Marco could have said so much more. He could have told Frankie his address, license plate number, and phone number right off the top of his head. It would be easy to explain Frankie's daily routine of waking up around 7:30, running over to WaWa and back to the house, where he'd watch TV until nine. At nine, he'd pack up and drive over to the warehouse on Upland Ave. Marco didn't know what went on inside the warehouse but he didn't have to know. All that mattered was that Frankie Corolla left that place every night around 7 PM and came straight here.

Robinson was stupid enough to raise, one of those guys who played just to stay alive in the game, but whenever he lost, he lost big. Frankie sneered as he laid his royal flush on the table before him. There was a look in Stuart's eyes as if he knew he'd be spending the next month digging for food in restaurant dumpsters. Leave, thought Marco. This would be easier without Robinson around.

"Shit, man," said Frankie. "Sometimes it doesn't work out. Know what I'm sayin'?"

Stuart Robinson pushed back his chair and reached for his coat. Corolla was enjoying his night of outplaying suckers and made his best effort to get Robinson to stay.

"Hey, I know. I know, man. It's tough. Stick around and play another game, I'll spot you some."

Robinson stood, took his jacket from the back of his chair, and draped it over his arm. It looked like he was about to turn and walk away, then he stopped. Just go, just go. Robinson was halfway to the door before he looked up and spoke.

"Nah," he said. "That's a...that's enough for me." He slipped on his jacket and left.

This was good. Witnesses were a pain. Robinson probably wouldn't have been much of a problem, might have enjoyed it a little, but his continued presence would be another complication, and the bald guy in the corner was already one difficulty too many. Every time he looked at the guy, Marco got the feeling that he was seeing a man who was definitely carrying a gun, but would rather smash with his bare knuckles. The guy was a bruiser, and guns were too impersonal for him. He'd met guys like Baldy before. Guys who thought that only pussies used guns and real men used fists.

"So, you still in?" asked Frankie. He was glaring across the small table at Marco, daring him to say no.

Marco said yes but declined Frankie's offer to deal the cards. After a quick shuffle, Frankie bounced the deck once off the table and began to deal. It wouldn't take him long, but his hands would be occupied the whole time. So, Baldy had to be first. He wasn't in the contract but guys like that had to be taken out as quickly as possible. They had a way of fucking things up. Marco slid his right hand casually into his jacket pocket and gripped the handle of his Beretta. Two shots. If he did this right, it would be over in a heartbeat. He looked at Baldy.

There was a hard impact in his gut, and the chair suddenly leaped out from under him. Marco crashed to the floor. His hands couldn't clench when he tried to pull himself back up. They felt like dead weight on his wrists. Fingers scratching uselessly at the cloth, he gurgled would-be words, then noticed his shirt was wet. He thought he had spilled beer, but he hadn't been drinking that night. Maybe it was Frankie's beer. That didn't make sense either, this liquid was too thick. His arms dropped to the floor out of sheer exhaustion, and he noticed that his fingers went numb. One hand landed on his stomach, and Marco watched in awe as redness enveloped his palm. He tried to speak, to ask what had happened, but the words wouldn't come. Metallic swirled in his throat and threatened to choke him if he didn't spit it out. As he rolled onto his side and coughed out the first of the blood, he caught a glimpse of Frankie standing over him.

"You dumb fuck," said Frankie. "You think I don't know what you're up to?"

Corolla bent over and pressed a gun hard to the side of Marco's face. Corolla's eyes bulged. The gun barrel felt surprisingly warm. Frankie said something that Marco couldn't understand, and then Baldy stepped in. *Chaz*, that was his name. He remembered that even as Chaz repeatedly slammed his fists into his face

"Hey," said Frankie. "I never figured you for a junkie."

Marco snapped out of it. He was unscathed and back in his spot, staring across the table at Frankie. The vision, what he silently referred to as a trip, couldn't have lasted more than a few seconds. He had been lucky this time.

Still, Frankie looked suspicious. That was bad, he had to clear his head quickly or suffer the fate he had just foreseen. Without giving himself any more time for thought, Marco slipped the gun out of his jacket pocket and fired one shot. The bullet drilled its way directly through Frankie's forehead and flew in a blast of brains out the back of his skull. Corolla's body flopped down and flipped up the card table. He slumped to the ground as Marco, still sitting, spun right and fired once at the oncoming Chaz.

It was just as Marco had expected. Baldy hadn't even reached for his weapon, like he'd forgotten about it altogether. Guys like him didn't understand, when it comes to killing a man, your ego can't enter into it. You've just got to put the son of a bitch down as quickly and cleanly as possible using the most efficient tools. Marco stood as the big man shuffled one, two steps closer, and then bent over, clutching the crimson stain that rapidly covered his stomach. It wasn't good enough.

Gut shots could take hours to bleed a man out, and Baldy was no weakling. Marco back-stepped, lined himself up with Frankie's former location at the table, and aimed at Chaz's head. This was the point at which guys in the movies would always say their coolest lines. Something like "Hasta la vista" or "See you in hell." That stuff was for the guys who had a flair for drama. Marco had always been of the mind that it was best to get in and get out as quickly as possible. The gun cracked once, and Baldy reeled back, his head banging on the white tiled floor.

There was a massive amount of blood spray. The hit had been messier than he'd in-tended, and Marco knew he didn't have time to stick around and clean it up. With all the noise, there was too much of a chance that someone had heard the commotion. Despite the silencer doing its job well, he had to get out of there before someone came to investigate. He had counted two guys in the warehouse next door when he'd pulled in at 7:30. They might still be out there. At least Robinson had left—there was that much to be thankful for.

Marco approached Frankie's body and re-moved the gun from his jacket. He wrapped the dead man's hand around the handle, slipped his fingers behind the trigger, and blasted three shots toward Baldy's corpse. One shot hit, the other two headed straight into the far wall. It was the best cleanup he could do to get out of this mess. Hopefully, the cops would walk in and see the situation as he wanted them to. For that to happen, he'd have to leave the money sitting on the table. What if they talk to Robinson? That was a big problem, but it couldn't be helped. Even with Robinson's help, the cops wouldn't find him right away. They'd be looking for Thomas Miller, a nonexistent bum from the streets of Philly. Marco put his gun back into his jacket pocket and walked to the door, sliding it open slowly to see if there was any commotion outside. All clear.

If you can't clean up the whole mess you made, then you get the hell out of Dodge as quickly as possible. That was one of Marco's rules for himself. Along with "Never drink on the job," he had few scruples he always worked by. These rules had helped him earn a reputation as a professional in an occupation filled with thugs. He started the car and drove east out of Philly. Not too fast or slow, just another dude going to his suburban house with his pretty blonde wife and two perfect children waiting for him. After a few hours with no trouble, he allowed himself to relax a little. What were the chances that the PPD would do an in-depth investigation into a scumbag like Corolla and his pet gangbanger? As he turned north toward Connecticut, Marco thought the odds were in his favor.

Got lucky tonight.

His vision had shown him that Frankie was wise to his plan. Aiming at Chaz first would have ended with Frankie's bullet in his stomach and a rainstorm of fists dropping on his face. The Trip had saved his life. This time. There had been other times in which these moments hit him so randomly that they'd put him in danger: The time in New York when he had a vision of being hit by a car in front of him, so he'd stopped short only to be hit by a different car coming up from behind. Then there was the time in Minneapolis when he'd predicted a rabid dog coming for him. In an effort to avoid the alley where he'd foreseen the dog, Marco had taken a long way around and wound up running into some muggers. He was starting to worry that his luck was just about used up. Frankie could have shot him easily while he was sitting there, lost in a vision of a possible future.

The problem with psychic powers is that they turn me into a sitting duck every time they come.

There was nothing to be done about it. It wasn't like he could check himself into a clinic, give them his birth name, social security number, and everything else the cops would love to have for Christmas. Things had worked out in his favor tonight, and he'd have to be happy with that. He took one more swig of water and started the car. Mystic would be a good place to stop, at least for one night. He made up his mind to continue north for the time being.

"Alright," he said to himself and drove into the night.

Chapter Two

Morgan's Mount, Wales

Brian had always believed the best way to tell what the weather was up to was to stand up straight and look at the sky. It was gray. Again. His father had told him long ago that a wise man didn't try to read the clouds. A wise man watched the birds; if they took cover, people should also find shelter. Something about the birds being able to feel shifts in weather patterns. Brian didn't necessarily believe that, but he couldn't help checking for birds. A far-off crow cawed three times, but that was all. Not a feather in sight.

The wheelbarrow was around the side of the building, and he still had two loads of mulch left to spread. Most of the grounds around the entrance fountain were already mulched with a thin layer but Brian expected a fair amount of it to be blown away before new plants took to the soil there. Birds or not, he wasn't taking chances with this.

Brian stood and turned back to the wheelbarrow. He had just gripped the wooden handles when a movement caught his eye. Something flashed quickly by the window nearest him. It was pure white. A face. There hadn't been anyone, other than that historian fellow, inside the castle for as long as Brian had worked there. Perhaps he hadn't really seen anything at all. He was an old man, and his mind liked to play tricks on him these days. Still…perhaps he had seen the face of a child looking at him from inside the castle.

It had been four years since Brian McAaron had entered Morgan's Mount. His hair hadn't been the silver it was now. The first time had been during his first week of work when he'd forgotten a shovel inside the greenhouse out back. He had only spent a few minutes inside, never even entered the castle proper, but he'd felt a heaviness, like a sheet of suffering, coming over him. There was a darkness inside those walls that brought back his little boy fears. He hadn't dared to enter after that. Now, as he pulled open the door, he told himself he had no choice this time. There was a child lost in there.

"Hello!" he called into the dark hallway.

His knowledge of the Mount was almost exclusively of the grounds around it. He had only a perfunctory knowledge of the interior. Brian knew he was looking down a hallway because he'd worked on both ends of it. Seeing the inside of it wasn't a possibility without bringing a torch along. He stepped in slowly.

"Is someone here?" he called.

A sound in the next room answered him. Someone had probably bumped into something. He peeked around the corner and could make out a square-shaped space with a picture frame on the far wall and a rocking chair. The rocking chair was moving. Back and forth. Back and forth. There was no one in the room. He wiped his forehead, fought for control of his breath, and moved on.

He noticed a door on the other side of the room and stepped carefully over to it. The face he'd seen had been here. He was sure of it. Whoever it was must have gone out in the other direction. The door opened onto the second-floor landing. A dusty painting of a fox hunt and a rotten old floor mat greeted him as he stepped out of the room into the open. He called out a third time and was answered by his echo.

To his left was a door, swinging slightly unless his eyes were playing tricks on him. He thought that was a real possibility in this place where things were shrouded in darkness. It was his ears that convinced him of the swinging. The rhythmic creaking of rusty hinges was unmistakable. He reached for the door. Stepping through, he found a long set of stairs and climbed to the second floor of the castle.

A metallic clang resonated softly in his ears. The sound suggested distance; something had happened far below. He turned, looked left to right across the vast space, and his old tired eyes saw the glint of something shining. An overturned lamp, perhaps? It lay in pieces next to a small wooden object he thought was a table. Brian took a step toward the second-floor railing to see the scene better. As he focused on the lamp down below, the door creaked open.

Darkness behind Brian coalesced and advanced toward his back. It reached out to him, a silhouette of a hand grasping his shoulder. A heavy presence settled on him; a dark angry entity, that considered Brian an intruder, unwelcome in its old ruined home. Smelling of ash and dirt, it drew ever closer to the old man. Brian had just enough time to turn around before his heart seized mid-beat. He stared deep into the darkness, and it crept into him, twisting his organs, infecting his thoughts. His eyes saw nothing but shadow. There was no time to shout. His heart stuttered, and he clutched his chest, trying to stop the darkness from tearing him up from the inside out.

Without realizing it, he had stepped away from the door, and his back now rested on the second-floor railing. An unseen pressure lifted him, his legs rolled swiftly up and over the rail, and he thought he heard laughter as he fell. The drop between floors was only fifty feet, but Brian was dead before he hit the ground. His heart had stopped.

Chapter Three

Boston, USA

The window overlooked a dark river far below. Neither the view nor the bustling crowd around him could tear his gaze away from his phone's screen. Pictured in a small photo, along with the headline, "Mafia Manhunt," was the face of Frankie Corolla. In the background, several figures that Marco recognized were milling around.

"Shit," said Marco.

Among the other men in the photo were a few mob bigwigs. Corolla had serious connections. Nothing in the information he'd been given on Frankie Corolla had indicated that he was connected to La Cosa Nostra at all. The article was about a police investigation of Corolla's death, and things had not gone as Marco had wanted. The cops were not just writing the death off as another shooting of someone who wasn't worth thinking about. They were actively looking for the killer. It was, however, not the police investigation that worried Marco so much as what the investigation suggested. Someone actually cared to look. He recognized one of the men in the photo, Joey Calvano, and had heard rumors of the cops he had on payroll. One of Corolla's gangster buddies could have infiltrated the Philadelphia Police Department far enough to get the search going, which would mean that the Mafia was looking for him. It wasn't as far-fetched a thought as he wanted it to be.

Suddenly, Boston didn't feel far enough.

He finally looked up from the phone, convinced that the multitude of people covering every space in the café could see the worry on his face. Finishing his drink in a swig, he grabbed his brown jacket off the back of his chair and walked out the door. He needed a plan.

It was a cold day, the kind of still cold that made it clear that Boston didn't care if you were dressed warmly or not. Marco wouldn't expect any more warmth from Corrolla's friends. The thought sat heavily in his mind as he dialed a number on his phone. It rang four times before it was answered.

"Hello?"

"I've got myself into a bit of a fix here. Hoping you can help me out. Look, I'm in Boston."

Harris suggested they meet in person later that day and gave Marco an address. An hour later, they were sitting across from one another at a small table.

"You, my young friend, have yourself a bit of a situation," said Harris, grinning as he spoke.

"I need you to appreciate the gravity of this,

alright?" said Marco. "I was given bad info on the guy. He was a made man. Where can I go that they won't be looking for me?"

Harris sipped from his glass, probably that fancy Argentinian stuff with the long name he always liked. He set the glass down and waved his hand in a 'settle down' gesture. Harris gulped quietly, savoring the aftertaste of his favored Malbec. Only then did he respond.

"You came to me because you need assistance, and you believe that I can give it," Harris said. "You were right. But if you think I'm going to throw you a lifeline without busting your balls first, then we really don't know one another as well as I thought we did."

Marco laughed despite himself. The old man was sitting across the table, fancy wine in hand, with a familiar I-know-something-you-don't-know expression on his face. Same old attitude housed in an older white-haired vessel. It eased Marco's mind somewhat to see how relaxed Harris was.

"What you need," began Harris, "is a big money job. Something that will allow you to hide out long enough for them to decide it's not worth looking any longer."

"But where can I go for that?" asked Marco. "California?"

Harris finished his glass and set it down on the table.

"No," he said as he motioned for a refill. The waitress was there in a flash. "I'm thinking something international. A working vacation if you want to call it that."

Marco had never had a job outside of the states. The thought of working in a foreign land seemed unbearably complicated.

"I don't know," he said. "I don't speak any other languages."

Harris smiled. He picked up his newly filled glass and downed the contents in one long sip. Marco was pretty sure that the old man had just broken some kind of wine drinkers' rule: Thou shalt not chug thy vino.

"I think I have something for you," said Harris. He stood up, placed money on the table, and walked to the door. "I have contacts in the U.K. Your unintelligible Philly accent shouldn't be much trouble for you there. Wait for my call."

Chapter Four

Martin Fisher's House, Cardiff, Wales

Small and decrepit, Martin Fisher's house sat by a backroad most people never cared to drive down. It was the muddy season, and deep tire tracks told of unlucky vehicles spinning their tires and lurching back and forth in earth that wouldn't let go. Nearby grass, formerly dark green, was now the shade of coffee with too much cream. The mud splatter from the cars had caked and dried it out. The house, however, remained unstained. It did not need the mud to supplement its broken form. No one would've guessed that the occupant owned a castle.

Martin Fisher, Fisher to all who knew him, walked across his kitchen floor and stopped at the counter. He scooped up the bottle there with a practiced grab. The cap was off in no time, and he sat, allowing the liquid to drain slowly down to him. He was neither tall nor short and had a forgettable face on a forgettable man. The liquid stains sat unnoticed on his blue shirt as he drank. The familiar burn was beginning in his stomach, promising comfort as it grew. He was snapped out of his reverie by a repetitive sound. The comfort was so welcome that he chose to ignore the phone for a moment and savor the feeling.

"Hello?"

"Hello, Fisher, my old friend," said the raspy voice of a man who'd enjoyed a good smoke on most days of his long life. "Am I to understand you're looking to resolve a situation in the mount?"

"Yes."

"I may have an idea for you."

Fisher scratched his chin, his eyes crinkling. Harris knew of his difficulties, but he couldn't see what solution his old friend would be suggesting. Surely, he'd already tried every possible method of fixing his problem.

"There's a fellow here that may be able to help you," said Harris. "Let's just say that he's special. He's done some work for me in the past. Never fails."

"What makes you think he'll be able to do anything to help me?"

"This man is more prone to belief than others, even if he doesn't realize it yet. He's effective and unrelenting, for the right price, of course."

"Is he in Britain?" asked Fisher.

"No, he's here," replied Harris. "If you're interested, I'll put the two of you in touch. I'd suggest you make it clear that it would be worthwhile. Financially, that is."

Fisher agreed, copied the phone number his

friend recited, and said goodbye. He hung up the phone and leaned back against the wall. What Harris was suggesting sounded crazy. Then again, crazy had become the norm in Martin Fisher's life lately.

He placed the half-empty bottle on the counter and dialed the number. It would be 3:00 PM in Philadelphia. An excellent time to call.

Chapter Five

Newport, Wales

Dinner had been lovely, and the restaurant
they'd gone to had proven an excellent choice.
They'd danced and drank fine Riesling from Corn-
wall until midnight. By the time they'd staggered
home, Alan was seeing double. Tomorrow's plans
involved a bit of shopping, then a day at the beach.
It was all planned so perfectly, but when the phone
rang, Alan immediately recognized the number
shown on the caller I.D., and knew it was about to
be ruined. He grunted and began to roll out of bed.

"Don't," said Maggie's muffled voice, her
face half-buried in a pillow.

"I've got to," said Alan. "It's Fisher. He
wouldn't be calling unless it was something severe."

Maggie mumbled something involving the
words "Fisher" and "nocturnal toad." Alan laughed
and delayed picking up the phone for the few seconds it took him to regain his composure.

"Hello?" he said.

Fisher's voice crackled briefly on the other
end of the line, and Alan was forced to ask his boss

to repeat himself. When he spoke a second time, the message was crystal clear.

"A man's been killed, Alan."

All thoughts of telling Fisher off for having woken him up at this ridiculous hour were driven from his mind. Alan momentarily put the phone in his lap and bowed his head. It was even worse than he'd feared.

"Sir?" he asked. "Who's been killed?"

"Do you remember Brian? The groundskeeper does the hedges."

Alan was shocked. Brian McAaron, the kind old fellow he'd worked with for the past eight years, was dead. The worst part of it was that he didn't even need Fisher to tell him how.

"Had himself a heart attack. But we know otherwise, don't we?" asked Mr. Fisher.

The sleepiness of the early hour, tied with the shock of this terrible news, wouldn't allow Alan to respond. He sat in silence until the gentle tickle of Maggie's fingers slid along his shoulder. Even then, he could only respond with a low grunt.

"I need you to come," said Fisher, "soon as possible. There's one last idea I've had and we need to discuss it."

"Sir..." began Alan. Fisher's insistent tone cut him off. Now his boss was emphasizing what he was still processing: the situation had become much worse than anything that had happened before. Whatever Fisher's idea was, Alan was sure he'd be opposed to it, but that seemed irrelevant

23

for the moment. Kind old Brian was dead, and this matter had to be discussed in person.

"Tomorrow," said Fisher.

Alan found his notepad and scribbled down the time of their meeting. Fisher hung up without saying goodbye. The phone hung in Alan's hand until Maggie slipped her fingers over his and took it. She wrapped an arm over his shoulder and kissed his neck lightly.

"You're leaving then?" she asked.

For a moment, he didn't answer. Then, he nodded and turned to face her.

"I'm off to Cardiff in the morning. I'm sorry."

She kissed him, then settled back into bed. Her silence betrayed her disappointment, but the caress of her fingers told him she understood. He had no choice.

Chapter Six

Cardiff, Wales

The pub was dingy, like an old run-down mill. He pulled into the back parking lot and slid into the faded white lines of a space. Herring Gulls covered the docks nearby, and Alan could hear them screeching even with the car door closed. The sound of the birds doubled when he got out of the car, and he was suddenly struck by the fact that he could be at the beach with his girlfriend but had come here instead. He silently cursed Fisher for calling him to this impromptu meeting when he'd had such wonderful plans in mind. Well then, Fisher would have to wait a little bit longer. Alan reached into his pocket and walked toward the docks.

The birds and the water were calming. Alan found a dock post that appeared to be void of excrement and sat. As he watched the waves lap in again and again to strike the seaweed-wrapped posts of the lower dock, he removed a small box from his pocket. He flipped it open. It had taken three years, but he had finally saved up the money to buy this.

All the toil, the arguments with Fisher, and the long hours were worth it. He'd known that all along. *Because she's worth it.* Waves rolled in and pulled away from him as he beheld the diamond ring that he'd gotten for Maggie. This would have been the perfect day to give it to her, but now…

"No, Brian McAaron's dead," he said aloud, forcing himself to face reality. Love would have to wait. Death ruled this day. He slid the ring box back into his pocket and stood. Making Fisher wait had been fun, but he decided that he'd punished the man long enough. Alan said a quick goodbye to the gulls and slowly walked over to the tilted wooden door of The Red Dragon Tavern.

The interior of the pub was no more glamorous than its shoddy exterior. Wallpaper was peeling, and Alan quickly noted that all of the stools stood at angles. It was dark too, but he didn't have much trouble locating his boss. A voice called to him from the brown dimness to his left. They had met here twice before, and although Alan knew Fisher liked this place for its utter lack of patrons, he decided to remind him one more time of how bad it really was.

"Lovely," said Alan, sitting down while ducking a low rafter. "Perhaps a bit of color on the curtains, yellow maybe."

"Yeah," said Mr. Fisher. "I'm well aware of your opinion."

"Just saying that with a little work, this place may even qualify as a worthy pub."

. Fisher didn't comment; instead, he grabbed the glass in front of him and gulped down the last of his beer. He motioned to the waitress and asked Alan if he wanted anything.

"The swill they serve here is tempting, but I think I'll pass," said Alan.

Fisher let a silent second go by before replying, "You remember what we're here to discuss, don't you? Have a pint."

Alan never would've admitted it aloud, but the old man was right. This called for a beer. He, too, placed an order.

"When is the funeral?" asked Alan.

Fisher gulped and said, "Thursday. It's in Swansea. You know that's where he was from originally, don't you?"

Alan nodded. They hadn't been friends, but Brian had always been a delightful character whose jovial attitude toward life endeared him to just about everyone. Alan expected his funeral to be heavily attended.

"Cardiac Arrest?" asked Alan. "What really happened?"

Fisher ordered himself another beer and, although Alan hadn't started his first, ordered a second beer for him. The glasses arrived quickly, and Fisher looked intently at his employee.

"Morgan was my mother's name," he said. "You know that. What you don't know is that I've never associated with my maternal family. Not really. The house was just something I'd inherited and put money into from time to time. None of it mattered to me until recently."

Alan took his first sip and paid clear attention despite the fact that he'd heard all of this before. McAaron's death must be hard for Fisher as well. He'd never show it on the outside, could internalize emotion like a champion, and come across as cold as a polar bear, but Fisher did care for his employees. And he cared for his castle just as much.

"I've been in a bad spot for quite some time, but I'm out of it," said Fisher. "You've been a big part of that, lad. But now this damned...it's ruining everything. Even my mother's name, Alan, her beautiful name."

Alan thought he saw tears starting to well up in the older man's eyes, but knew better than to mention it. As castle historian, it was Alan's job to know everything about not just the building itself but all those who had lived there. Fisher's family, the Morgan line, had lived there for just short of five hundred years on and off. The castle had passed to other proprietors in its time but always came back to its original owners. In the end, it had always belonged to the Morgans, whether they wanted it or not.

"Brian fell from the stairway on the second floor. Doctors claimed heart failure, and that's a fair enough diagnosis, as his heart stopped before he fell. But I know why it stopped. He saw Aldryyd. I'm certain of it."

"Are you sure? You think Aldryyd killed him?" asked Alan.

Fisher swigged down the rest of his beer and wobbled over to the bar to order another. As he stumbled back into the booth, Alan realized that he was much drunker than he'd initially thought.

"I don't think. I know he killed him. Popped right out of a wall or something and made his heart outright stop pumping. Might have pushed him himself," slurred Fisher.

"Sir…" Alan began. He was promptly cut off.

"I want him dead, Alan," Fisher barked. "This has gone on too long, and I've made a decision. He's got to go once and for all this time."

"Listen to yourself," said Alan. "You just said—"

"I know what I said! I'm not an idiot, am I? A drunk who never should have been trusted with his family's precious castle, yes, but an idiot, no. We've tried everything else already."

Fisher was getting redder by the second and Alan couldn't help but be reminded of a few years before when his boss's drinking had nearly lost him everything his family had left behind for him. He had a terrible feeling that there was more to the story than Fisher was letting on. McAaron's death was one thing, but there was something else.

"Yes," agreed Alan. "We have tried everything. You have made every effort to restore and protect your family property. They would be proud of your work."

"Your work," said Fisher. "Without you, I never would have made it this far." He leaned back in his chair and called up to the bar for another pint before going on. "Look at me, I'm a fifty-seven-year-old drunk, no good to anyone. All I've got is that damned castle and money I don't deserve. Got to do something decent with the rest of my days, don't I?"

A waitress placed a drink in front of Fisher and gave Alan an inquiring look. He responded with a look that he hoped sent the message that everything was ok. *Just having a bad day, is all.*

"Here it is," Fisher said. "I've got no children and no more family I know of anywhere. Morgan curse took 'em all away, didn't it." He allowed Alan no time to try to comfort him. "Someday, I'll be gone too, but that castle...bloody rock will still be around. Ruining the pretty view of Welsh countryside. Someone's got to watch over it."

All of a sudden, Alan knew what was about to happen. His boss was on his last legs mentally, making a last-ditch attempt to use his wealth and inheritance to do something good even if it meant something as minor as assuring the preservation of a ruddy old building.

Fisher raised his glass and said, "It's all for you. Every last drop of it. The castle, the grounds, and all the shit left inside. You're not family but it couldn't pass to better hands. Never let it be said that Martin Fisher didn't look after his mummy's precious shithole." With this, he drank.

Alan couldn't believe it. Fisher was leaving everything to him. The whole lot. Such generosity coming from a man he'd argued with day after day ever since he'd been hired on. He thought of the cracked windows, crumbling walls, and broken staircases of the castle, and couldn't help but smile. He loved it all. Every last worthless bit of it.

"But first, there's Aldryyd," said Fisher. A dark look came over his face, and the shadows from the bar wrapped him in their blanketing arms. "I know a man. He did some business in America. Boston. Things went bad for him, and he required a certain type of professional. A mechanic, if you will. To fix the problem."

"Sir, this is Aldryyd we're talking about here," said Alan. "You can't just get rid of him like—"

"Yes, I can!" shouted Fisher. "In two days, this man will come. You'll meet him and tell him what he needs to know. Help him get the job done, will you?"

"I don't know what you're suggesting, but it's not going to work, whatever it is. Let it go, sir, we can just—" Alan stopped there. For the first time, he realized that he was out of ideas. Fisher sounded like a madman but at least he had some kind of plan. *Isn't a crazy idea better than no idea at all?*

Fisher continued as if Alan hadn't spoken.

"It's happened before and you know, Harriet, remember? There's more too, it's all in the notes in my chest. I'll give you my key so you can look. You'll find there were five deaths you don't even know about in there. And it's all Aldryyd. He killed every last one of them!"

Alan couldn't believe he was hearing this. He would take Mr. Fisher's offer of checking his family documents for five unreported deaths as quickly as possible.

"Meet the yank and give him the tour, the history stories, everything. And he's going to want the money day one. Give it to him. You'll want to do this job right, Alan. Do it and see what I give you after. You finish and take that pretty girl of yours to the most beautiful fuckin' island in the world. Promise me that."

All of his dreams were being dangled in front of him. The castle, the money, the opportunity to have the life he'd always wanted with Maggie, all sitting there waiting for him. Alan wanted to sit and daydream on that beautiful future but his rational mind slowly crept back to him and imposed itself on his blossoming hope.

"It's just not possible. None of it." Alan felt terrible about laying the facts down in this cold manner, especially with his boss in such a state, but the man was clearly mad. He needed to hear it.

To Alan's surprise, Fisher leaned forward and smiled.

"Aldryyd's not possible either."

For a full minute, neither man spoke, until Fisher, who seemed to have momentarily sobered up, said, "This American. My friend tells me he's got this...he can see things. Knows things he can't possibly know. So just maybe he can do something for us here. It's my last idea. If you've got a better one, do tell."

Alan noticed that his glass was empty, but he didn't even remember drinking his beer. It had been that kind of conversation, so undeniably interesting that it drove out all thoughts that were not directly related to it. He ordered another beer. The dark brew again. They sat and drank for another half hour with only the normal banter of two guys getting soused in a pub. Business talk was unofficially over. Nothing to do but sit back, relax, and wait for the American to show up two days from now.

"What's the yank's name?" asked Alan.

Fisher laughed and smiled.

"I spoke to him shortly. I asked him his name, and he told me, 'My name is Marco.'" Fisher performed this last part in his best American accent. "So then, I asked him his surname and you know what he said?"

Alan shook his head.

"Polo," said Fisher as he burst out into raucous laughter.

Marco Polo. Very clever, thought Alan. The perfect answer for a man who didn't like to answer questions. An unsettling feeling was creeping up in his stomach, but he didn't think it had anything to do with the drinking.

Chapter Seven

Morgan's Mount, Wales

Marco was riding in style. This Fisher guy was sparing no expense. Marco had expected to get a cab from Cardiff Airport, but he'd found a driver in the terminal waiting for him. He didn't know what kind of car he was sitting in, some shiny little European thing, but it was comfortable. Considering the money on offer here, he wasn't even very disturbed by the fact that Fisher hadn't told him much about the job. It was as if the guy was willing to pay up just to have Marco come and listen to his spiel. If he played this right, he could walk away from Wales a rich man. Things were great and he decided not to dwell on business, choosing instead to stare at the rolling green landscape outside the window. One giant emerald green golf course interspersed by the occasional cluster of trees.

The car turned and slowed as it began to wind down a long dirt road, leaving the small town they'd been passing through. The driver, Peter, had said it was somewhere west of Cardiff, but that's all he could remember. There were more trees in the woods away from town and the golf course appearance quickly gave way to dense forests. Shade from the trees made the world outside a little darker, but for a city boy like him, it was still beautiful. Peter took a sharp right turn, and that was the first time Marco got a look at the castle.

"Welcome to Morgan's Mount," said Peter.

The first thing Marco noticed about the castle was that it resembled one of the big manor houses he'd seen when driving through some rich area of upstate New York. Three stories of gray stone sat atop a small mountain. Long thin boards featuring curved brown shingles ran down each corner of the roof and stretched their eaves to hang over an 80-foot drop to the thick cobble below. Excepting some light beige siding, the castle's color scheme was summed up by gray and brown. It reminded Marco of those old photos in which everything was sepia-colored. Even the grass of the castle lawn was a dull grayish-green. It had the look of sick plant life, and the bones of the rotting bushes lining the expanse of garden told a story of neglect.

"Here we are," said Peter. He stopped the car in the circular driveway and stepped out to get Marco's bags. Marco walked to the front of the building and stared at the heavy wooden front door. A large bronze knocker hung askew on the door's right side, and Marco couldn't help but think about the scene in *The Christmas Carol* when Scrooge's door knocker had turned into the face of Jacob Marley. He laughed at the thought. Still, he had to admit that he was wary of that door, as though touching it would be a mistake. He turned and saw Peter placing his bags on the lawn opposite the castle.

"Why are you putting them there?" asked Marco.

"Mr. Fisher didn't want you entering alone, sir," said Peter. "Best to wait for his man to come and lead you in."

Marco shrugged his shoulders. Whatever. It was Fisher's dime. Lots and lots of dimes. He walked over and stood next to his bags, getting a better view of the castle. There were ornate windows with faded red panels rounding the second floor, and small statues jutted out from in between each set. As he walked around to the west side of the castle, he got a glimpse of a greenhouse extending out behind it. Beyond that, he saw only deep, dense forest far below. The opposite side of the mountain dropped off at a much steeper grade. Eyes flitting between the few twisted trees on the lawn, the gray grass, and the building itself, Marco was left with a feeling of staleness, as though all of the vitality had been drained away from the location. He looked over at Peter and saw him speaking to a tall, thin, blonde man. They shook hands then Peter got in the car and drove away. The blonde man walked toward him.

"Hello. My name is Alan Basset. It's a pleasure to meet you."

Marco introduced himself and shook Alan's offered hand.

"You're Fisher's guy?" he asked.

"Aye," said Alan. "Mr. Fisher thought we might have a short discussion before rushing you off to your hotel. Peter will return in an hour to take you anywhere you like."

Alan led the way to a circular stone table just to the side of the driveway. He was lean in a way that made Marco suspect that he was a runner, arms dangling as he walked. They sat across from one another on flat blocks of stone. While rifling through a small folder, Alan implored Marco to admire the weather, insisting that days like this were a treasure in the rainy Welsh countryside. Eventually, Alan found what he was looking for and slid some papers onto the stone table.

"I'm certain you have questions, that's understandable," Alan said. "If you'll bear with me for a bit, I can explain everything. I am Martin Fisher's castle historian. My job involves the study of the grounds, record keeping of matters of historical significance, and knowledge of the building's history as well as its former inhabitants."

"The Morgans are his family?" asked Marco.

"Aye," confirmed Alan. "His mother's side. He inherited the Mount from her and has tried to preserve it. As you can see, it's not very healthy at the moment."

Marco was, once again, struck by that feeling that all life had been taken away from this place. He took note of a crumbled bit of the outer wall and the rock pile beneath it. A light wind swayed the tall chimney rising from the far side of the roof.

"Yeah," he said. "So, what does he need me to do?"

Alan slid the opened folder to him and spun it around so he could see clearly. Marco picked up the paper on top and held it up to the sun. It was a print of what had been an oil painting originally. The left half of the print was a solid dark brown that faded to gold as it led the viewers' eyes to the middle. A dark-haired man stood in the center, one arm propped atop a long object that stretched to the ground. A ceremonial saber. The most striking part of the painting was the bright red coat the man wore. It was long, falling well below his waist, and featured large circular buttons of rich yellow. The colors of the coat drew the eyes to it first and were so pronounced as to keep the viewers' eyes from wandering off to examine the other features of the subject for a time. However, Marco forced his eyes to look elsewhere. It was the man's face that interested him.

"That is a man named Aldyrdd Morgan," said Alan. "He is a Welshman and one of Mr. Fisher's relatives. Mr. Morgan was a fisherman. He spent his childhood working long days on his father's boat, hauling in the loads of fish and crabs his father and brothers caught. Eventually, he became quite the fisherman himself, made a decent living at it for a while in Cardiff, Pembroke, even as far away as Holyhead. He traveled widely and became a rather transient figure in this area. Aldryyd never stayed long, claiming that his family was a thankless lot unworthy of living in such splendor. All except for his beloved mother, whom he adored. The Mount was quite fantastic then. It was the most precious part of Aldryyd's life."

Marco had made his way up to the eyes of the man in the painting. The eyes of Aldryyd Morgan. Heavy dark brows arched over strangely small eyes that didn't show any noticeable pupils. The brown of the eyebrows bled down to the blackness of the eye sockets. Only a mysterious light source from something outside of the painting's canvas made it possible to discern any color within those eyes. From the depths of the shadow eyes came a hint of blue.

"Is this the guy?" asked Marco." A photo would be better. I can't work from a painting."

"Yes," said Alan. "However, I'm afraid that I have not been able to get you a photograph.

Please give me a chance to explain the difficulty we are facing here. Aldryyd Morgan stands accused of eight murders. Four within the past year alone. He's killed three women, four men, and one child. A little girl. Back when he first arrived at the Mount..."

"Look," said Marco. "The history lesson is great, but I need current stuff. I don't want to be rude 'cause your boss is paying me a hell of a lot of good money just to meet with you. But if you've got info on this Aldryyd guy, it's got to be up to date. All this old stuff isn't going to do me much good."

"Six hundred thirty thousand five hundred eighty-four pounds," said Alan.

Marco nodded. That was the agreed number exactly. Roughly one million dollars, just to show up and hear whatever Fisher wanted him to. It wasn't the way Marco usually did business, especially when he didn't know the people involved, but Harris had given a thumbs up when Marco asked about the legitimacy of Fisher's offer. He hadn't worked in Boston for years, but when he did, it was always a job for Harris. It was hard to find honest contracts in this line of work. Like any other kind of freelance job, there were all too many people trying to get you to put out maximum effort for shit money, so if Fisher was vouched for, then the trip was certainly worth it.

"That's correct," he agreed.

"You have every right to be suspicious. In fact, you'd be a fool not to be," said Alan. "The first half of the money is on the property, and you'll receive the rest upon completion of the task. I can assure you that Martin Fisher's offer is genuine and that you'll receive the discussed payment regardless of your acceptance or denial of this…job."

That pause at the end of the sentence told Marco quite a bit about the man opposite him at the stone table. Bassett was a regular guy, a worker bee like all the everyday folks of the world, but who happened to work in a medieval castle. What could a guy like that know of Marco's world? Of guns and killing for money? Bassett was probably pissed at his boss for making him present an offer to such scum of humanity. Perhaps the poor guy was even a little bit afraid. It probably wouldn't do any good to tell him that he was safe because there was no financial benefit from his death. "Job" was as good a word as any for such subject matter. Marco decided to adopt this term since it seemed to make Bassett a little more comfortable doing business.

"But, with this kind of money on offer, you'll understand that we can't simply hand it over until we've presented our situation in full," said Alan. When Marco nodded understanding, he continued. "The most up-to-date information I can give you is that Aldryyd never leaves the Mount. Finding him will not be an issue."

His patience was wearing thin, but Bassett was making an attempt to impart relevant information for once, so Marco bit his tongue. However, those last few words he'd heard were sitting in his mind. "Finding him will not be an issue." That was good. But this expression also warned Marco that he was about to learn what the issue actually was. On the plane, he'd had plenty of time to question the situation. Why offer an American guy a bunch of money to hop on a plane, come to your country, and hear your employee give a presentation when you could have easily found some gangster for hire running around the streets of London?

"The reason we are prepared to offer such payment and that we have specifically contacted you is twofold," said Alan. "Mr. Fisher believes that you have a certain ability that may prove useful in this situation. Do you know which ability I'm referring to?"

Marco nodded. Tripping is how he usually labeled it, but that wasn't accurate. That he was being asked about this was not surprising in the least. It had happened many times.

"You know how sometimes you have a dream, and you know that you're having a dream?"

Alan nodded.

"It's like that. It might give me some hint about the past or future. I sometimes don't know which. But, it's kind of like being aware of your dream but not being able to do anything to control the outcome."

"Do you blackout?" asked Alan.

Bassett's directness was surprising. He had dropped his oh-so-proper manners and was finally getting straight to the point. This was an important subject to him.

"No," answered Marco. "It's not a blackout at all. In fact, it's perfect awareness with every sense. I can see, smell, hear, feel, taste—all that stuff. It's just I can't move until it's over. Not a seizure, but I'm sure as hell not going anywhere until it ends."

Alan nodded again. He wrote something quickly on the back of a paper, then stashed it in his bag.

"What's the second thing?" asked Marco.

Alan didn't answer right away. He sat and looked at his hands folded on the table. When he finally started talking, the first words were inaudible.

"...come before, but it never works out. Priests, nuns, and paranormal whatnot. You'd probably call them ghostbusters. We've tried exorcisms. Once, Fisher even hired a gypsy woman to hold a séance in the main hall."

Marco was growing more and more curious by the second. All of this talk about ghostbusters and priests made him think there was some kind of satanic cult involved. The money on offer was good, but there was no way he'd agree to take on multiple jobs at one time. There were too many unknowns for that.

"Frankly," said Alan, "we contacted you because we've already tried everyone else. You're a last resort, you see. And as I sit here considering what Fisher wants me to tell you, I admit that I have almost no doubt that you will laugh, say something about how sorry you are that you must be going, and then rush off down the road as quickly as your feet will carry you."

"Just. Tell. Me," said Marco. Behind his sunglasses, his dark eyes were squinting in anger. If this guy didn't get to the point soon, he would threaten to stomp off down the road for sure but he wouldn't be saying sorry about anything.

Alan tore his gaze away from his own hands and set it on Marco. His hands remained as they were. Folded. They had tightened a bit.

"There is a perfectly good reason that I am unable to give you current information on Aldryyd Morgan. There isn't any. Aldryyd Morgan died in 1786."

Marco glared across the stone table and fought the urge to flip it over. This whole thing had been a waste of time. It was all just some kind of hoax to promote castle tourism or something like that. He'd get the money and then get the hell out of there. He'd done some fucked up jobs before, but no one had ever wasted his time so boldly. Fisher had some balls, getting him all the way out here just to say that he'd been hired to kill a guy who was already dead.

"You're kidding me," he said. Marco rose from his stone block and took a step away from the table. It was the first time Alan understood how big the man was; a towering presence in a brown leather jacket. "I don't know what your angle is. For all I know, you think you can lay this ruse on me because of my special skill you're so interested in. Hey, the stupid American will fall for the ol' ghost in the castle routine because he's dumb enough to believe in supernatural stuff like ESP."

"If you'll give me a moment—" said Alan. He was abruptly cut off.

"I've given you and your damn boss as much time as I'm willing to give. Ok? So, thanks for the trip. The plane ride was fun, and the country is pretty, but you should've chosen a bigger sucker for whatever it is you're trying to pull. And do I even need to stress the fact that cheating a guy like me out of money is a very bad idea?" He walked around to the other side of the table. His temper was rising quickly, but he wanted to keep it at bay for the time being. Attacking Bassett probably wouldn't get him his money any faster. Experience had taught Marco that it was best to deal with tricksters like this guy when he had had a chance to form a plan.

"But...don't you bel..." stammered Bassett. "Don't you think it's possible that there are things in the world that we..." Upon seeing Marco vigorously shake his head No he stopped.

"Do you understand what I do, pretty boy? You read your little books all day, and I dispose of unwanted people. Is that term comfortable enough for you? I am a fucking expert on looking into a man's eyes as he falls for the last time, and nothing I've ever seen has made me stupid enough to believe that there is anything left over afterward. It's lights out, buddy. Once you're gone, you're gone."

Basset slumped and did not reply. His face, the set of his shoulders, and his stillness all told of his utter resignation on the topic. He had realized that it was impossible to pull a ghost story over the eyes of a man who spent day after day taking lives away from others. There was only one thing left to do.

"I'm sorry that things have turned out this way," said Alan. "Though, I must say that I more or less expected this exact reaction. I imagine you'll be wanting your money now."

Marco nodded and took a step back toward the stone table. The mention of money helped him relax.

"Fine," said Alan. He turned and walked away. Just as Marco began to think that Bassett was trying to run out on him, he said, "If you'll follow me inside, we'll get you paid and send you on your way."

Marco didn't move.

"It's inside?" he asked.

A faint "Yes" floated back to him. Bassett was standing near the large door knocker at the front of the building. For a moment, Marco hesitated, not understanding why his legs were loath to carry him across the yard. He thought about the money and managed to get himself moving. As Alan was gripping the door knocker, Marco stepped up beside him. Alan rotated the knocker counterclockwise, and the door slowly swung open. With a nod from Alan, Marco walked forward and entered Morgan's Mount for the first time.

Chapter Eight

Harriet's Chamber

He would never have said this aloud, but Alan always agreed with Fisher when he referred to Morgan's Mount as a house. There'd been days when people had draped tapestries along the walls of the great hall and held extravagant parties in the ballroom. Ladies in feather boas and men you wouldn't have been able to look at without thinking of the word Gentleman had graced the bottom-most floors regularly. Those were the times before the stone above the massive fireplace had cracked and shed its fragments across the wide floor, only to roll their way into the kitchen, bedrooms, and throughout the main hall. People had cared back then. No Morgan would have walked by the gaping break in the ceiling, having leaked itself open one especially wet winter, without immediately seeking to patch it up. The shards of roof tile would not be covering the floor of the main hall, and the maroon carpets, now gray with time and dust, would be inviting with their brightness. A gowned woman floating her way down the second-floor staircase with a Clark Gable look-alike on her arm would have looked right at home. But those people no longer came here. The parties would not be held and there would be no imaginings of noblemen drinking champagne in the courtyard. It really was just a big house these days, not worthy of the illustrious title of castle. The past had slowly squeezed its breath away until poor investments stole money from it, war ravaged its grounds with the pain of human grief, weather beat its wings until the walls could barely stand against the wind, and murder.

That had been the final blow. After all that the castle had endured, it was the killing that finally brought it to its knees.

Aldryyd Morgan did not realize that this once spectacular home had been damaged as much by his actions as by any other detriment. At the moment, the only thing he noticed was that the voices of two men were echoing through the west wing hallway.

"This way," said Alan, stepping aside as they took a left turn in the corridor.

The doorway was set oddly close to the corner and was almost too small to walk through. Marco pushed the door open and noticed its light-weight. Most of the doors he'd seen on the way in had been thicker and heavier than this one. Many had occluded bits of rooms that looked quite large when seen without obstructions. This was not such a room. Its door flapped open with just a touch, and it measured a space not much larger than the typical office cubicle. A lace-blanketed bed was pushed against the far wall but took up most of the room. Marco looked up and noticed three tattered pink curtains hanging from the window. He had just noticed the gold-rimmed mirror standing at his waist level when Alan brushed by and walked to the far end. There was a short bureau standing there, covered with statuettes of horses. Alan was careful not to disturb these as he slid the top drawer open.

"Here we are," said Alan.

Marco looked away from the mirror just in time to see Alan lift a large envelope. He took it and leaned against the wall. You count your money as soon as possible, and if something smells rotten, you do whatever you have to make the money man pay up. At first glance, it all looked good. There was plenty of paper in there, but closer scrutiny made him question what was going on.

"It's all small bills," said Marco.

Alan nodded.

"We thought it would be less suspicious. And since this is one of the more comfortable rooms of the castle, we thought you might like to sit here as you count it."

Marco shrugged and began to count the notes. He removed his sunglasses and compared each one to the money he'd exchanged at the airport, only setting them aside in the Counted pile after he'd assured himself that it wasn't counterfeit. Marco was no expert, but there were people who knew that stuff. Harris had some guys in London who could check for him. He was thinking about this, but mostly just trying to keep track of his counting when he heard something. Bassett had been sitting on the bed, being politely silent as Marco counted. Now he was muttering, and it was distracting. *Three hundred thousand eighty pounds, three hundred thousand two hundre...*

"Come, dear," said Alan, his voice nearly a whisper.

"Shut up," said Marco. *Three hundred thousand five hundred seventy.*

"Come back, dear," whispered Alan. "We need you now. He's not bad. Promise."

Marco gave Alan his best evil eye glare, but it went unnoticed. He tried to ignore Alan and went on counting. The money seemed to be on the level, but he was not about to let anyone distract him now.

"Once I knew a little girly, awfully bright and just as silly, whence she came to comb her mane, she looked to me a right fine filly," recited Alan.

He couldn't believe it. After all the nonsense he'd dealt with from this guy, Marco had to put up with this chatter. It would probably be better to grab all the money and go across the hall into a more private room. Bassett wouldn't be able to annoy him then and he'd be able to pick up where he left off. He'd lost count somewhere around *Four hundred thousand ninety-five.* As he pushed off of the wall and turned toward the door, he caught a glimpse of Alan. He was staring across the room as if there was something of importance on the mattress. Marco looked and didn't see anything significant. He chalked it up as more craziness and walked toward the door.

"Did thou write it?"

Marco stopped in his tracks.

"Aye, I did," said Alan. He looked directly at Marco, but only for a moment, quickly returning to his focal point near the bed.

"What did…" Marco saw one of the pink curtains moving from the corner of his eye. He looked at the window and saw that it was closed.

"I wrote it for you," said Alan. "Lovely ladies deserve lovely poems. I'd be happy to write more for you, but first I need you to come and meet a friend of mine. What do you say to that?"

Marco wanted to ask a question that began with Who. The words that came after Who wouldn't really matter. He saw Alan staring at nothing, speaking to no one, and almost asked. Had the voice not cut him off mid-breath, he would have.

"From whence comes the wanderer?" asked the voice.

The voice that came from nowhere was breathy and light, clearly a child. Marco began to think that leaving the room was a good idea for reasons other than privacy, but his legs were locked in place. He had to know. To see.

"This is Marco," said Alan, "my friend from America. You know all about America, don't you?"

"America?" asked the voice. It was loud this time. Excited.

An onrushing car couldn't have moved Marco from his spot where he stood, staring at the space above the little bed. His gaze was locked on the same spot as Alan's. A few inches above the mattress, the dark stone color of the wall paled little by little. First gray, now white, and whiter still. The colors twirled slowly together in a hypnotic fashion, and although Marco wanted nothing more than to ask Alan what was happening, he found himself unable to produce words. The whiteness was no longer swirling but stretching vertically.

"I've missed you," said Alan to the whiteness.

A misty appendage grew from one side of the gaseous form and soon came a second. The form stopped expanding and solidified as the appendages grew small digits and the bottom of the shape unrolled into the flowing likeness of a bell.

"And I thou," spoke the voice.

When he was ten years old, Marco was hit by a car. He had been young and spry and was able to roll off the hood without much more than a few bruises. There had been some pain, but it was negligible. What he remembered now was the way he felt when he realized that it was too late, the car would hit him, and he would be hurt. A tightening of the stomach matched with an awareness that something that couldn't ever happen was about to occur. The feeling came back to him in full force. Whatever he was about to see was going to hit hard, in one way or another. There was no mistaking the silhouette now. No mistaking those five little digits on each of the moving extensions sprouting from the form. And the bottom was not a bell. It was like rippling lace, complete with floral designs at the edge.

"Marco," said Alan. "I'd like you to meet an old friend of mine. Lady Harriet."

The white faded to grayness in three distinct areas as the arms, still in flux but having overcome their previous formlessness, reached up top and caressed long lines that dropped down the sides of the dress. The hair was done up in numerous tight braids that remained in place even as the matter that constructed them continued to flow inside, across, and around. The two uppermost circles of grayness deepened and Marco was drawn to them by a certain knowing that had nothing to do with a sixth sense.

"Dost thou hail from California?" asked Harriet.

The eyes were amorphous swirls of gray and were undeniably set on him. Marco could feel them. They had a pull that would not allow him to look away. After a passing moment of silence, he was no more capable of speaking to the apparition than ignoring it, and he began to feel strangely comforted. This was not a formidable entity. The gray eye spots that looked upon him were not intimidating but round and wide in a way that suggested curiosity. But there was something more than the pull. Something deeper he had yet to identify.

"Please pardon my friend," said Alan. "I don't believe he has ever met anyone quite like you. The answer to your question is, No. Marco is from a city called Philadelphia."

The specter tilted its head to the side in a manner that reminded Marco of some dogs he'd seen. A look that expressed a lack of understanding or a desire for information. It had spoken to him directly and he'd been unable to reply.

"Uncle Philip has gone to America," said Harriet, her voice hardly above a whisper. With the silence in the room so palpable, the men heard her easily. "King George sayeth they were naughty there."

"Yes," agreed Alan. "Only it wasn't a nation then, was it?" Alan turned toward Marco. Marco, however, did not look away from Harriet at all. "Harriet's uncle Philip fought and died long ago. She had a rather large family once, didn't you, my dear?"

Marco couldn't believe it. Had it...*no, she, really been talking about what I think she was talking about?*

"Harriet knows a lot," said Alan. "She's a very smart girl."

Marco surprised himself by taking a step forward. He told himself he'd look for projectors, screens, anything that could produce the effect he was seeing, knowing full well he wouldn't find anything of the sort.

Alan coughed once and stood as though preparing himself for something to come. His smile faded as he addressed Harriet again.

"Marco is here to help us. He's trying to stop Aldryyd."

Harriet stopped her playful movements abruptly and began to retreat. Her head bowed, and the words she spoke were nearly unintelligible.

"No, Alan. They all fail. He'll fail as well, and the man will be wolfish." Harriet began to sob quietly, her hands covering her face.

"Harriet," started Alan. "We have an idea. Mr. Fisher thinks—"

"When angered, he bites!" shouted Harriet. Her hands dropped, and her face snapped up as she eyed Alan; despair and anger set into the swirling stare of a young spirit. Grey circled and darkened as her eyes focused more intently.

Alan showed his hands, placating the child. He stepped forward slowly and sat on the edge of the mattress, reaching out as though she could take his hand.

"Aye," he said. "That's why Mr. Fisher hired Marco. He makes bad people go away." Alan shifted his gaze to Marco. "Is that a fair enough description of your work?"

Marco looked at Alan, then back to Harriet. He tried to speak and couldn't. A short breath, he closed his eyes and decided to try again. The ghost didn't give him time.

"He's a vile man. Please make him leave me be." With these words, she stepped back and faded into the wall behind her.

Silence in the chamber. Marco stood still, an unasked question on his lips. Alan rose quickly and reached out his hand once more. His chance to say goodbye was denied by the child's sudden departure. She didn't believe this would work. But, for one moment, she had hoped.

They walked to the front door in silence. Marco stuffed the money into his pocket. He'd count it later. As Alan opened the door, Marco turned to take one more look at the great hall.

"That," said Alan, "was Harriet Vale. Aldryyd's fourth victim."

He pushed the door open to find the car waiting out front. A small figure in a black suit and tilted cap stood in the driveway. Peter waved, unseen by Marco. Alan turned and walked toward his vehicle, and as Marco headed for the car, he heard him say one more thing. He got into the car, hardly acknowledging Peter at all. Alan hadn't said 'Goodbye.' It was something offhand. Something spoken quietly, as though Alan thought it wouldn't matter to him.

As the car pulled out of the driveway, Marco was glad to see Morgan's Mount shrinking into the background. Peter got them onto the main road and headed for the hotel. The castle was the size of a shack when Marco realized what Alan had said.

"She was eight."

Chapter Nine

The Hotel

Chaz would've bled out from that gunshot, but it might have taken a few hours. He'd have been just as dead in the end, but only after the most excruciating pain he'd ever felt. That part didn't matter to Marco. He'd just wanted a clean kill. One more shot to the skull had made it a nice, efficient Brain Death; a complete cessation of the respiratory and cardiovascular systems. Nothing left to do, over and done with.

He'd never be foolish enough to say that killing people was easy. It wasn't. Marco had certainly had his share of close scrapes, but he was still amazed by the simple oversights people could make, even when they knew there might be someone out to get them. Doors, for example. Countless people never thought to look behind a door before passing through it. Like the guy in Montreal. He'd walked in, gone straight to his kitchen, and never had any inkling of Marco coming up from behind the parlor door.

One of the easiest methods of concealing oneself was simply to hunker down in the back of a guy's car. If he fails to check the backseat and sits down, you've got him right where you want him. If he checks the seat, you get him while he's looking.

Marco was no expert in poisons but he had once taken a card from the old ninja playbook and crushed up a load of Poinsettias into a man's drink. He'd died the next morning. Marco considered that one of his more creative endeavors. These days, he preferred efficiency; the quick, clean kill.

Alone in the room with nothing but his thoughts, he picked up the decanter and flopped down on the bed. Two swigs, then he laid back. None of it mattered.

"Because you can't *kill* a guy when he's already dead," he said aloud.

He rolled over and placed the decanter on the table again. One thing about Wales, the whiskey sure was good. Marco dropped back onto the pillow.

A cool night breeze blew in through the window, and for a few minutes, he closed his eyes and listened. A few car horns in the distance, some fellow guests of the hotel chatting on the steps below, but otherwise, there was not much to be heard. Not the hurried pace of city life he'd grown used to. This was a town that valued its small size and old-timey way of life. It held a certain ambient quiet that Philadelphia couldn't hope to duplicate. Ever since the ride back to the hotel, he'd hardly spoken a word to anyone. He thought he'd said "bye" to Peter but wasn't sure. Otherwise, he'd eaten, then wandered up to the room. It had been a quiet day, and this quiet night made sense.

At least my jet lag isn't too bad.

He laughed at the thought. After the day he'd had, an issue as trivial as jet lag was nothing but a joke. He'd been paid a shitload of money, met a dead girl, and then learned that he'd been hired to kill a ghost. More whiskey was required.

"To Alan,"he said as he raised the decanter. "Al, you smooth sumbitch. Getting me in there to meet Harriet like that. Made a believer out of me."

It was true. He did believe. There had been no projectors or special effects in that room. If he told others, they'd almost certainly tell him there had been hidden cameras or that it was a trick of mirrors. Maybe Alan had a computer-savvy friend who'd designed a Harriet character in an animation program. He'd heard about tricks like that. *Harriet the Ghost by Pixar.* But he'd been in that room. He'd felt…something. Inside him.

Please make him leave me be, she'd said.

Those words had seeped into him, made his bones shake. No special effect could do that. If she was real, why couldn't Aldryyd be real? Her fear had felt real enough, she'd run off at the mention of Aldryyd's name. But what could he do about it? You can't kill a ghost.

His mind kept arriving at that same thought. A dead end. He stood and walked to the window.

A swig of whiskey and a deep breath. Another cool breeze wafted by. Had this been a normal job, he'd be following his regular procedure of gathering information on the mark. Perhaps that was the best course of action now. Observation. Find Aldryyd and watch him. Learn about him.

As he placed the empty decanter on the table, he laughed one more time. Slipping into a fast sleep, he mused on the thought that he had never seriously considered leaving.

He'd call Alan in the morning.

Chapter Ten

Morgan's Mount, Wales

Alan turned the corner and walked up the short staircase. Marco followed.

"He likes the east tower," said Alan. "Spends a lot of time here with his heirlooms. Old family quilts and such."

Another turn, quickly followed by a second small staircase. Then again. And again. They entered the tower proper, turning ever upward. Marco wondered how high they had to climb.

"What's your plan with that?" asked Alan.

It took Marco a second to realize what he was referring to, then noticed the other man's hand pointing at him. Waist level.

"Couldn't hurt," said Marco. "Has anyone ever tried to shoot Aldryyd before? I brought it because, well…you never know until you try."

Alan nodded. "You'll get no argument from me."

He'd been told about the priests, their bibles in hand as they shouted and tried to cast Aldryyd out. Morgan's response had essentially been the 1700s Welsh version of "Fuck you!" and then Father Owen had been speared through the chest by a flying fire stoker. Immediately afterward, Father Whittaker and Sister Cunningham had been barraged with an attack of chairs, glass shards, and flipping tables, all tossed about by a relentless invisible force. Whittaker had escaped with numerous lacerations in his back and had been confined to a wheelchair for the rest of his days. Sister Cunningham never made it outside. The heavy wooden front door had slammed itself on her head at the last second.

The ghostbusters hadn't lasted more than eight hours. After a while, their cameraman, Charlie, had started choking their techie, Susan. By the time their boss Nigel had arrived on the scene, Susan's face was blue, and Charlie was straddling her on the ground, saying, "I dunno what happened. I dunno." Nigel is reported to have beaten Charlie to death with a hiking boot.

They stopped, and Marco noticed that there was only one more level to the staircase. Alan pointed upward.

"He may not be there, but it's a good bet that he is," said Alan. "Likes the view."

His voice seemed drained of strength. For a moment, Alan stood and looked up the stairway. Then he turned to face Marco.

"You might want to get that thing ready now."

Marco flipped the safety catch off the Beretta.

The top floor of the tower was cluttered with everything from books and paintings to blankets and worn old tapestries. It was surprisingly well-lit, the sun's rays hitting the narrow-slit windows at the perfect angle this time of day. Alan sorted through the mess, looking for nothing in particular. Marco stepped over some ripped sheets and kicked aside a broken pot, gun in hand all the while. Alan stopped in the middle of the room and stood still. He waited a moment, then spoke something in Welsh. Then he immediately turned to Marco and said, "Shoot him!"

Alan didn't wait. He ran straight back to the stairway, jumping the corners as best he could while trying to land safely on the twisting steps. Marco had just enough time to marvel at the speed of the historian before he heard the thrashing noise from across the room. A bookcase shifted, a table fell on the opposite side of the room, and Marco realized he was cold. So cold.

The white shape was large. It appeared to move even while standing still. Flowing white and gray lines, shooting and shifting all around its form. That it was standing, he had no doubt. Those were legs on the bottom. They held up a broad torso and long moving arms. Marco had no idea where this thing had come from, but he had no question about who he was looking at. Unlike the eyes in the painting, these held no hint of blue. He was staring into two holes of obsidian night.

Aldryyd Morgan charged.

The room spun around him, and everywhere was filled with thunder. He tried to run, but the sound made him stumble. His mind didn't understand until his hand reminded him what it was holding. He didn't remember firing the gun, but its report had nearly deafened him in the confines of the tower. His rational mind fought to reassert control as he berated himself for being so foolish. He considered lying there on the floor a moment longer, but he couldn't. As he got his feet under him, the room turned again, and he thought, *Run.*

Aldryyd covered the distance of the room at top speed, managing to catch the lapel of Marco's coat. Marco shrugged and fought, twisted sideways, and broke free of the grip. He moved forward, still disconcerted, and slipped on the spiral staircase. He fell. As Aldryyd began to close the distance, Marco struggled to right himself from the fall. Planting his feet on the ground and pushing his body laterally, he managed to crash himself into a corner wall. It stopped his momentum, and he leaped to his feet. He started running again. It was an effort to go at speed in the close quarters of the stairwell while negotiating the tight corners and steep small steps. He came close to falling again but saved himself by grabbing the wall. The steps didn't appear to be a problem for Aldryyd. He was quickly gaining. Marco only dared to look behind himself one time and was unnerved by what he saw. Aldryyd's feet weren't even touching the stairs.

The turns kept coming and coming, relentlessly twisting, always down, down, down. Marco knew he had to be near the bottom of the tower. The house had three floors, he recalled. Once on the top floor, he'd have options, places to go to. If he could just get out of the tower.

"Marco!"

The voice came from somewhere below. *Alan can't be far*, he thought. The tower twisted sound and made it hard to find the voice's location, but he had to believe that he was almost out. He felt phantasmal hands brushing along his back, and he found new speed. Down the steps. Everything a blur. A corner. And out!

The expanse of floor spread wide in front of him. He wanted to dash right out onto it, but which way should he go? Marco stopped, looking left, looking right, searching for a sign of a way out. Aldryyd emerged from the tower behind him. A flash of red amidst the dark walls of the third floor. *Alan's shirt!* He sprinted toward the color in time to see Alan peek up over the edge of a railing.

"This way!" shouted Alan.

A rising wail began behind him as he followed Alan down the grand staircase. Marco had always considered himself a fairly fast runner, but there were too many steps. Aldryyd would close the distance before they reached the bottom. He would feel the touch of a ghost.

Alan made a loud noise and pointed left, over the railing. Marco didn't understand. Then Alan planted his hands on the railing and vaulted off of the staircase and out of sight. Aldryyd roared, the chandelier began to shake, and Marco jumped, following Alan. He smashed heavily onto a large oak table several feet below the staircase. The impact of the landing shook him up, but he was grateful for the table and the potential crash landing it had saved him from. He rolled off the table and ran. Alan was heading for the front door.

Aldryyd had continued straight down the steps and was nearing the door, when Alan grabbed the handle. He pulled with all his might and dove outside. Marco ran as Aldryyd rushed up on his right. *He's trying to blindside me.* He tried to run faster but couldn't. His lungs were burning, his feet leaden. There would be no getting around the ghost.

"Get out!" shouted Alan. "He can't leave the castle!"

The door was open. He darted straight for it and was almost there when the specter floated in front of the doorway. There was no stopping and nowhere to go but forward. Aldryyd lurched at him, arms snapping like a vice, and Marco dropped. The ghost swiped his hands in front of him in the man-catching movement of giant pincers, while Marco slid by along the floor. The vice hands closed on nothing and Marco's momentum carried him outside. Alan slammed the door.

Moments later, they were sitting on the front lawn, both men breathing heavily. Marco fell back onto the grass. The point of the encounter had been to observe the ghost and to try to learn something from the experience. He said so, and Alan laughed.

"You can't watch Aldryyd. You can only run from him. He'll never give you any other option."

"Great," groaned Marco.

"We're hoping that you can help us learn to fight him," said Alan.

Marco didn't hear him, his mind lost in a half-memory. He must have pulled the trigger, but the movement was so quick he'd done it without thought. However, he could recall one thing right before Aldryyd charged at him: Two dots, the bullets, racing directly through the ghost's chest. The smoky figure hadn't even slowed down.

"Hey, Al," said Marco. "Up there in the tower, you said something. What was it?"

Alan shrugged and said, "Just something farmers around these parts say to one another sometimes."

"What's that mean?" asked Marco.

Alan smirked.

"More or less," said Alan. "I called him a dirty pig cunt."

Chapter Eleven

The Study

Low wooden rafters crisscrossed above a long dark table. In an old padded chair in the room below sat a man who no longer required the use of furniture. He had no body with which to sit. Once, people had spoken of the way his light blue eyes could hold a person in place with their stare. Now, sightless holes that held nothing but white peered up from the chair at a hanging quilt. A patchwork design, the quilt had been sewn long ago by Constance Morgan: Aldryyd's great, great grandmother.

His mind wandered from one family member to the next, thinking fondly of few, disgusted by the others. They'd been fools for the most part. Not since the days of Constance had the Morgans been a force in the world. The likes of his sainted mother, Lillian, were now being insulted by the only living remnant of her line: Martin, who'd sought to dissociate himself from the family to the extreme of adopting the name Fisher. Such an ordinary surname, it probably came from Martin's peasant-ridden paternal line.

This could all be traced back to Martin. The new man who spoke like a Yankee was a hired gun. A big fool. No weapon could harm Aldryyd. Didn't they realize that people had tried such tactics before? He wasn't sure they'd return to try again, but he hoped so. The chance to prove once again that he was king in this domain was irresistible. He salivated for it. The challenge was accepted if the challenger dared enter the ring for a second round.

It was, however, not the American that truly weighed on Aldryyd's mind. It was the other one. Alan. For years, Alan had been in and out of the mount, studying, searching, talking to the girl, but never posing a threat. He had, in fact, been responsible for much of the castle restoration. As Aldryyd could no longer care for the building himself, Alan had become a tolerable guest. Better to allow the man to pass safely through these halls than let them fall to ruin.

Things had changed. The caretaker was now an active opponent. It tasted of betrayal. There would be no more safe passage given in Morgan's Mount.

Alan Bassett had become an enemy.

People had tried to rid the castle of Aldryyd before, and he delighted in their inevitable failure. They tried religion first, and the look in the priest's eyes, upon realizing that his faith would not get the job done, would stay with Aldryyd forever. It made him smile. The gadgets of the scientists had been no more understandable than their academic approach to the haunting. Had they truly believed Aldryyd would allow them to enter his home, analyze every inch of it with cold indifference, step on his sweet mother's old rugs with their filthy feet, without suffering retribution? Now, there was something new, even stranger than the others. This new man had pulled a high-tech weapon, some sort of revolver from outer space, and shot him with it. The absurdity of it made Aldryyd laugh. Firing a gun at a ghost was every bit as useless as reciting from a bible or taking temperature readings of the tower rooms. His powers were far beyond their comprehension, but he would make them understand.

Chapter Twelve

The Ballroom

They'd spent the next two days discussing tactics. They were going back in, that was decided, but the gun hadn't helped at all, and Marco didn't have any reason to think that a knife would be any better. Aldryyd was, essentially, a gas. Somehow, he was able to touch things while remaining untouchable himself. This thought led Marco to another. *If we can't damage him, maybe we can, at least, contain him*. Alan said he thought that the ghostbusters were thinking along similar lines until tragedy befell them. They never had the chance to spring their trap.

In their search for a container, Alan and Marco came across some large plastic bags. The bags held air well and ballooned up easily. Perhaps they'd hold in the misty substance that Aldryyd was made of. They bought many of the bags and sat down to decide which part of the castle to use.

"We need a room with space for us to run," said Alan. "He's guaranteed to chase us again."

Marco nodded, adding, "And there needs to be a limited number of entrances and exits. We want to know where he'll come from while still leaving ourselves a way out."

"The ballroom," said Alan without hesitation. "There's plenty of space and it's on the first floor. We can close the doors, there's only the one set, but I doubt they'll keep him inside. However, we can always climb out the windows if things go wrong." He was silent for a heartbeat. "And they might."

Marco agreed. It seemed unlikely that they'd be able to trap the ghost in the ballroom, but that wouldn't matter anyway if the bags didn't work. Ultimately, he thought the plan had a chance because of what he'd learned about Aldryyd.

"He's a madman," said Marco. "Attacks anyone on sight. This is not a discerning killer we're dealing with. You said yourself, he's killed women, children, the kind of victim doesn't matter to him.

He'll stay in the room because that's where we'll be."

The location was chosen, and they'd worked out a detailed plan. They sat on the front lawn, repeating the schedule aloud until they both had it memorized. Now it was well past noon, and any more delay would just breed excuses. They walked into the ballroom and sat in a corner near two large open windows.

"Say it again," said Marco.

"But I know—" said Alan.

"Say it again."

Alan sighed.

"1:30, I leave the ballroom," Alan began. "I have twenty minutes to get back, at which point you'll go out looking for me if I haven't returned. After leaving, I'll attempt to draw Aldryyd toward the ballroom by pretending that I'm on the way there to meet Fisher. He hates Fisher."

Marco nodded. Alan had told him all about the ghost's opinion of his only living descendant; the drunk who'd allowed the family castle to fall to ruin. Fisher would be a prime target.

"At 1:50, assuming I've been successful, I'll come through the door. If I think I'll be late, I'll send you a text reading my estimated time of arrival. But a phone signal is no guarantee here, so if the phone doesn't work, I'll get the bullhorn from the storage closet and announce my E.T.A. from the grand staircase. So, upon entering the ballroom, I need to remember to duck immediately. If we trap him, then all is well. If not, I'll grab the next set of bags and attempt to net him."

"Deadline?" asked Marco.

"As you said, 'If it don't work, it don't work.' There's no reason to run around like idiots if the bags fail to contain him. The cut-off time is 2:00. At that time, we have either succeeded or escaped via the two left-corner windows." Alan took a deep breath. "How's that for a recitation? Not exactly Shakespeare but almost as wordy."

Marco suppressed a retort. The Brit was acting like an annoying brat, but he had agreed to take part in a plan that required tremendous courage. Alan knew the plan and was well aware of the potential consequences. It would have to be enough. Now, it all depended on the bags.

"He can't leave the house, right?" asked Marco.

"No, I don't believe he can," Alan replied.

"So," began Marco, "say we catch him. What do you think would happen if we toss the bag out the window? Would he just…woosh?" Marco performed a theatrical magician's disappearing gesture.

"I don't think it works that way," Alan said. "His remains are physically bound to this building, and therefore, his ghost must stay as well."

They sat in silence, each man speculating on the success of their plan, wondering if there was something better than what they'd come up with. They were up against a murderous spirit, armed with two cell phones, a bullhorn, and some plastic bags. Marco hadn't bothered to bring the gun this time. Alan was about to comment on this when Marco spoke.

"1:30," he said.

Alan nodded once and stood. He gave a nearly imperceptible wave and then walked to the door.

"Last chance," said Marco. "You can still—"

"No," said Alan. "No, I can't. Because you need me." He stood in the doorway, looking out into the great hall. "For this at least, you need my knowledge of the castle. Because I'm the one who has devoted the past 10 years of his life to this bloody place, and because, frankly, I don't think you can do this without me."

Marco stayed silent. He should never have suggested it to begin with. This really was a two-man plan. Alan walked out, and Marco took his position behind the ballroom door.

He couldn't help but wonder why anyone would ever care so much for a rotting old place like this. This was no Tower of London. It wasn't even an official castle. It was a ruin on the edge of town but for some reason, Alan was risking his life for it. But he didn't need to understand. Alan could have his reasons. For Marco, the money would do just fine. It always had.

As Alan climbed the grand staircase his confidence in the plan decreased. The American was Hotheaded and too quick to seek confrontation. Alan had wanted to argue but, as with the conversation with Fisher, he'd been unable to offer an alternative plan. Aldryyd had backed them into a corner in which every option looked foolish. Now he had to go along with Marco's scheme to trap a homicidal poltergeist in a bag because it was the only plan on offer. He groaned about Fisher having hired the killer, to begin with.

He heard something.

Alan told himself it was a board creaking or wind pushing over a candelabra. This old house made all kinds of noise. The more nervous one was, the more noise it seemed to make. Not every sound could be accounted to Aldryyd, but Alan had a feeling that was not the case this time. He summited the staircase and looked toward the east tower, remembering their close call two days before. Breathing deep, he wished silently for success, then turned. This time he walked west toward the sound.

1:34

They'd gotten a bit of a late start, but Marco wasn't ready to worry yet. He'd keep a cool head until it was time to move, one way or another. To pass the time, he checked, then rechecked the ropes around the doorframe. Secure. The far windows were open wide enough. The question now was what he'd do if he did manage to trap the ghost in the bags. Based on Alan's response, tossing it out the window didn't seem likely to help. He couldn't exactly beat Aldryyd to death inside the bag. The bags would have to be in layers, at least ten of them at once. A cage of plastic wrapping. Later, the bag cage could be buried somewhere or locked away in the deepest part of the castle. He checked the ropes again and wondered how Alan was doing.

The west wing of the mount was unlike the east tower. Darker. The entry corridor was significantly wider because the west tower had collapsed in 1908. Lillian Morgan, Fisher's great, great grandmother, had tried to rebuild it once. It stood three days longer before being blown to pieces by a lightning bolt. Martin believed his family was cursed and, in this place, surrounded by gray rubble and creeping drafts, Alan considered that he might finally believe it too. He inched along the corridor. A room was there. He drew in a deep breath and spoke into his phone. There was no one on the line.

"Hello, Mr. Fisher. Aye, I'm here. Certainly, I'll meet you there momentarily."

Alan put the phone back into his pocket and walked back toward the staircase. He stopped at the top to listen. The sound came again. A quick rustling, wind brushing cloth. It had worked. He started down the steps, careful not to go too fast. Aldryyd needed to be right behind him when he arrived at the ballroom.

1:48

The Brit was cutting it close. Marco hated to walk away from the doorway but he needed to be sure Alan hadn't sent a message and the signal was better near the open windows. He flipped open the phone. No messages. He put the phone back in his pocket and returned to his post by the doorway. There was still a little time, he didn't want to worry himself too soon. Alan was a smart guy, he could pull this off. Marco forced himself to recite the alphabet five times before checking the time again.

1:52

He started for the door.

"E's—ear!"

It was Alan. His voice sounded close, but Marco couldn't make out the words. Something was clearly wrong and there was a commotion outside the room. Footsteps rushed toward the doors. As much as he wanted to run outside and find out what had happened, Marco thought it was best to stay in the room for a moment longer. *Stick to the plan.*

The doors burst open. The starting gun had sounded. Marco pulled the rope he was holding. Alan crunched himself into a baseball dive, heading for the table behind Marco. The rope rushed painfully through Marco's hands as it released the layered bags above. They swooped down, and the white shape of Aldryyd loomed up in front of them. Alan reached the table. Marco watched. He saw his trap envelop the specter like a large net. He saw the shroud descend upon Aldryyd and cut off the ghost's piercing screams. He shuffled sideways, grabbing the tail end of the bag cage, closing the last opening it had.

Alan stood.

All was still.

A white hand shot out of the bag and grabbed at Marco's throat. He managed to dodge before it took hold. Aldryyd began to slip, head first, out of the bags, closing on Marco, but Marco refused to release them. It didn't matter. The ghost was almost halfway out, only his left arm still inside.

"He's got a spear!" shouted Alan.

Marco heard but understood only as Aldryyd's hidden arm emerged from the bags, the head of a boar spear gripped in its hand. He instinctively stepped back, dropping the bags in the process.

There was no time for any further reaction. The spear drove forward and caught him hard in the shoulder. White lights flashed before his eyes as he dropped to his knees. Marco gripped his shoulder. Wetness. It wasn't until he looked up that the pain hit. Aldryyd floated many feet above, free as ever, happy with his work, judging by his mad grin.

As the ghost descended, Marco kicked and fought. His first attempt to stand up was thwarted by a sharp pain through the side of his body. He fell again, and the spear came free as he went down. Aldryyd reached out a misty hand, and Marco punched. His hand went through the ghost, as ineffective as the bullets had been two days before. The ghost shoved him backward and lunged with the spear. Marco turned and swung a haymaker. It passed directly through Aldryyd's skull, doing no damage. He couldn't hurt smoke. The spear drove forward once more. It missed. Marco knocked it aside, then tore it from the ghost's hands. He immediately turned it around and thrust the boar spear into Aldryyd's heart. Aldryyd's gray eyes glared, and he struck a glancing blow on Marco's arm. The weapon was useless. Marco was forced to drop it and run. *You can't kill a ghost.*

Aldryyd advanced, then abruptly stopped when everything went black around him. He turned and clawed in the darkness. He was high above ground, but not far enough to be among the tapestries. He realized the other one, the caretaker, Alan, had done this. They were using the same trap that failed in the doorway. Aldryyd was furious. Their useless traps posed no problem, he'd be out in a second. The first one had been sprung in the doorway by the dark-haired man. It had done no more than come as a surprise. But now Alan Basset was attacking. For the first time, the little historian was being offensive.

Alan never saw it coming. He was thrown back into the middle of the ballroom and crashed down on its musty burgundy carpet. As he looked over his body parts, trying to assure himself that they were still functional, he pondered the fact that he had never been hit before. Not so much as one single boyhood fistfight. Still, he realized, even after being tossed like a useless sack, he had sustained nothing more than a few bruises. Alan Basset, historian, scholar, was not fragile.

"Get up!"

It was Marco. Alan came to and looked in the other man's direction. Marco was pointing to his watch. That pointing finger indicated 2:00. That finger marked failure. He stood and ran without looking at the speeding shape behind him.

Aldryyd growled something that Marco would've found unintelligible even if he did understand Welsh. Despite the danger, he found himself laughing. Alan was too fast. The ghost would never catch him.

"Out!" shouted Marco as Alan ran by. The look in his eyes left no room for argument. Alan reached the window first. As he swung his leg over the sill, Marco turned to face the ghost.

"Keep coming, asshole. He's almost…"

Despite the failure of the bags, Marco had allowed himself that one brief moment of cockiness. Alan was safely outside where he couldn't be touched, and Marco himself was only a second behind. Or so he was until his fear came true.

The Trips always began with a numbness of the body. He'd try to move an arm and find it unresponsive, or he'd gesture without feeling his movement. This time, it began when he lifted his foot to the window sill. It rose halfway and then flopped down again as if it had no energy. The car was coming. There was no time to move, nothing left to do but take the hit and hope for the best. Aldryyd was flying unimpeded across the ballroom.

The room was dark. And long. Too long. So, no, it couldn't be a room. His view panned the space around him and showed walls stretching on into darkness. Paintings on the far side: the little boy in the hat fishing in a pond. The lady in the red dress, riding the horse. He recognized that one. The red dress. The horse. He'd seen that…*The second floor.* This trip was showing him Morgan's Mount. He was in the second-floor hallway and his hands felt heavy. He must be holding something. There was a wet noise, and he turned toward it. Alan's bloodied face looked up at him. Marco lifted his hand and saw the dim light painting it red-going-black. They were not alone, but he couldn't look away to see the others. Alan coughed, and the blood trickled from his mouth, down his cheek, and pooled on the floor near his arm. There was a spot of red, a wound, in his stomach.

The slightest crack of light came into view, like peeking sunlight through a window at dawn. Marco couldn't let it in. It would take him back to the world, and he couldn't go yet. This was important. The vision was showing him something, and if he could learn from it, then just maybe, he could do something about it when the time came. He fought the light, but struggling against the dawn sun is futile when the window couldn't be closed and the blankets couldn't be pulled up. If he could just get a moment longer. There must be something. *Weapon?* he thought. The light invaded more and more, but he seized the thought. There must be a weapon in the hallway somewhere. Alan was lying on the wooden floor, the blood trailed from his stomach, across his slacks, reddened his belt, and passed a short object on the floor. The light grew brighter. The object was…More light. It was…

The hand that grabbed his collar yanked him upward with a jolting force. As he came to, he saw a blurry shape and was sure it was Aldryyd. The damn Trips had finally sealed his fate. He wondered what it would feel like to be killed by a ghost.

Chapter Thirteen

Peter's Car

Hills rushed past the window. Marco leaned his head against the glass and fought to control his breathing.

"Sir, are you ok?"

It took Marco a few seconds to process the question and realize that it warranted a response.

"Um, yeah," he said. It was a default answer.

"Mr. Basset looked rather distressed when I arrived. Something I can help the two of you with?" asked Peter.

Marco looked at the back of Peter's head. He could see the driver's bald pate clearly from his backseat. He was a diminutive man, made smaller by sitting in a car so often.

"We ran into some trouble," Marco said.

"What kind of trouble, sir?"

Marco tried to speak but couldn't find the words. He could say, "We got attacked by a ghost," but that would just make Peter think he was crackers. He thought of explaining that there was a killer inside the castle, but that would certainly make the driver speed straight to the nearest police station, and cops would only complicate things. He decided that it was best to be vague.

"The kind Fisher is paying me good money not to talk about."

"Fair enough," said Peter.

The rolling green hills were getting farther and farther apart. They were entering town. It wouldn't be long now.

"Hey, Peter," said Marco.

"Yes, sir?"

"What can you tell me about Alan? He comes across as this pencil-pushing nerd, but I'm starting to rethink my opinion of him."

Peter chuckled quietly in the front of the car.

"Mr. Basset is not the sort of man who'd deny his nerdiness. I do believe he embraces it."

It was Marco's turn to laugh. It felt good, and his residual fear eased slightly.

"I mean, there's more to the man than I first thought. He's got guts."

"Guts, sir?"

"Yeah," answered Marco. "He's brave, you know. Helped me out a lot back there."

For a moment, neither man spoke.

"Sir."

"Call me Marco."

"Marco," began Peter. "If I may tell you something that I think will help?"

Marco nodded, realized that the driver couldn't see the nod up there in the front of the car, and said, "Yes."

"Before my employment for Mr. Fisher, I was in the royal navy. In my first year, a simple cadet, my ship was attacked off the coast of China."

They turned a corner and Marco saw the run-down blue house they'd be pulling into.

"I'd been shot in the side and as the water rose around us, I thought that was the end of it for me. Nineteen years old, and I was convinced I would die on a sinking ship half a world apart from everyone I truly cared for."

"Shit," said Marco. It seemed an appropriate response.

"A fellow cadet, whom I'd never met, patched my wound and managed to calm me down long enough to get me into a lifeboat."

He stopped talking and stared out his driver's side window for a moment. Then he resumed his story.

"Charles Hopkins was his name. I learned this later. He was killed by an incendiary device on his next tour. I never had the chance to repay him for what he'd done, and I regret that."

Marco leaned forward to hear better. He couldn't see where Peter was going with the story.

"I don't know what you and Mr. Basset are involved in, sir," said Peter, "but when the pair of you came out of the castle door this afternoon, you looked like you'd been in a battle. Mr. Basset had to support you as you got into the car, and I heard you thanking him profusely. I am unaware of your purpose for being here. It seems to me, however, that you and he are involved in a conflict of some kind, and I hope you can appreciate his help. He is a nerd, as you call him. He is also, like Charles Hopkins, one of the best of us and deserves whatever help we can give him, as long as we are able to offer it."

"Message received," said Marco. "But what if I can't save…"

He immediately decided to banish the thought. It would do him no good and it would distress Peter. The car pulled into Martin Fisher's driveway.

Chapter Fourteen

Martin Fisher's House, Cardiff, Wales

The ramshackle blue house gave no hint of its inhabitant's wealth. The past eighteen years had been spent shelling out endless amounts of money for the upkeep of one ratty old castle. While Morgan's Mount had its staircase repaired and its window panes replaced, the paint on Martin Fisher's little home flaked off into the wind. The money had barely sustained the castle. It had kept the house running only on fumes.

The truth was that the old Morgan family treasury was a bit light these days, the result of an alcoholic owner who'd decided to invest it in the castle only after realizing he was the last of his family who could. It's a hell of a thing to be the one that killed your family's five-hundred-year-old ancestral home.

Fisher knew his existence mattered no more than his decrepit old house did, but that did not mean that he would fail his family. The mount would stand. If he had his way, the home would outlive the family.

He poured whiskey into the glass and pushed it across the table. Alan did not reach for it. Martin didn't respond, just stood, hand on the glass, staring at the younger man. It was always the same with Alan; that need to be perfect on top with the rougher man waiting beneath. It was all for the woman he loved, Martin knew. She was delightful, and she'd still love this uptight fool even if he got a bit tipsy tonight. Martin withdrew his hand and sat. After a moment, Alan took the glass. Always the same with him.

"How is he?" asked Alan.

"Don't worry about him," said Fisher. "He's been in tougher spots than this, man in his line of business."

Alan nodded and arched his back in a stretch. It still hurt after heaving Marco's large frame up and out of the window. Marco hadn't snapped out of his trance until crashing into Alan's thin body on the castle lawn. The ghost had been so close. Alan drank.

"I think he's going to leave," said Alan.

Fisher nodded as though that's what he'd expected to hear.

"Be wanting the rest of his money then."

Fisher poured more whiskey into Alan's glass and received no resistance. He put down the bottle and folded his hands on the table.

"He needs hope, Alan," said Fisher. "The man's a professional, but think about what this situation does to his mind. He's up against something he doesn't understand." He took a drink, then went silent for a moment. Finally, he said, "It was wrong of me to hire him."

The two men sat. Only the sounds of Marco's movements in the adjacent room filled the quiet.

"I think you know who can help," said Fisher.

In all the years they'd known one another, Martin had never seen Alan lose his temper, but the look on the young man's face was undeniable. Fisher was nearing dangerous territory, and Alan's glare told him to go no further. It didn't matter. Glare or no glare, Martin had to continue. This crackpot scheme was his last idea, and he owed it to the Morgans to apply every resource he could.

"She knows things," he said.

Alan was having none of it. He pushed the glass away and stood. Marco entered the kitchen as Alan began walking out.

"What's up his butt?" asked Marco.

Martin didn't reply. Instead, he got a large glass, filled it with the remaining whiskey, and handed it to Marco. Marco nodded his gratitude.

"Well," said Martin, "certainly can say you've given it your best shot, my good man."

There was an old chestnut cabinet to Marco's right. Martin walked to it and pulled open the main drawer. When he walked away from the cabinet, he held an envelope in his hand, similar to the one Alan had stored in Harriet's room. Marco started to speak, but Fisher waved it off. He handed over the envelope, then pointed to the couch.

Marco flopped onto the couch while Fisher settled into his old green armchair. Marco leaned forward and placed his whiskey on a low glass table while he stared at the brooding historian.

"Alan," said Fisher. "You've done a fine job. Thank you for all the assistance you've given Marco."

No response.

Marco raised an eyebrow at Fisher. Fisher ignored him and turned to Alan.

"It's all I've got left," said Fisher. "You know that. Once this castle falls, it's just me and this stupid ol' hou—"

"She's not getting involved!" Alan shouted.

Marco leaned forward on the couch.

"Who is she?"

The other men ignored his question. Martin stood, emptied his glass, and walked back to the kitchen.

"Then, it's over," he said.

"Look," said Marco. "If I could lay a hand on the guy, hit him, shoot him, set some kind of trap, I'd keep trying. For some reason, he can hurt me, but I can't do a thing to him. You have to understand that this is not my usual gig. Aldryyd is something completely new to me. Maybe you thought I could do something because of my Trips but…"

"Your what?" asked Martin.

"It's what I call the visions I get," Marco said. "You might refer to them as psychic flashes or something."

Fisher nodded. Alan looked up.

"You had one in the castle, didn't you?" Alan asked.

When he met Alan's gaze, Marco found himself unable to reply at first.

"What did you see?" asked Fisher.

He was glad that Martin had asked the question because it gave him a reason to look away from Alan.

"It's, umm. It's still unclear in my head," said Marco. He'd prepared the lie the night before on the drive to Cardiff. It was a politician's response, an answer that was no answer. "Sometimes I need time to figure out what I've seen before it makes any sense."

They accepted that response, but Marco was uncomfortable with the subject. He wasn't ready to discuss it yet, therefore, he chose to return the conversation to its previous topic.

"Who are you two keep talking about?"

Alan stared at Fisher but said nothing. Martin shook his head.

"He deserves to know," said Fisher.

For a moment, Marco thought that Alan would charge his boss and knock him off the stool. The atmosphere in the room was tenser than ever. Alan walked toward Fisher. Martin didn't budge. Alan stopped at the table where Fisher sat, took his boss's drink, and walked out to the deck without a word. Fisher slumped a little on the stool. He looked older than before.

"She," he began, "is Maggie Warlow. A brilliant young anthropologist. It's my belief that Maggie has enough expertise in cultural studies of death to be of help to us."

"Ok," said Marco. "So why is Al so dead set against bringing her in? I meant what I said before. I'll keep trying if I can figure out what to do next, and if she can help, I'll welcome any crazy idea she has."

"Maggie is his girlfriend. I expect I'll be saying fiancé soon," Fisher said.

Marco understood. He took a drink and got up.

"Probably best to let him have some time to himself right now," Fisher said.

"Nah. It's cool. I need to have a little chat with him anyway." Marco walked out onto the deck and leaned on the railing, an arm's length away from Alan.

The air was heavy and lacked any breeze. It held the portents of rain. Night was settling in quickly.

Marco intended to start gradually, small talk, then some kind of joke. Get Alan to relax a little, then thank him for getting him out of that window in time. He was surprised when Alan spoke first.

"Why are you doing this?" Alan asked.

Marco shrugged.

"You know why. It's just what I do. Some guys build things, some mix chemicals in labs. I, pardon the expression, earn a living by providing a service that people are willing to pay a lot of money for."

"No," said Alan. "That's not good enough. If that's all you are, then I'll be glad to escort you to the airport in the morning."

Marco wanted to get angry but didn't. He was still dwelling on the thought that Aldryyd would have gotten him if Alan hadn't been there. You don't shout at the guy who just saved your life.

"Alright," said Marco. "I owe you, so here it goes. A better answer." He placed his hands on the railing and tapped his fingers on it a few times before continuing. "I told you the truth, I do this because I can. I'm good at it. When I'm not shooting at a goddamn ghost." He laughed.

Alan looked like he was about to respond, but Marco held out a hand.

"Other guys," Marco continued, "they do it to make some kind of statement, or sometimes they have religious reasons. But the worst guys are the guys who kill for fun. Because those guys don't care about the cash at all. You fail to come up with the cash, I back out of the deal, that's the way I work. But those guys...the money is just a bonus for them. They want to do it anyway."

There was silence. Marco was staring into the dark while Alan looked down, hoping that the killer across from him would say the right words. Whatever they may be.

Marco continued. "As I see it, there are men who deserve to die and men who don't. Aldryyd, he definitely deserves it. You are the latter. Most guys I kill have screwed somebody out of money, or they cheated the wrong guy in a deal, I don't know. I don't concern myself with that. My point is there are levels to this stuff. For example, I wouldn't kill a guy like you."

"Wouldn't you?" asked Alan, incredulous.

"Ok," said Marco. "If you don't believe that, I'll put it a different way. I would never kill a little kid. Aldryyd did. Guys like that have to be held accountable. Now I'm probably one of those men who deserves to get killed, but since I'm not going to do it myself, I'd rather spend my time here paying that son of a bitch back for what he did to Harriet."

Alan turned to face him. His stare was cold.

"Let me tell you how I got into this stuff. Back when I was twenty-five, I worked on a loading dock. Hard work that paid shit. One day, this guy at work starts going on about his buddy. The buddy had a daughter. Twelve years old. She got shot by some guy because she called him names."

Alan looked skeptical.

"Anyways," Marco continued, "the guy says that the shooter was picked up by the cops but got off on a technicality. So now his daughter's killer is walking around free. The dad is so pissed about it he's thinking about going to the mob for help. He wants revenge."

"So, you stepped in?" asked Alan.

"There's big money in revenge. And I saved that guy a lot of trouble. Those mob guys don't mess around once they've got their hooks in you. And the cops? Imagine this. You're a city cop. You've got a full caseload on any given day. Suddenly, a guy comes out of nowhere and offs a known child killer. How hard are you really going to search for the guy?"

"Why are you telling me all of this?" asked Alan.

"I'm trying to tell you that I don't do this stuff indiscriminately. I'm not some kind of terrorist. And I don't kill kids."

"Can you protect?" asked Alan.

"I'm not sure what you're asking," replied Marco.

"Maybe Fisher is right, Maggie might be able to help us," said Alan. "This woman is my life. You need to know that."

Marco didn't know what to say.

"You will make me a promise now," Alan said. "It's either that or you leave."

"Ok," said Marco. "What is it?"

"You will give me a vow that you will guard her with your life," said Alan. "If I ever think you are failing in that respect, she and I will leave you behind without a thought."

Alan took another step forward.

"Hey," responded Marco. "Do you know why I insisted you climb out the window first? I was playing interference, trying to buy you time while I faced off Aldryyd." Then I watched you die. "So, yes. I can protect. And if I do it for you I'll certainly do it for her."

Alan turned and began to walk back inside. He was holding an empty glass.

"Good," said Alan. "Your top priority is no longer killing Aldryyd. It's protecting Maggie."

And keeping you away from the painting of the woman in the red dress.

He went back inside, leaving Marco standing alone on the deck. Marco looked up at the dark sky. The air felt heavier. Rain was coming.

Chapter Fifteen

Maggie's Apartment, Cardiff, Wales

"You look uneasy," she said.

He didn't know how to ask and wasn't sure if he could. Alan just sat, slumping in his chair, a half-drunk cup of tea in his hand. Maggie came up next to him, playfully poking him in the side.

"Might as well tell me what's on your mind. You know I'll just annoy it out of you otherwise."

Alan laughed and looked up at her.

"It's just that," he began, "this situation at the mount has proven far more difficult than we're prepared for. And Fisher thought that you might be able to help."

He regretted saying it the moment the smile appeared on her face.

"Yes," said Maggie. "You know I've always been interested in the castle. I'd love a chance to explore it."

Alan turned toward her and put his hands on Maggie's shoulders.

"I need you to understand," he said. "This is dangerous. You could get hurt."

Maggie gave him a small empathetic grin and hugged him. When she withdrew, she spoke again.

"Alan, love. I'm sure it'll be alright because we take care of one another. Don't we?"

He nodded noncommittally.

"I could never forgive myself if..."

Maggie's kiss stopped him mid-sentence. Once again, she withdrew from him, then walked to the other side of the kitchen table, where she picked up a bowl and began eating. Alan drank his tea, and for a minute, neither one spoke.

"There's something more," said Maggie. "I can see it in your face."

Alan laughed. He had never been able to hide anything from her. His efforts to spare her from dealing with his problems always failed. Maggie had a way of finding parts of him that were hidden.

"Let's walk," Maggie said.

She slipped her arm through his, and they went outside into a damp misty morning. They couldn't see much more than a few feet in any direction, the mist separated the two of them from the rest of the world.

"It's this man, Marco," Alan said. "I'm wondering if I've judged him unfairly."

"How so?"

"He kills for money."

Maggie stopped walking.

"He insists that he's different from Aldryyd. That it's only a job he does, nothing more."

"Does he believe that makes him any better than a serial killer?" asked Maggie.

"Aye, I think he does." Alan nodded.

"What do you think?" asked Maggie.

Alan laughed quietly.

"That's what I'm trying to figure out. This man is awful, but I can't see him doing the things that Aldryyd has done. I don't believe he would ever hurt a child."

"I suppose that is better," said Maggie, "but it's like comparing a smaller pile of rubbish to a larger one."

Alan looked her in the eye.

"The crazy thing is that I'm starting to think he may be exactly the one we need."

Maggie brushed a finger along his cheek, then took his hand again. Her tug on his hand prompted Alan to resume walking. She looked up into the misty sky.

"Have you considered, and hear me out, just leaving it all? You don't need to stay attached to that castle," Maggie said.

Alan wasn't exactly shocked by what she said, but the impact of her words was visible on his face as his eyes grew wider. He knew he couldn't do what she suggested. Squeezing her hand tightly, Alan turned toward her.

"That castle is all Fisher has left. I'd be leaving him on his own with a ruin no one cares for and a problem he can't solve. The poor man deserves at least one friend in this world."

"He's a grown man, Alan," said Maggie. "He can take care of himself. You don't have to babysit him."

"That's not what I mean," Alan said. "He's got this fascinating place. A ruin, certainly, but I'd love to see it restored. Wales is filled with large castles for tourists to flock to. But it's these smaller ones, like Morgan's Mount, that truly get us in touch with peoples' history."

"I can see that," Maggie replied. "The Morgans were wealthy but not royal. Closer to the earth, as it were."

"Aye, and closer to the people as well," Alan said, "but that's only the smallest bit of it."

She looked into his eyes.

"Tell me the rest."

"That bloody old ruin, ghosts and all, is our ticket to the life we've been dreaming of. Fisher told me as much. If we can help him save it, he could set us on course to move on to something better."

"Something better?" she asked.

"We could start our lives together."

The words were out before he knew it. She had stopped mid-step and was staring at him. It had been a mistake on his part. He'd never meant to hint at his thoughts. Alan was not carrying the engagement ring but he suddenly felt the weight of it in his mind. She was looking at him with an expectant intensity, and he wanted to propose to her right then.

Not without the ring.

Alan had thought about his proposal endlessly and he wanted it to go perfectly. It wouldn't do to propose without the ring. As difficult as it was, he would have to wait. He lifted her hand to his lips and kissed her finger. He then let go and stepped away.

It was not lost on Maggie that he'd kissed her ring finger.

Chapter Sixteen

Caretaker's Cottage, Morgan's Mount, Wales

As far as Marco was concerned, the only good thing about the cottage was the coffee machine. It was a compact drafty little place constructed of densely packed round stones that failed to hold in heat. He'd drunk three cups of coffee by the time the door opened, and Alan walked in, and he was still shivering. A rush of biting air wafted toward him and was not cut off until another form huddled in behind Alan. As he placed his mug on a table, Marco spotted lengthy blonde hair.

"Hello," said Marco. He stepped forward, offering his hand.

"Just a minute," said Alan. He turned and helped Maggie remove her long coat. "Cold out there today."

Maggie smiled but made no effort to shake hands. She couldn't.

"What's that?" asked Marco, pointing to the bundle in her arms.

"This," she replied, "is Oliver."

Something peeked out from underneath her jacket, and when she placed the jacket on the coat rack, it climbed onto her shoulder. There sat a small orange cat, silently observing the strange new surroundings.

"Please," said Alan, as he stepped toward a small wooden table and pulled out a chair near Maggie. She sat and smiled up at him. Alan sat as well. Oliver maintained his shoulder perch all the while.

"So," began Marco, "I've heard a bit about you, but I didn't know you'd be bringing your little buddy along."

Maggie reached into a bag and withdrew a metal thermos, from which she took a long sip. She then handed it to Alan and placed her hands on the table. She looked like she was exactly where she wanted to be.

"And dear Alan has told me about your situation here at the castle," she said.

"Hey, Al," said Marco. "Maybe we should introduce her…"

Maggie waved a hand in the air.

"I'll be glad to meet Harriet, but it's not necessary. I believe already."

Marco saw a thin smile on her face. Maggie reached up and took Oliver off her shoulder, placing him on the table. The cat was orange with brown stripes that were only visible in strong light. It strolled back and forth on the table, keen eyes taking in everything at once.

"But, gentlemen," she said. "I would like you both to meet our new friend."

Oliver meowed.

"Aye," said Alan. "I meant to ask you when you stepped out of the car. Why have you brought that mangy old cat?"

"He's not mangy," snapped Maggie. "He's my sister's."

Marco could've sworn he heard Alan mutter, "Your mangy sister," as quietly as possible. Maggie didn't notice.

"Many cultures throughout the world," said Maggie, "notably the ancient Egyptians believe that cats are capable of sensing the presence of the paranormal. Our little friend Oliver is here to act as our alarm system."

Marco had no idea whether she was right or plain old-fashioned out of her mind, but these past few days had pushed him into realms of thought he'd never ventured to before. A cat as a warning of ghosts? *Sure. Why not?*

"So, how does Oliver let us know when Aldryyd is coming?"

"I imagine some hissing and spitting going on," replied Alan. "Followed by a wild scamper about the castle in which many fine artifacts will topple and…"

Maggie glared him into silence.

"Ever since Alan told me about this situation, I've been playing the same question over and over in my mind. Why is Aldryyd still here?" Maggie said. "It's a widespread belief that ghosts exist for particular reasons; fear of moving on to whatever comes next, unaccomplished goals, or something they're trying to find."

"So, we need to find out what he wants?" asked Marco. "What if it's something we're not willing to give? Guys like him want the worst."

Maggie stared questioningly at Alan. She received no answer.

"Great," said Marco. "We have an alarm cat and a dead guy with a mysterious goal. None of that changes the fact that he always has eyes on us, and we can't see him most of the time. We need some kind of leverage this time, or he'll get us for sure."

Alan nodded and looked at Maggie.

"I've been thinking about what you said in the car, love. About spirits encased in bodies. "

"It's got to be there," said Maggie. "The spirit cannot be present unless the body is somewhere ne…"

"In the basement," interrupted Alan. "Aldryyd died in the castle basement."

"We go down there and find the body," said Marco. Ok, then,what can we do with it?"
Alan looked dour. He held a placating hand out to Marco before speaking.

"We must not get our hopes too high. Morgan died in a fire, and the body was never recovered. No one cared enough to look. We just don't know what we'll find down there."

"Fair enough," said Marco. "But has anyone got a better idea? I know I don't."

Maggie looked directly at Marco, her green eyes catching the light.

"I won't pretend to be some paranormal expert. I don't think anyone really is. But in thousands of years of world myth and legend, a body-to-spirit connection is an extremely common belief. And I believe that if we find that body, we will finally have the leverage you say we need."

"It makes sense that he wouldn't want anyone messing with his body. Even if we don't believe in this spiritual mumbo-jumbo," said Alan.

"How so?" asked Marco.

"You've looked around the castle a bit. What have you seen? What kind of objects are there?"

Marco mentally replayed the few calm moments when he had not been running for his life through the castle halls.

A lot of sculptures. Hmmm…candlesticks, vases, tapestries, and a lot of paintings," he said.

"Heirlooms," confirmed Alan. "Most of the objects in the castle are left over from Aldryyd's family, and some are just things he had a fondness for. The biggest sculpture in the castle is a gargoyle near the former west tower. It was donated by a family friend in 1861. But most things, like the candelabra, came from the Morgans themselves. The place is rife with Aldryyd's grandfather's old carvings and paintings of his mother."

Marco looked at him quizzically. He crossed his big arms.

"All this tells us what, exactly?"

"He's incredibly sentimental," replied Alan. "Those things are all he has left of his past. I recall one day when a statuette fell off a table and broke loudly on the floor. I heard such a wail as to make me deaf and before I knew it, I was lifted up and thrown out the front door. I did not knock that statue down. It could've been a rat or anything else. Anyway, my point is, that if he causes such an uproar about one little stone carving, imagine the fuss he'd get up to if we had custody of his body."

"He'd fight us harder than ever."

Alan was lost in thought.

"I didn't dare go back to the castle for weeks after that incident," he whispered.

The coffee pot was running low, and Marco simply couldn't allow that, so he walked away from the table and searched the cupboard for new filters. Maggie put an arm around her boyfriend.

"What I often wonder," said Alan, "is why Aldryyd has never killed me. He's frightened me more times than I can count but never truly tried to do me harm."

Maggie stroked his arm.

"I think you've answered your own question, love. He is sentimental, and you're the only one he has to care for all his old stuff. He can't do it himself."

Marco placed the newly ready coffee pot on the burner and returned to the table.

"So," he began, "even after all the killing, the shithead still needs someone to keep house for him?" He sat and drank.

Oliver meowed at the window. The sun was at its zenith.

"I agree with the cat," said Marco. "It's getting late in the day. And although I am caffeinated enough to stay awake for the next week, I prefer to do my underground corpse hunting in the daytime."

Alan stared at him fixedly. "Is the big tough hitman scared?" he asked, laughing a little.

"You're damn right I'm scared," said Marco. "That's why I've managed to live this long."

"If it makes any difference," said Maggie. "I don't think it matters to the ghost whether we come in daytime or night. He doesn't need sleep. And once we enter the mount, we're encroaching on his territory. But I agree with you, Marco. I'd be more comfortable going in the daytime."

Alan stood, and offering his hand to Maggie, helped her out of her chair. As they put on their coats, Alan said, "Tomorrow it is. I have some equipment for us. Shall we say, 9:00?"

Marco agreed. He couldn't stop looking at Oliver perched on the window as if studying the castle outside. His ears were perked up, nose twitching.

"I think he likes it," said Maggie.

"I don't," said Marco. "I think he's studying it now because he thinks it's an enemy. Smart cat."

Gently, he lifted Oliver off of the window sill and handed him to Maggie. He nodded good night and returned to the kitchen table. As he heard the car drive away, he considered the situation; Maggie seemed like she had a good head on her shoulders, and she was full of ideas they hadn't thought of before. That was all good. But, as his old boxing buddies would say, "It's all decided in the ring."

How would she fare tomorrow inside the castle? He finished his last cup of coffee and put it down. Alan, he thought, had proven himself time and time again. Simply having the guts to spend so much time in that building was impressive on its own. But did Aldryyd still value him as he did before?

"No, said Marco aloud. "No predator would tolerate a weaker animal fighting back."

Tomorrow they'd go underground and, hopefully, locate the body and destroy it. He left the cottage, called a taxi, and tried to rest assured of the likelihood of there not being any paintings of women in red dresses in the basement.

Chapter Seventeen

The Basement

"Gloves, the thick woodworking kind. Flashlight, eight plastic bags, that's all we have leftover, and a shovel just in case."

Alan had brought provisions, and Maggie had prepared food. They were going into uncharted territory. There were no maps of the castle basement and not even Alan knew its layout. This had the potential to be a long search.

There was a soft purr.

"Don't forget the cat," said Marco.

Maggie lifted Oliver from the car and held him out to Alan. Alan stepped back.

"I don't want your sister's smelly pet."

"Oh, stop it," said Maggie. "I carried him all day yesterday. It's your turn." She thrust the cat into his arms. He grudgingly accepted. Oliver looked as disappointed as Alan did.

As Marco inspected the flashlight, he asked, "What can you tell us about this place?"

"It's all enclosed," Alan said. "Supposedly, it's a bit of a maze down there. Lots of narrow corridors, poorly lit. I expect numerous side rooms. The body could be in any one or in multiple rooms."

"Exits?" asked Marco.

Alan shook his head. He held out a pair of gloves to Marco. Marco declined.

"Messes with my accuracy."

"Why is that a concern?" asked Alan. "After all, you're not carrying your gun."

A fact that Marco was acutely aware of. The thought of descending into utter darkness with no weapon at all was unnerving. He was heading into the unknown against an enemy he couldn't fight. It was a fear he had not felt before. At least the flashlight was decent, a long solid metal police-man's torch. It would've made a fine club against any other opponent. He tucked it into his belt, Alan struggled with Oliver, and Maggie walked by his side carrying the pack.

They entered the castle and immediately turned right. Just past the kitchen was an old wood-en door, thinner than the others. It was locked, but one light hit with the flashlight cracked its rusted old hook. Marco creaked the door open, and they descended into the castle basement.

"What caused the fire?" whispered Maggie.

A moment passed before Alan realized she was addressing him. He'd been lost in thought. For the first time since beginning his career, he was entering an unfamiliar part of Morgan's Mount, and he felt as though the darkness cast a shadow over his knowledge of the building. The light in front panned left and right. Down the steps. They reached the bottom, and only then did Alan answer.

"Ummm," he began. "Some sort of heating problem, I think. They used gas back then. One spark went awry, and all hell broke loose. I guess it wasn't maintained well. So, Aldryyd went down to fix it, and…"

"Not much of a handyman," said Marco.

"No," said Alan. He gave a nervous laugh.

"Guy kills all those people and dies because of poor heater maintenance?" said Marco. "If that's karma, it's got a sick sense of humor."

A dark hall stretched before them. Outside of the light beam, they could make out shades of black against the gray of the walls. They stepped slowly along the corridor, looking into each room as they advanced, Marco in the lead. One room showed pieces of an old wheelbarrow. Another held remnants of discarded furniture. Most of the rooms were empty. They reached the largest of the rooms and walked inside.

"What do you think?" asked Marco. He shined the flashlight across the ceiling and down the walls.

Alan looked about and nodded, not realizing at first that the others couldn't see him.

"Looks like the most likely spot for a heating system," he said. "Let's look around here."

It didn't take long for them to find old metal bits and washers scattered on the floor. There were fragments all over. Maggie picked up one in particular. She tapped Marco on the shoulder. He shined the light on the object.

"I wouldn't bet my life on it, but I think this is bone," she said as she examined the piece.

"I'm not dumb enough to argue with an anthropologist about what is or isn't bone, so I'll take your word for it," replied Marco.

They began to search the floor in earnest. More rusted metal, a few more chips of bone, but most of the floor was simply caked in dust. Maggie made a noise.

"No," she said. "It's not all dust."

"What is it?" asked Alan. His voice quivered. Oliver meowed grumpily in his arms.

"It's dust mixed with ash."

"Ash?" inquired Alan. "As in human ash?"

"Yes."

"How can we possibly clean all of that up?" asked Marco.

"We can't," Maggie responded. "There's too much. The ashes are inextricably mixed in with the dust by now, and we can't possibly get all of the dust out of here." She hung her head.

"Alright," said Marco. "No point in staying down here if we can't do anything about it. Let's get back to the surface again. We can make a Plan B when we get topside."

They headed back to the main corridor.

"If I'm correct," said Alan, "going further on would've taken us to the intersection of rooms under the first floor. There were pipes that…"

He stopped talking.

The others continued walking back the way they had come, but Alan stood still, staring downward intently.

"Don't go that way," he rushed.

Marco and Maggie turned and followed Alan's gaze. Oliver was climbing onto Alan's arm. The flashlight revealed raised hair on the cat's back, and ears laid flat against his head. Oliver began to hiss loudly.

They followed Alan down the hallway in the opposite direction. Marco cautioned silence but worried it might already be too late. Maggie moved in behind Alan, and they pressed slowly down the corridor. The cat stayed on Alan's arm, hissing incessantly.

As Marco looked behind him, he stretched his arm out to Maggie.

"Here, Maggie. Take the light."

She turned. Then she screamed.

"Run!" Marco shouted.

Maggie and Alan ran off down the corridor. Marco followed, knowing their progress would be slow without the light to guide them. Just as he began to gain speed, he was knocked to the ground. With one hand on the flashlight, he softened the fall by catching a jagged chunk of the broken wall, slicing his hand in the process.

He tried to turn, only to be jarred by an unseen force again. He collapsed to his knees. The flashlight crashed to the floor but did not break. It rolled to the wall and stayed there, glowing lowly to reveal the misty figure of Aldryyd floating above.

Marco's hand had been bloodied on the wall, and he had to roll on his shoulder to look upward. The light of the beam flashed on the deep gray circles of Aldryyd's eyes and the white arm rising above his head. The arm came down, a smoky fist at its end.

Without thinking, Marco raised his bloodied hand in defense. Aldryyd's arm drove toward him, as Marco reached out.

For the first time, Marco thought he could see an expression other than hatred on the ghost's face. He saw confusion. Aldryyd's fist was now tightly in Marco's grip. His reddened hand had caught the spectral arm.

"What?" was all that he had time to say before the ghost wrested his arm free and floated upward. Expecting a second attack, Marco rose slowly to his feet and held his bloody hand out in defense. Aldryyd lingered for a moment, unsure. Then he floated right, and when Marco lunged, he went high and flew off down the corridor, following the others. Marco caught a quick breath, then ran after Aldryyd.

"We're almost at...Ow!" Alan shouted.

Oliver dug his claws tightly into his arm, and Alan dropped him. The cat gave a low growl, then dashed ahead on his own. Alan continued running.

If Maggie had been two inches taller, she would have been the one to fall. However, she passed unknowingly beneath a dangling old steam pipe. She was about to announce that she'd found the intersection when she saw Alan go down. He had lost the cat and looked back for a moment, unaware of the metal danger the darkness had hidden in front of him. She saw him fall before she heard the dull clang of his head on metal.

"Alan!" she cried.

Aldryyd looked down on Alan. The caretaker had been injured, grabbing his head and sluggishly trying to stand up, and Aldryyd wanted to teach him the price of betrayal. But the ghost hesitated. A person had made physical contact with him. That had never happened before. Aldryyd had always been untouchable to the living, but an attack on Alan Basset now would leave him directly in the path of the man who'd done the impossible. Aldryyd Morgan would never admit to feeling fear, but he didn't move, his formless body refusing to go toward Marco.

Aldryyd looked down the corridor in the direction Maggie had gone. She did not know the castle, and her death would devastate the historian. He flew swiftly after her.

As hard as he ran, Marco was gaining little ground and watched from down the dark corridor as Aldryyd passed Alan by and flew straight toward Maggie. She had no time to think. With Alan holding his head in his hands, Maggie was left with no choice but to run off down the corridor. Alone.

Marco caught up to Alan, who reported that his head was swimming, but his consciousness was clear. He stood as if he were being tossed about on a ship and could not right himself despite his efforts. His questioning was incessant. Where was Aldryyd? Was he coming down on them at that moment? Where was Maggie? Alan tried to steady himself against the wall.

"Al! Hey, Al!"

Alan snapped to attention, only to find that he had slid halfway down the wall. Marco had hold of his lapels, pulling him back to his feet.

"What's…where's Maggie?" asked Alan.

"Don't worry," said Marco. He grabbed Alan's head in his hands, turning it side to side. "No blood. You're ok, buddy. You just got a bit rocked, that's all."

When Alan's eyes focused on one spot, Marco felt it was safe enough to let go. Alan shrugged once and slowly stood up.

"Where's…where's…"

"I don't know," said Marco. He regretted it as soon as it was out of his mouth.

"You don't…you do…" Alan stammered. "We've got to find her! Where is she?"

Alan was shouting and pacing back and forth in the darkness. It was still possible that his head had suffered severely from the crash but Marco couldn't be sure. He only knew that Alan's craziness would make matters worse.

"Listen," he said.

"No! Where is she?" shouted Alan. "You promised to protect her. You said it. And now you…"

"Look, Alan," replied Marco. "You need to calm down."

It was the wrong thing to say. Alan advanced quickly.

"You worthless scum," he said. "She's lost, and you did nothing! Maggie! Maggie!" His cries grew as he paced the intersection.

Maggie was alone and in immediate danger. There was no time for a breakdown now. Marco grabbed Alan by the back of the head and jerked his face toward him.

"Listen," Marco said as quietly as he could manage. "Losing your mind does not help her. You need to get back to smart-guy mode right now and listen. I'm serious. Shut up and listen for any sounds that will tell us which way she went."

That got through. Alan nodded then Marco released his grip. Alan backed up to the middle of the intersection, head raised high, like an animal wary of predators. He remained silent as Marco shined the light along the floor. There was a thick layer of dirt and dust over the stones below their feet. When he pointed the light down the right corridor there was nothing out of the ordinary, only the same widespread dust cover. He pointed the flashlight down the other corridor. Immediately, the light showed a large smear in the dirt at the corner of the intersection. Marco tapped Alan on the shoulder and pointed down the left corridor.

"They went this way," he said.

She'd gone left twice and right once, or so she'd thought. Maggie wasn't sure anymore. Everything was twists and turns, and she had no light to help her. All she knew was that she had to keep moving. The ghost was always there, just around the corner, chasing her like a cat toying with a mouse in a black maze. She dashed across a hallway, bumped into a wall, and turned the other way. She ran down another hall. Aldryyd was flying toward her. Maggie backstepped and sprinted to a corridor she had passed before. As Aldryyd approached, she saw a crack of light in the wall six feet above the ground. Without slowing, she rammed her way through the space of the door and into a small room. She stopped and looked left, then right. He was floating up behind her, and she had no idea how to get out.

At the opposite end of the room, a door flew open. She hadn't seen it at first. A large disused furnace was in the way. She ran straight for it, and Aldryyd followed. Beyond the doorway was a staircase. It spiraled upward. She began to ascend. Aldryyd pondered for a moment. He had an idea.

The men were far behind. They'd been checking corridor after corridor, room after room, but the trail had gone cold. Marco could not find any indication of Maggie's direction. Alan began his frantic pacing again, his previous madness threatening to reappear. Marco leaned against a wall, his mind reeling. Then he heard a soft sound. He stepped over to the next hallway to see. A moment later, he walked back to Alan.

"Come see this," he said.

The two men walked together to the nearby hall. They both stood, staring down the hallway at the calmly waiting cat. Oliver was sitting and looking up at them.

"I thought he ran away," said Alan.

Oliver walked a short distance down the hallway and sat again, staring at them.

"This is going to sound crazy," Marco began, "but I think the cat knows which way to go."

Alan posed no argument. He was lost in emotion. Marco took his arm and led him down the hallway, following Oliver.

The cat led them straight for a few minutes, then turned right. After a short walk in that direction, he sped up. It seemed to Marco that Oliver was running toward something he would enjoy finding. The men had to go faster just to keep up. Oliver stopped short of another intersection and ran through an open door. Marco and Alan walked in. Alan stopped in front of a large, worn old furnace while Marco kept watching the cat as he ran to the opposite side of the room and leaped into a pair of small white arms.

"Good kitty," Harriet said as she stroked Oliver's soft fur. Oliver luxuriated in her ghostly touch. Alan had finally seen her.

"Harriet!" he shouted in excitement. "Where is…?"

She cowered at the intensity of his voice but responded nonetheless. She pointed to the stairway and spoke one meek word.

"Up."

Alan sprinted to the stairway. As he followed, Marco offered "Thank you" as quickly as he could. The men disappeared up the stairway, and Harriet remained below, petting Oliver, her new friend. She hadn't seen a kitty for many years. She didn't know how long. Oliver was content to relax in her arms, but she found that she could not keep her mind off of the current situation.

"Kitty," she said. "What will happen in the castle?"

***

Maggie's lungs were burning, her legs leaden. The staircase was a tight spiral filled with old shallow stone steps. She ran ever uphill, with the ghost gaining from behind. He did not need to run, and he didn't tire. He floated closer, and she saw something. It was an opening and she registered a moment too late that it was an exit to the first floor of the castle. It would've been a way out, a way to an exit or a hiding place. But she had passed it. An attempt to leave the staircase now would bring her into direct contact with Aldryyd. As she continued her upward run, she would escape to the second floor, if the staircase presented an opportunity.

***

"Oh," said Alan.

"What," said Marco mid-run.

"I know…where this…goes," puffed Alan.

"Where?" Marco asked.

"It's the…" Alan was having difficulty talking during the steep run up the steps. "Old staircase. Goes to…East tower."

Marco thought about that.

"Shit," he said.

"What?" puffed Alan.

"Don't you get it, Al? He's leading her there like a sheepdog. There's no exit from the East tower. Once she's there, it's a…" he barely avoided saying dead end, "trap."

"No!" said Alan. "Couldn't she exit onto one of the floors?"

Marco was silent for a moment.

"If I were Aldryyd," he said, "I wouldn't give her the chance."

***

The second-floor exit had to be close by. With all the turning and rising on the steps, it was difficult for Maggie to judge distance but she considered the height difference between the windows on the outside of the castle and figured that her second chance at an escape was coming soon. It would hurt her exhausted legs to make a run for it, but there was no choice. She had to get out of that stairway. She looked up and saw the steps ahead. There were two whole steps followed by a larger flat one and light emanating from an unseen source to her right. She sped up and ran for the second-floor exit.

Aldryyd had been expecting it. He swiftly floated in front of her. She stopped and tried to sidestep him, but he lashed out, hitting her shoulder. She spun. He swung at her again but missed. She was faster than he'd expected. However, he was easily able to shut out all her attempts to pass him. In the end, he left her no choice but to retreat into the stairway. Aldryyd silently congratulated himself on returning the woman to his trap.

Upon her return to the steps, Maggie slipped and banged her knee.

"Try again."

It was the voice of a child.

Maggie found herself shaking her head as if testing it to make sure it still functioned properly. It felt like the voice was speaking straight into her ear. She was slowing down, and Aldryyd had gained considerable ground. It would not be long before he caught hold of her shirt or her hair. The voice wanted her to try again. She would appease it.

After what felt like an eternity, the exit for the third floor came, and Maggie ran. Aldryyd moved to get in her way and she wondered if she had the speed to rush past him. He rose to face her.

A long object came hurtling through the air and Aldryyd could not move away in time. It passed unimpeded through his chest and clattered onto the floor below. Curiosity overtook him as he looked back and saw an old-fashioned hobby horse lying near the stairway entrance. Its aged brown face looked up at him with a taunting eye. At first, he didn't understand, but when he looked back toward the third floor, it became clear. The woman had been able to make a mad dash out to the floor while he'd been distracted. He laughed. The little trick didn't matter. Aldryyd saw as the woman unknowingly turned away from the direction of the grand staircase and tried to hide in the old library. He'd catch her soon enough.

Maggie ran into the room and shut the door behind her. She had no idea which part of the castle this was, but it felt great to be out of the stairway. Her aching legs needed the' rest. Something had happened back there. The voice. Then something had attacked Aldryyd, although she hadn't seen what it was. She'd been too busy sprinting to the safest spot she could find.

The first thing she noticed in her new hideout was a large wooden table on the far side of the room. It was covered with a mess of books and candles. There were high shelves with books around the room's perimeter. On a smaller table, she saw some old mariner's maps and assorted papers. Near the room's two large windows was a gold-framed painting of an old woman with a bouffant hairdo. It was the most prominent object of all. She had just enough time to acknowledge the lack of doors before she saw that her predicament was not over.

Doors were no problem for Aldryyd. He seeped through to the other side. Maggie watched in frightened awe as his white shape slowly emerged in the room. Upon entering, he floated upward and seemed to wait for a moment, if only to lengthen her fearful anticipation.

She looked quickly around, knowing she hadn't seen any other doors the first time. There were books, candles, papers, and an assortment of old junk lying around. Otherwise, there were only the two large windows and that painting. That hideous painting of the old woman.

Maggie tore the painting from the wall and held it in front of her like a shield.

He's sentimental.

"I'll break it," she threatened. "I swear I will." Her voice was shaking. The picture was large and unwieldy.

The ghost's gray eyes grew smaller, pinpoints of anger.

"Fy mam," he said.

She was right. It was a painting of his mother.

"Yeah," she said, feeling a bit more confident. "Don't you come over here, or I'll break precious mommy."

His anger was palpable, and she doubted her plan would buy her much time. She had to get out of the room. Even with the painting held hostage, Maggie did not think she could reach the door behind him. The only way out was through the window. She inched slowly over to the nearest window and was silently thankful that it was so large.

As the ghost glared on, she discovered a latch on the windowsill. She tried to hit it. Aldryyd made a move, and she held out the picture, directly above her knee.

The ruse worked, and he did not charge.

Struggling with the large picture, while fumbling with the window latch proved difficult. She couldn't drop it or risk putting it down. It was her lifeline. Her arms were heavy with effort.

Finally, the window snapped open. She managed to swing one leg up onto the window sill and sat back as far as she could. As soon as she dropped the painting, she had to be up and out of the window as quickly as possible. Maggie breathed deeply.

"Here!" she roared as she tossed the painting across the room.

She didn't see the painting fall, nor did she witness Aldryyd's frantic dive to catch it. The sound of breaking glass was nothing more than distant background noise as Maggie planted her left leg onto the windowsill and stood. She had to shuffle her feet minutely to get away from the open window without falling. The windowsill was large and allowed her space to stand.

As she looked at the top of the window frame, she felt something brush roughly against her foot.

Alan had told her that the ghost was incapable of leaving the castle. He'd been mostly correct. White arms were swiping at her feet from inside the library, and for a moment, she was falling backward. She had to grab onto the open window for support. It was a heavy window, but it swung wide as she dangled from it, far away from his searching arms.

Hanging allowed her a brief respite, but her arms were growing tired from gripping so tightly. She would need to move as soon as she could. Maggie looked to her left, past the windows and the room where Aldryyd still waited. That way was not an option. She looked right. There was another set of windows, but she did not dare try to get to them. Even on the slim chance that she made it there, Aldryyd was bound to be waiting somewhere nearby.

She looked down.

There was a sheer sixty-foot drop between her window and the hard cobblestones below. An experienced rock climber would've been able to identify handholds and footholds along the way, but Maggie could not. She saw only uneven stone walls with bumps and occasional cracks. A climb down was a risk she could not take.

She looked up.

Above the window frame was a small stone ledge. It continued around the perimeter of the castle and was the seat for the gargoyles she had seen that morning. One gargoyle, a squat, sour-faced creature, sat glaring out at the forest beyond. That was her only option. She had to go up.

There was no more time to rest. She managed to hook one foot onto the crosspiece in the center of the window. Kicking out the glass would have provided more of a hold, but she did not think she was capable of such a feat. Maggie pulled herself up the side of the window frame while pushing upward with her foot on the crosspiece, her right leg swinging freely.

She stood on the top half of the window, both hands gripping the corner tightly. She allowed herself to briefly lay her head on her hands before the last push of the climb.

There was a creaking sound. The window hinges were giving way.

Maggie had years of experience walking through excavation sites for hours at a time, and she'd gained the arm strength of a frequent digger, but as she readied herself for the next move, she heartily wished she'd spent all that time in the local rock gym. She planted her right foot on the crosspiece with her left, the window now bearing her full weight. Biceps straining, she pulled herself up as far as she could. A hinge snapped as she jumped.

It had not been quite as far as she'd thought from below. Her left hand banged painfully against the gargoyle's side, but she bore the pain and held on, right hand firmly gripping a stone wing. Maggie hung from the statue, unable to reach any kind of foothold. She kicked out to gain momentum and tried not to think about the drop below. Her left foot swung toward the statue and bounced off. With the remaining momentum, she forced herself to try again, and this time, she hooked her leg around the gargoyle's arm.

The gargoyle was a solid grumpy piece of stone salvation. Its downturned mouth showed a couple of sharp teeth peeking out the side.

Maggie hugged it out of necessity and kissed it out of gratitude.

"You're gorgeous," she told it as she planted her right foot on the statue.

She gave one final jump and rolled over the lip of crenellation onto the castle roof. There was only one more thing to do. Collapse. Everything hurt; her legs, arms, gut, and her bruised hand, but none of it mattered. She was on the roof, officially out of the mount, where Aldryyd could not go. It was the safest place she'd been since entering the castle. She'd be content to spend the next year resting right in that spot.

As she studied the gray sky, she heard a crack of thunder. The world darkened around her and rain started to pour steadily down. It spattered the castle roof, and she saw no cover to run to. So, she stayed, lying near her gargoyle friend, laughing half from joy and half from madness as the water quickly pooled around her.

***

Marco exited the castle first.

"Let's check over here," he said, walking to the east side of the castle.

They'd indulged their worst fear first and headed straight to the tower where they'd seen no sign of activity. On the way down, Alan had spotted Harriet's hobby horse on the landing and remarked about how strange it was for her to leave her toys lying around like that. They had taken it as a sign and searched the third floor. Marco had noticed the library with its closed door and gone inside. The broken painting on the floor and open window prompted him to look outside, hoping not to see her body on the stones below. After that, they'd immediately rushed outside.

"Maggie!" shouted Alan.

The rain picked up, and their shouting had to keep up with it. Marco looked for any sign of a fall; blood on the ground, broken bushes, anything at all. Alan was bent on shouting, and it kept him occupied. With each passing second, Marco's fear of finding Maggie's broken body somewhere outside the castle grew.

"Maggie!"

"Hey!"

Alan looked toward the voice and smiled brightly. The look on Alan's face told Marco everything he needed to know. He looked up and waved at the soaked woman on the roof.

"Would one of you gentlemen be so kind as to lend a lady an umbrella?" Maggie asked.

Chapter Eighteen

The Hotel

"Good day, sir."

Marco heard the voice and did a double-take as he walked through the hotel door. A squat woman of about sixty years old sat beaming at him behind the front desk. She stood and held something out to him formally, using two hands.

"Message for you, sir."

Marco reached out and took it. He nodded his thanks and walked up the stairs.

"It sounded urgent, sir. He wants you to call right back," she shouted as he walked away.

Out of curiosity, Marco stopped halfway up the steps and unfolded the paper. The message was short: **4:47 PM, Marco: call Harris**. He made his way up to the room, sat on the bed to take off his shoes, and stopped for a moment. This situation was getting crazier by the minute. He couldn't recall any job that had been more complicated than this one. Before finding out what Harris wanted, he needed to catch his breath.

His mind wouldn't let him rest. It spun with memories and speculation: Running through the corridors searching for Maggie, wondering if they were too late. Alan's temporary madness in the basement. What could Harris possibly want? That and more nagged at him as he lay on the bed. He had never been a man who was able to sit still when there was work to be done, so he grudgingly sat up, picked up the phone, and dialed. Harris picked up quickly.

"Hey," said Marco. "What's up?"

"I have good news, my young friend," said Harris's old man rasp. "Remember your dilemma we discussed in Boston?"

"Of course."

"Turns out that situation is now resolved," Harris began. "The whole thing has been pinned on a man seen leaving the scene a few hours before the incident was discovered."

"Who?"

"A man named Robinson," said Harris.

Marco remembered well. Stuart Robinson was nothing but a down-on-his luck guy who'd played cards with seedy people. How could anyone think he was a killer?

"He didn't do it, Harris," Marco said. "Robinson left before."

"I'm sure he did," said Harris. "But that's not the point. The point is that you're in the clear to come on home."

Marco remained lost in silent thought.

"Marco?"

"Robinson doesn't deserve what's coming to him," said Marco. "He's just a poor gambler who was in the wrong place that night."

"It already came to him. He was killed in prison last night. Hanged with a bedsheet."

Marco was in shock for a moment.

"They got him," he said. "Corolla's buddies."

"It certainly seems that way," said Harris.

No one spoke until Harris broke the long silence.

"So, when do you plan to return? Are you about finished in Wales?"

"No," replied Marco. "Things here are more complicated than I thought they'd be."

"Do you plan to finish it? I promise Martin Fisher is a man of his word. You will be paid."

Marco didn't know how to explain things. He'd been hired to kill an unkillable man. The money was great, but for the first time in his life, he wasn't sure he could finish the job. He had no answer to Harris's question and simply said "Bye", then hung up the phone. He sat on the hotel bed, thinking.

Stuart Robinson, an innocent man, had been killed in prison for something he'd done. Many people had died by Marco's hand, but this was different. It struck him in a way no other death had. This was an unintentional killing brought on by his failure to cover his own tracks. Robinson had never been guilty of anything more than being unlucky. Despite his years as a hitman, the death of a truly innocent man bothered Marco. He couldn't accept it.

Alan is an innocent man.

The Trips came and went as they saw fit; Marco couldn't control them. He'd tried in the past and unequivocally failed every time, but he still questioned whether or not he'd ever be able to thwart them. Alan didn't deserve to die any more than Stuart Robinson did. The Corollas and Morgans of the world deserved what he gave them. The Robinsons and Bassets should be left to grow into their eighties and die in their sleep with wives by their sides in their own cozy homes.

The idea of leaving came to him. The vision of Alan's death couldn't possibly come true if Marco wasn't there. Every vision he'd ever had featured something he was there to witness when the time arrived. All he had to do was get on a plane and leave the job unfinished, and it might be enough to save Alan's life. There was only one problem with that thought.

It would mean he'd have to forgo the second half of the money.

Harris said that Robinson's death had wrapped up the investigation in Philadelphia and that Marco was free to return home. He believed Harris; the old man didn't lie about such things. The jobs would be available back home just as they always were, and he could pick up where he left off. He no longer needed Fisher's money to hide out long-term. Still, he wanted it all the same.

After years of spending many of his days and almost all of his nights in the company of the world's worst people, Marco felt he deserved something more than the occasional paycheck. He was finally getting paid what he was truly worth, and it was about damn time.

He stood up and walked to the window. A glass sat on a tall table by the windowsill in the shadow of a bottle of whiskey. Marco picked up the bottle and poured it into the glass. He drank deeply, and the warmth spread throughout him. His breath came in slow, easy puffs.

What did he really owe Alan? A warning, certainly. But he was not about to give up the biggest score he'd ever been offered for a man he hardly knew. He couldn't even be sure the vision would come true. Could he? Perhaps there was a chance that the Trips would be wrong about this one.

They've never been wrong before.

He filled the glass again and sat by the window, overlooking the bay. Distant boats hauled in their daily catch. Far away, fog rolled in, and ships raced away from it, hoping to make the bay before it ensnared them. It was both serene and ominous. He tried to lose his thoughts in the fog, hoping it would blind him to the possibility that he was enabling the death of another innocent man.

Chapter Nineeen

Alan's Apartment, Cardiff, Wales

The rain hadn't stopped. The gray weather had continued throughout the day, pelting Alan's deck relentlessly. The sky was the shade of old steel, and small puddles sought entrance into the flat. For now, the glass door was keeping them at bay, but Alan worried about water damage. He'd been running back and forth, plugging the doorway with towels then rushing to the kitchen to prepare the tea. Marco and Maggie sat by the door, staring out at the speeding raindrops.

"Lemon?" Alan asked.

Maggie and Marco said yes.

"I've been trying to figure something out," said Marco. "I'm hoping you can help me."

Maggie looked at him. Inquisitive.

"There was a moment this morning. He came after me, and I made contact with him. I mean that I actually caught his arm in my hand."

She leaned toward him; her eyes wider than before.

"I have no idea how it happened," Marco said. "I just know that I fell, cut my hand, and then he was on me."

"You couldn't touch him before?" asked Maggie.

Marco shook his head.

"Curious," Maggie said. "What was different about this time? Consider the factors: environment, time, your condition. What had changed?"

Marco nodded and sat in thought for a moment.

"We were under the castle, so that was a location change. It was the earliest we'd gone in, so, different time, and I was wounded. Otherwise, I just don't know."

"Which hand did you catch his arm with?" asked Maggie.

"My right."

She pointed at the bandage on his hand.

"It was bleeding, wasn't it?" She didn't wait for an answer. "Blood. Maybe that's the reason."

"Why would that…" he left it unfinished, intrigued by the look on her face.

"Blood is the essence of life," she began. "Without it the body cannot function, therefore, the more blood you lose, the closer to death you get."

"Is this another one of those cultural beliefs of the Yadayada people of Whateverland?"

"No," laughed Maggie. "Think of it like this. In all of the vampire stories vampires drink blood, right? They do that because it's like drinking life itself. If you lose your blood, you lose your life, and in that moment, when you caught Aldryyd's arm, you were just a bit closer to death than usual. At least, your right hand was."

Marco looked out the window, lost in thought for a moment. He silently stared as the raindrops pelted down on the porch. The rain was picking up speed.

"Do you think that a ghost can touch another ghost?" he asked. "Since they're both dead."

"Yes, I do," she said.

"Harriet is in trouble," Marco said. "Aldryyd will punish her for what she did today."

They had told Maggie about the help Harriet had given her that morning and she was frightened by Marco's words. She had never even met the ghost girl but feared for her safety.

"But," she began, "he couldn't possibly kill her. Could he?"

"He wouldn't have to kill her to punish her," Marco said. "Besides, figuring out how to 'kill' a ghost is what I've been thinking about all along. This thing about the blood has my head spinning. Maybe we can use it."

Alan walked over with teacups on a tray. He handed one to Maggie, one to Marco, then sat on the couch beside Maggie. He took a sip, then gestured to Marco.

"I heard that last bit," Alan said. "Harriet is brilliant at hiding. There are places she can go that Aldryyd would never make it to. Plus, she has Oliver with her. And, as we know, that stupid feline actually did prove useful as a warning system."

Maggie punched his shoulder.

"But eventually," insinuated Marco.

"Aye," agreed Alan. "Eventually. Harriet can't hide forever, and Aldryyd certainly knows what she did to help Maggie. Which does not give us much time."

"Not much time until when?" asked Maggie.

"Until we have to go back in," said Marco. "Because I think Harriet is in trouble. Because I think ghosts can touch other ghosts."

"As do I," said Alan. "What do we do next time? We need a new plan."

Marco nodded to Maggie.

"You just gave one to me."

They sat calmly for a while, drinking their tea and discussing lesser matters like shopping and weather. It failed to take their minds off of their predicament. It wasn't long before Maggie declared herself exhausted and walked off to take a nap. Marco was glad. He didn't want her here for this conversation.

"There's something I need to tell you," said Marco. "I didn't tell you before because I didn't think it would matter in the basement."

"Look, Marco," said Alan. "You're a lovely man, but I just don't feel that way about you."
He laughed.

"Shut up," said Marco, unamused. "This is absolutely serious. It's about what I saw in my vision the other day."

Alan clammed up and sat back in his chair, curiosity plain on his face.

"I saw…" Marco began. Then he stopped.

How do you tell a man that you saw him die?

It had to be done. Marco began again.

"I don't know which part of the castle it was in, but there is a place I don't want you to go. I saw something bad happen to you there."

"Which part?" asked Alan. He seemed to be taking it seriously, which heartened Marco a little.

"I just know that it was sort of a dark hallway, and there was a painting on the wall with a woman in a fancy red dress."

Alan nodded.

"Second floor," Alan said. "The painting is of Lillian Morgan going to a ball."

Good. He knew the place.

"You've got to promise me you won't go near it," said Marco. "Better yet, don't go back into the castle at all."

Alan sipped his tea and sat in silence for a moment. When he was finished, he placed the empty cup on the table and shook his head.

"I thought we already had this conversation," said Alan. "This matter means more to me than it does to you. I am going back to the mount whether you approve or not. Especially since Maggie is involved now. Your help is invaluable, but you can't be everywhere at once, and whatever theory you may be developing, the fact is that you still don't know how to stop Aldryyd. So, at this point, I'd say that Maggie is just as safe with me as with you. You don't think I'll leave my girlfriend behind, do you?

"Ok," said Marco. "I get it. But I at least need you to promise me to stay out of that area."

"Fine," agreed Alan.

A crash of thunder followed the word. The storm had moved beyond simple rain.

"Are your visions ever wrong?" asked Alan. "Do they always...come true?"

Marco thought about the question.

"They act as sort of a warning system for me. I think they show me what will happen if I don't respond appropriately. The trick is that I don't always know what I need to do to change it."

"Well," said Alan. "Thank you for telling me. And I will heed your warning."

"What else could I have done?" asked Marco.

"What else could you have done?" asked Alan. This time, the question was rhetorical.

With this, Marco stood. He waved goodbye and walked outside to call a taxi. Alan sat in silence, staring at the half-open bedroom door where Maggie slept. He thought of her in there, with the blanket pulled all the way up to her chin, the way she always slept. He considered joining her, instead, he just sat and reached into his pocket. His fingers found the ring box, and gripped it tightly.

The taxi pulled into the hotel around nine. Marco said hello to the receptionist and went upstairs to his room. He sat and removed his jacket. The pouring rain obscured the view of the hills outside his window.

He slipped off his shoes, then knelt next to his suitcase. As he opened it Marco began to think about the envelope Fisher had given him. It was safely stashed away, and he'd counted every pound. Fisher had paid as promised. What was to stop him from leaving? The money was all there, and no one would get in his way if he simply left.

As he took the plastic container out of the suitcase, he thought about Alan. That stubborn fool would be sure to go back to the castle even without him around. He'd get himself killed and Maggie right beside him.

Marco reached for the box he'd brought from the store. He took the package off the bed and unwrapped it. He threw the wrapping in the trash can, grabbed the container, and walked into the bathroom.

There were professional reasons to stay: mainly, the job wasn't done. There was, however, another reason. He was curious. For the first time since arriving in Wales, he had the feeling that he was on the right track. The ghost had seemed to be genuinely intimidated by him last time.

He rinsed out the plastic container and placed it on the sink. Then, he put his left arm across the sink and held the syringe in his right hand.

Alan would go back in, he was sure of it. As Marco lowered the syringe, he realized that he'd already decided to stay. Men like Alan didn't deserve to die. After all, Alan himself had declared that Marco's priorities had changed from killing to protecting.

The syringe slipped in gently. Marco squeezed down on it, and it pumped full of blood in a second. He withdrew the needle and wrapped it tightly before disposing of it. After pouring the blood into the container, he capped it, then put a band-aid over the pinprick on his arm. He placed the container on the table.

He walked back into the bedroom and switched on the TV. As he lay back on the bed, a game show came on. Men and women were answering embarrassing questions about one another, and it was mildly amusing. He rested his arm on the pillow and decided to call Alan in the afternoon. That should give him enough time to recover.

Chapter Twenty

The Car

They sat in the car as the rain blasted the windshield. Marco told them his idea, and they nodded along, not sure what to think. They promised not to allow themselves to get separated this time. Their mission would serve two purposes: an attack on Aldryyd and a search for Harriet.

"I knew a guy," said Marco. "Big guy named Cyrus. We were in the same business."

Alan and Maggie leaned in from the back seat.

"Cyrus used to mess with his marks. Torture. He'd talk about a guy's family as he died or make a guy eat his own fingers as he chopped them off. Real horror movie shit."

Maggie recoiled.

"Anyway," Marco continued, "I never could figure out why he did that stuff. The job doesn't call for it. You do what you need to do, then you walk away and get paid."

"What's your point?" asked Alan.

"My point," replied Marco, "is that I think Aldryyd is like Cyrus. He just likes it. What if the only reason he stays in the castle is so he can continue the killing?"

Maggie shivered as though hit by sudden cold. Alan put his arm around her, and she changed the subject to the first thing that came to mind.

"What about Harriet? Why would she stay?"

"Fear," said Alan. "She's still a little girl. She's afraid to move on alone. This castle is all she knows."

"But she's trapped in this place with…him," said Maggie. "Forever."

"I don't get it," said Marco. "She's been here for two centuries, and in all that time, she never tried going outside once?"

Alan leaned back and folded his hands on his lap, a historian in his element. "Let me explain the situation."

***

She woke to the sound of rustling. Casting a look around the chamber, she saw the white curtains were still. The noise was coming from beyond her bedroom door.

Mother.

The girl quickly donned her softest slippers and opened the door to find her mother wearing her blue robe, posed in mid-knock. Mother smiled down at her and announced that breakfast was being served in ten minutes. The girl went back inside to change. She took a moment to enjoy the view of the forest far below her window. The mass of trees was endless. She wanted to run out into it to see how far she could go, but it was time for breakfast, and it wouldn't do to be late.

As she walked downstairs, she tried to recall all of the red things in the tapestries on the bottom level of the castle. It was a challenge Father had given her. She thought it was a memory game.

The tall man was at breakfast again. It was the third day this week he'd dined with them. He dressed in the fine clothes of nobility but his brown beard never quite fit in with his clothes. It looked unkempt. Shaggy. He always kept his hair short, and it contrasted with the beard.

Having repeated all of the red objects in the tapestries from memory, father congratulated her on a job well done. He issued a new challenge. Now she was to count all of the statues on the entire property. It would take some time. There were statues around every corner.

As Mother joined them at the dining table, the tall man said something the girl couldn't understand. Father stared at the man with disgust. They exchanged heated words in Welsh. She did not understand. The language was unfamiliar to her, much like the castle she lived in. The past few days had made her doubt that she could ever feel at home in this place. It was overwhelmingly gray. A cold place.

Father stood, slamming his fist down on the table, his face going red. The tall man did not react. His eyes remained expressionless. Mother took

Father's offered hand and stood to walk with him. She was beckoning the girl to follow when a clatter interrupted her. Turning toward the sound, the girl could see the table crashing to the floor, plates and ceramics sliding and shattering on heavy stone. The tall man stood. He kicked the table aside and walked over to her parents.

Her mother ran to her side and took her hand. The girl was pulled along behind as Mother began to rush up the staircase. They had only just turned the first corner when a loud bang resonated off the walls around them. It came from below. Mother put the girl in her room, closed the door, and told her to hush. The girl would've done so if her mother had not walked out into the corridor, letting go of her hand. She called out, but Mother didn't return. Through a crack in the door, the girl saw her mother walk toward the second-floor landing and look down at the dining room. Mother's scream was the loudest thing she'd ever heard in her eight years of life; a nightmare's song. She watched as mother dropped to her knees, wailing.

A flash of scarlet outside her door. The tall man. He paused for a moment, as though he considered something, decided against it, and continued down the corridor. The man walked to the landing. To her mother.

She watched as he walked up behind her sobbing mother. She watched as the man wrapped his hands around her mother's neck. She watched as her mother tried and failed to scream. By the

147

time he let go, the girl had looked away. She didn't see the moment her mother stopped moving.

As she sobbed into her pillow, scarlet showed up at her door once again. A creak told her the door had been opened. The girl turned as a large hand reached towards her.

***

302, including the gargoyles on the roof, this was the total number of statues in the mount. She had counted them all just as Father wanted. There was no doubt in her mind that he would've assigned her another task, so she decided to complete one of her own design. She would learn the names of all the children that had lived in this place before.

The tall man came to her again and again. Days passed. They got worse. Crying was no use, so she stopped. She continued her projects of exploring her new home because daddy would want her to. One of Mother's old dresses provided good material for new curtains, so she cut them and hung them up in her room.

On her last day, the girl was hoping to complete her task of finding all of the mouseholes the castle contained. She was exiting the greenhouse when his shadow loomed across her path. His legs were so long that he caught up with two steps. She was still trying to run when he lifted her off the ground.

As he lifted her, she heard a strange noise. A squeak. There was a mouse nearby. That meant there was an undiscovered hole near the green-house. She had to find it—had to complete the tasks like daddy wanted her to. The man was in-terfering. She hadn't seen what he'd done to Fa-ther, but in a deep part of her that she didn't like tapping into, she knew he'd done the same thing he'd done to Mother. The look on Mother's face as the breath was squeezed out of her would nev-er leave the girl's mind. And now he was deny-ing her the mouse! The girl fought and kicked, but the man's grip was unbreakable. For the first time, her fear melted away. Her vision went red, and she screamed a challenge at him, while she twisted her tiny body and scratched as hard as she could. His shout hit her at point-blank range. She was already flying through the air before she noticed the new-ly-opened gash below his eye. When she crashed through the glass of the greenhouse's front door, she wondered where the mouse had gone.

The girl had no recollection of hitting the ground. In time, her memories of coming to as formless smoke began to fade. She learned about her new self and continued her projects. Not know-ing why her parents hadn't stayed behind as she had, the girl passed each day trying to make them proud so they'd be happy when they returned from wherever they had gone.

The front door of the castle would occa-sionally speak to her in whispers. It wasn't Welsh. It wasn't any language she could identify, but it spoke all the same. The door wanted to be opened by her. But her parents had brought her here. Perhaps if she stayed in this new form, and diligently continued her exploration of the castle, they would return. They would take her with them to wherever they had gone so long ago.

Then one day, the tall man became like her. He could hurt her all over again. The days passed. They got worse.

* * *

"That's what she told me," Alan finished.

Maggie and Marco looked at one another.

Alan sighed and peered out the car window. "I've wondered for so long what happened to her parents. Why didn't they stay in the castle with their daughter when they died?"

"Shitty parents, abandoning a kid like that," said Marco.

"No," said Alan. "I don't believe that. I think perhaps they went to look for her outside, hoping she'd escaped. She was fond of the woods, after all. Then, they learned the tragic fact that they were unable to reenter the mount once they'd left."

"Do you think that's how Aldryyd learned not to leave the castle?" asked Marco.

"Yes," said Alan. "I think that's exactly what happened. But we can't forget the biggest reason he refuses to leave. In his mind, the mount is his, and that everyone else is a trespasser. He believes he's protecting his property."

Chapter Twenty-One

Morgan's Mount, Wales

Marco checked the bandage on his hand. It was dry and well-wrapped. "Alright," he said. "We're staying together this time. No splitting up. We follow Alan's list of Harriet's hiding spots, and if we encounter Aldryyd along the way, we'll see if this theory is any good or not. Ready?"

There was no response, so Marco opened the door and got out of the car. The others followed, and they walked together to the castle door. It was a moment before Alan's soaked hands undid the lock, but they made their way inside and stepped into the gloomy main room.

The first place on their list was the greenhouse. Alan said that Harriet loved remembering all the flowers that had once been there and that she would stand for hours on end staring out of the glass at the outside world as though she wanted to be part of it again. It was a small edifice and they left after a short search.

Next came the master bedroom. Harriet's parents, English nobility, had stayed in the room during their short time at the mount. Alan thought that Harriet liked to curl up in the bed and pretend the pillows were her mother and father.

There was no sign of her. They turned back and walked into the hallway. Marco had brought cheese along to throw down in hopes of attracting Oliver. Perhaps he could lead them to the girl as he'd done before. He had not shown up and as he entered the hallway Marco wondered if mice had eaten all the cheese.

Alan pointed down the corridor. A white shape floated in the darkness, and Marco reached into his pocket.

"There," Marco said. He withdrew the plastic container from his jacket with a shaking hand and held it out in front of him. "Get behind me," he whispered to Alan and Maggie. They did so.

At the far end of the corridor, Aldryyd floated and stared as though he had not decided when to make his attack. Marco's hand went to his belt and slipped a buckle loose.

"This," he said as he showed his hand, "is called a Bowie knife. Popular with cowboys. People say Buffalo Bill used to carry one of these."

Aldryyd inched closer but Marco could feel his apprehension. Their last encounter had shaken the ghost, and Marco's newfound confidence unsettled him. He held out the plastic container.

"But the knife isn't what scares you, is it? The stuff in this little cup is what you're really afraid of."

Aldryyd was halfway down the hallway. He stopped, glaring.

Marco opened the container and dipped the Bowie knife inside. He rotated the plastic to slather the blade with blood. Careful not to let the blood wet his grip on the knife, Marco held out the red blade for Aldryyd to see.

"Let's see what happens this time," he said.

The anomaly two days before was not enough to offset hundreds of years of perceived invulnerability. Aldryyd charged. Doors rushed by. Lights rattled in their wall posts. Marco lashed out with the bloody knife.

A beastly roar echoed through the hall and reverberated off the walls. Alan and Maggie covered their ears. Aldryyd's formless body kicked and retched at the end of the hall before turning to face them. They saw a large red opening on his torso.

"Got ya," Marco said to himself.

As though his voice were its cue, the gash in Aldryyd's side began to close. Smoky white swirled inward and filled the red hole. The ghost looked down, and Marco knew exactly what it was doing. When you get wounded, you need to assess yourself to see if you're ready to engage the enemy again. Aldryyd looked ready. In fact, he looked no worse than he had a few moments before. The bloody knife wasn't much more useful than the gun had been. Aldryyd looked up.

Marco's attack had not been as effective as Aldryyd had feared, so he set his gaze on the caretaker. It was time to change tactics. He would tear them apart from the inside out.

Alan felt a distant tug on his shoulder. He hardly noticed it. The eyes of the ghost held him, transfixed and immovable. Aldryyd's shape was breaking apart slowly and floating toward him.

"Let's go!" Marco shouted. He began to walk back down the hallway. Maggie took two tentative steps toward him, then stopped. Alan had not moved. He was standing in the corridor, enveloped in the smoky substance that had been Aldryyd moments before. The ghost seemed to have vanished, only a residual mist remained. Marco walked over to Alan and tapped him on the shoulder.

"Hey," he said softly. "You ok?"

Alan said nothing but acquiesced when Marco started leading him down the hallway. They hadn't gotten far when Alan stopped walking and stood still again, staring silently at Maggie.

"Is something wrong?" asked Maggie.

Marco wondered if Alan's head wound from the previous day was taking its toll. He began to search his pockets for his small stash of medical supplies. When he looked up again, he saw that Alan's gaze was now directed at him, specifically at the knife in his hand.

"You want to see it?" asked Marco. He saw no harm in handing over the knife. Perhaps the cold reality of the metal would snap Alan out of his stupor. He held it out, and Alan took it from him, observing it like a scientist with a new specimen. Maggie and Marco exchanged a confused glance.

Maggie walked over to Alan, her hand reaching out to soothe him. Her fingers brushed his hair, and an ethereal white shade suddenly overtook his natural blue irises, distracting her as the knife came down. Her scream filled the corridor, and Marco was forced to cover his ears. As Maggie stepped back away from Alan, she held out her bloody hand and stared unbelievingly at the space where her index finger had been.

"He's…he's…" she gasped.

Alan raised the knife again and walked toward her.

Marco couldn't believe what he was seeing. He was frozen, but he forced himself out of it and followed Alan down the corridor.

"Don't," said Maggie. "It's not him!"

Marco understood.

With that, Alan slashed down again and Maggie had enough space to jump back in time. She covered her bleeding hand in her shirt and looked back quickly. She was almost to the end of the corridor, and Alan stepped progressively forward.

"Al!" Marco shouted.

Alan turned and stared at him. It was just enough time for Maggie to run out of the hallway. She burst through the door of an old bedroom and descended a small staircase on the opposite side.

Alan's eyes were unnaturally white. They held a misty quality Marco recognized easily. Maggie was right. Alan was no longer in control of his mind. As Alan stepped toward him, Marco prepared himself. Knife or no knife, he was confident that he could defeat Alan in a fight. But with Aldryyd in his mind, the attack would be relentless.

I don't want to kill this man, he thought.

Alan stopped moving, and his white eyes cleared. A flash of blue shone through them, and a pained expression appeared on his face.

"Marco," Alan pleaded.

Then as quickly as it had vanished, the whiteness covered his eyes again and Alan rushed through the same door Maggie had used. Marco followed, not knowing what he'd do. Upon turning the corner into the room, he crashed into an old bureau by the wall. The bedroom did not have even the dim light of the hallway and he had to step back and take a moment to adjust to the darkness. As he oriented himself, Marco hurried to the small staircase beyond the opposite door, hoping that Alan hadn't caught up with her yet.

There was nowhere to run to. Maggie had turned in a random direction after leaving the bedroom and rushed off down a corridor into darkness. She had tried the door to a room only to realize that it was an old closet she could not fit into. As she looked around, she realized she was at the end of the corridor. Three walls surrounded her, and Alan was still coming up from behind, waving the knife in front of him.

"Alan!" she shouted.

It was as though he didn't care. As she cried out, Alan increased his pace and raised the knife. Marco came running out from behind him. Alan heard him enter the hallway and turned to look.

"Al," said Marco. He stepped slowly forward, aiming to close the distance as much as possible.

There was nothing he could do from far away. "Your head is messed up right now," he said. "Aldryyd is in there screwing with your brain, and you can't let him do it."

Alan remained in place, staring at Marco.

"Yeah," Marco continued. "Point the knife at me but look at her. Go ahead. Look."

Alan did look. Maggie was backed up against the wall and doing her best not to get pushed into the corner. There would be no way out from there. She wasn't aware of her tears, but Alan could see them clearly.

"Alan," she repeated, hoping the sound of his name would make him himself again.

"That is the woman you love," said Marco. "Aldryyd is trying to ruin your life in the most effective way he can think of. He wants to make you kill her. Then she'll be dead, and you'll be too devastated to continue."

His gaze remained fixed on Maggie, but Marco thought he saw the knife lower slightly. She dared a small step forward. By this time, Marco had inched close enough to get involved physically, but this was not a physical battle. The battle was not his at all.

"Al. This is a contest of wills. He is in your mind, and there's only one thing you need to do. Listen carefully. Now kick. Him. Out."

The blade lowered a fraction more, and sweat began beading visibly around Alan's neck. He was gritting his teeth as though in pain. Two minds clashed in a space where only one could exist. Ruthless violence made every attempt to grind down the weaker opposition. Yet, the opposition was learned and adaptable. It sidestepped and swayed in ways the violence could not foresee. It could stick and move when all Aldryyd's mind could think was to hammer, hammer, hammer it down.

"Alright, love?" asked Maggie.

That was it. Her voice. The words she'd spoken built a wall beneath him and Alan could not be hammered any deeper. Aldryyd would have to exhaust himself before that would ever happen. The battle of wills was over.

The knife clattered to the floor.

Crisis averted; Marco slumped back against the wall. He caught breath he hadn't realized he'd been holding and saw Maggie slide down into the corner in his peripheral vision. Alan looked exhausted yet resigned to the situation. Aldryyd was clearly no longer inside him. The white mist had seeped out of Alan's eyes and mouth to form a cloud near the ceiling. It was amorphous, save two gray points of darkness looking down on them. Intangible and angry.

"You ok?" asked Marco.

Alan nodded and sat.

Marco looked toward the mis, which was swiftly reshaping. He looked to the floor and then he saw it. The knife.

There was something on the ground next to Alan's body. I couldn't see…

"*Gadael!*" the ghost boomed.

With one last rush of energy, Aldryyd launched himself toward the ground and scooped up the knife in his formless hand. His lupine eyes focused pointedly on Maggie. The possession had taken its toll on his stamina. Both the living and the dead suffered in a battle of wills, but the ghost was ready to give it one last push. Aldryyd raised the knife and flew toward Maggie's corner.

Even as he moved, Marco knew he wouldn't make it in time. The ghost had one last burst of surprising speed and would reach Maggie first. All in one moment, he saw her eyes widen in fear, and then the sight was blocked by descending blue. Alan's shirt caught the light from the single hall-way window as he expended his own final rush of energy. The blade sped towards Maggie and came down heavily underneath the blue collar. It welled up in a sickening Rorschach design as the color changed to a liquid black in the dimness. Alan fell to the floor. With a final cry, Aldryyd rose into the air and vanished. His plan was foiled, and yet, the traitor had paid his due.

In the narrow corridor, there was no avoiding the ever-widening puddle of blood. It pressed up to the walls on both sides and stained Maggie's knees

as she held Alan's head in her arms, speaking unintelligible words through her tears. Wounds were
nothing new to a contract killer, and Marco immediately found himself assessing the extremity of the cut
and his chances of mending it. He stared at the wash
of redness on his shoes and estimated the depth of
the stab wound. Blood erupted from Alan's mouth,
and his chest sank slowly. Sometimes knowledge is
no help at all. Marco sized up the wound and did
the only thing he could think of. As Alan strained
to see his love's face, Marco took hold of his hand.
A gesture of recognition, if not friendship. A way of
saying, "Goodbye." Alan's eyes stopped their incessant staring and closed halfway.

"Don't," mumbled Maggie.

Marco missed the time of death. His eyes had
been drawn to a large golden frame. As he raised
his head to see its contents, fear crept through his
body more than it ever had before. Twisted hair
and bright lips on display, the portrait of Lillian
Morgan stared down at him from above, her red
dress prominently vile.

Chapter Twenty-Two

The Third Floor

He couldn't keep up. No matter how quickly he ran or how far he jumped, Oliver could not gain on the strange human child. She didn't move in the normal human ways. Her paws never touched down, and she moved more like a sky animal than a land creature. Even with his limited feline vision, Oliver was convinced he had seen the girl pass through a wall and emerge a moment later from the other side. He thought she had gone upwards but didn't know how far.

There was another like her, shaped like a man. That one was wrong. His presence reeked of anger that remained in place even when the man was not around. He was the kind of human that would swat at him whenever he came near. Oliver could recognize the type and did not want the girl to be near him.

To protect the child, he would first have to find her. Oliver went up and up. The steps were endless. He'd begun to lose hope when he noticed a strange thing nearby. It was out of place in a large room. As he crept slowly toward it, Oliver saw that it was old and brown. And it had a head! He drew back.

After a moment, he observed that it didn't move. Perhaps it was dead. He moved up next to it slowly, studying each detail he could make out in the dim room. The creature had a stick for a body and a raggedy malformed head. As he circled the thing, Oliver managed to pick up a scent coming off of it. The stick beast smelled like the girl. She could be nearby.

His nose was of limited help. It wouldn't do him any good to sniff around the floor trying to locate the smell of her. Oliver sat, perked up his ears, and listened. Wind. There were small critters scuttling behind the walls, but he didn't have time for them now. Water dripped from an unseen place. Nothing else of note. He would need to check each room on the floor.

Oliver heard a squeak. It was not one of the wall critters. This was a loud sound that echoed for some time. It must be the girl! He dashed toward the place he'd heard the sound coming from and had to stop in his tracks when he found the way blocked by a large wooden door. Oliver pawed at the door and called out again and again. The door creaked open, and Oliver squeezed himself through the gap before it was fully ajar.

"Kitty."

The strange girl bent down low to greet him. She spoke, but quietly, like a prey animal worried about hunters. As she scooped him up in her arms again, Oliver realized the child would need his help finding a better place to hide. He had found her easily. The bad human could find her as well. He decided to make a detailed search in and out of the building to find a place for her, seeking out spaces the other could not go. Places only a cat, or perhaps this strange child, could hide.

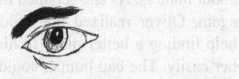

Chapter Twenty-Three

The Study

There'd been a time when Aldryyd had gotten hurt running down a hill. He'd been six. A fox rushed by, and he decided to chase it. The fox dashed away before he could grab it and disappeared into the high grass. Aldryyd had chased the fox into the grass and found himself tumbling over and over in an endless spin, only to come to a jarring stop against a hidden rock and, in a bit of a daze, tried to stand up. He'd noticed that his hand couldn't support his body weight when he leaned on it. A quick look showed him that his knuckles had dislodged and were now set too far back along his hand. Two of his fingers hung uselessly from the knuckles. It was a hand from an abstract painting, and it terrified him. As an adult, Aldryyd had figured that he'd probably been in shock at that moment. This memory appeared to him as he contemplated what had just happened.

There was a hole in me.

He floated to the room's far end and settled near shelves filled with old parchment. His hand touched his stomach as if checking to see if the hole had returned. Like his broken hand, the hole in his stomach hadn't hurt, but it certainly shocked. The hole had sealed itself up soon after appearing, but that did not ease Aldryyd's mind at all. He'd still been hurt. For the first time in hundreds of years, the first time since dying, someone had caused him harm.

If the man could hurt him once, he could do it again.

He waved a formless arm through the air, and parchment flew across the room. At that moment, he felt what the living would refer to as a shiver, something a dead man should never feel.

Papers on the floor. A broken chair in the corner. The castle was slowly collapsing around him century after century. Now, the caretaker was gone . Damn him for getting in the way! Killing Alan was not part of the plan. It was supposed to be the woman. He scanned the room, looking for nothing in particular. He had doomed the castle. Alan was the only one who'd truly cared for Morgan's Mount. Without him, the building would fall into permanent disrepair, and no one, certainly not that worthless Fisher, would do anything to stop it. The best he could hope for was that the ruins would never be swept away by time or by man. The thought of being without the castle was unbearable.

Then a thought struck him with unexpected force. What if he couldn't exist without the castle? He wasn't capable of leaving. Doing so would mean giving in to what comes next and releasing his hold on his precious home. He would never do that. But if the castle left him behind, would he be forced out into the beyond?

The true horror of his situation weighed on his mind for the first time. He was in danger of losing his home. **His** castle. That man had come, and then Alan had proven untrustworthy after all, pushing Aldryyd out of his mind like that and forcing him to change tactics. The fool brought about his own death. The woman would've died, and the men would have run out, broken, never to return. Now Aldryyd could do nothing but wait and wonder if they'd come back.

Let them come.

Aldryyd looked out the window, over the long acreage of his family land.

It had all started going wrong when the American arrived. If the man came back, he would end it quickly. There would be no more chases, no more nonsense with traps. The man, Marco was what they called him, would finally understand who he was up against: Aldryyd Finneas Morgan, captain of the Seastar, survivor of war, and owner of this bloody castle! Aldryyd would tear the man's guts from his body and force the girl to watch all the while. She would know then, this man was no rescuer, but just another invader like the others before him. He would smile as Marco fell and take great joy in watching the blood seep down into the stones in the floor; another addition to the mass of lives he had taken to bring joy to his endless unlife.

Let him come.

Chapter Twenty-Four

Cardiff, Wales

The man in the cap slipped an arm around her shoulder. An onlooker would assume a father-daughter relationship. That onlooker would be incorrect, but the mistake would be understandable. She was red-faced and fought back inevitable tears. He knew they would come. The tears would get the best of her as they had with him the night before. He would not tell her about that. At the moment, she needed his support, and he would not allow himself to fail. The woman's head pressed on his gray coat as they entered the parking lot.

"Well," Fisher began, "rain finally stopped."

"Exchanged itself for the cold," Maggie said.

They came to the car, and Fisher opened the door for her. She slipped into the passenger's seat and stopped all movement; didn't reach for the seatbelt or the door. Maggie looked like a woman out of ideas, nothing left to do but stay in one place until someone nudged her along to the next destination.

"Who's driving you?" asked Fisher.

"Carrie."

Fisher nodded, placing a hand on her shoulder.

"That boy was like my son, blood or no. Don't think he told you, but I offered him the mount."

She looked up.

"And now I'm making the offer to you. It's all I have to give."

Through tear-stained cheeks, there came a flashing grin, entirely lacking in mirth. Her eyes went cold.

"All I'd do is hire a wrecking crew to knock the bloody thing down. I never want to see that awful place again."

He saw in her eyes that she meant every word of it. The castle had taken everything from her.

"Could be that's exactly what's needed," he said. "Finish the place once and for all."

A woman with short red hair walked toward the car.

"That's Carrie," Maggie said.

Fisher nodded and stepped away from the car.

"If you need anything...anything at all," he said.

She waved to him as Carrie got into the driver's seat.

Fisher turned away and walked down the hill, past the bushes, and out of the cemetery. He bundled his long coat up against the cold. Where thoughts of sadness had recently prevailed, thoughts of destruction were now forming. He could finish the place once and for all.

The drive to Betws y Coed was long, so Carrie was annoyed when a large man in a brown jacket stepped in front of the car, blocking her in.

"Hey you," she began.

"Please," he said. "Maggie?" He held a placating hand in the air.

Maggie knew the voice and considered not answering. She did answer though, for one simple reason. Marco's voice had never sounded so kind.

She made no move to leave the vehicle despite his clear invitation to walk with him. This conversation was a big deal to him. It was an annoyance to Maggie, and she wanted to be sure he understood. After a moment, he crouched down next to the car, resting his forearms on the frame of the open window. He had lowered himself, a supplicating gesture, if not a conscious one.

"I know," he began. "You need to get going. I won't take much of your time."

Carrie started to retort, but Maggie stared her down.

"I just want to ask you something. But it's a little weird."

"Out with it," Maggie pushed.

He nodded.

"I have a...not really a theory. Just an idea. Half-formed."

She glared, and he knew he'd only have one chance to get her to listen.

"Do you think," Marco resumed, "that the bloody knife is evidence of something bigger? I mean, it didn't stop him, but it sort of worked, right…" A moment passed before he found the words he needed. "What if that was evidence of something that could work, but I just interpreted it incorrectly?"

Maggie sat in silence for a long time, staring ahead, still as a post. Then, "There was something, yes. Maybe a knife wasn't the way to go. But the blood part makes sense. That's the essence of life itself. It could be it takes a certain ritual or perhaps you were thinking small scale. Some people think the best way to get rid of evil spirits is to get a large group of people and drive it out by standing in a circle and holding hands."

"Ritual?" Marco asked. "But exorcism failed. Al told me."

He hadn't realized what he'd done until Maggie's head drooped, and she began to bite her lip. Saying Alan's name had been an emotional punch in her gut.

"I don't know," she said as she fought to hold back the tears. "The good news is, you don't have to care, do you?" She nodded to Carrie, who immediately pressed the gas pedal, and Marco was shaken off the window and left in a cloud of brown dust.

As the car turned onto the paved road, Marco stood in thought.

***

The counter was a long mahogany-stained solid block with a stack of peach-colored trays high on one end, offsetting the drab clothing of the morose girl on the cash register. She checked her phone for the eighth time that hour. Five hours left on her shift. She'd cash out at seven and hoped to be home, showered, cleaned up, and kitted out for Elsie's place by eight. A regular customer, an obese man named Todd or Ted, walked by, waving a chunky arm at her. She returned the wave half-heartedly. It was always good to keep the regulars happy, even if her feelings about seeing them didn't match the joy they felt at seeing the buffet tables. Todd or Ted waddled to a table near the window, slid out a plastic chair, and plopped himself down to gorge on the largest pile of mashed potatoes Catherine had ever seen. She checked her phone. Still, five hours left.

"Excuse me," said a voice. "Did a tall guy in a gray coat recently come in here?"

The man's accent snapped her out of her daze. She looked up to see a large man in a brown jacket looking down at her from behind a pair of round-framed sunglasses.

"Umm," Catherine started. "Yes, he's sat by the corner."

"Thanks." He began to walk away.

"Are you American?" asked Catherine.

"Yeah," he said.

Catherine couldn't help herself. Before he had taken more than a step, she blurted out, "What's it like in Times Square?"

Marco, who had never been to Times Square, replied, "Big and loud, I guess." He spotted Fisher and wandered over to him.

"Wanker," Catherine muttered. She quickly spit-shined her glasses, then poured herself a drink.

Fisher didn't look up as the other man approached. He continued sipping his coffee and pointed to a chair opposite him at the table. Marco sat. For a moment, neither one of them spoke.

"What's your plan then?" Marco eventually asked. "I'm curious."

A small brown bird flitted by the window. It landed on the branch of a nearby tree. He was still staring at the bird when Fisher finally replied.

"This whole thing was foolhardy to begin with. I'll call the wrecking crew tomorrow. Time to end this."

Whatever he'd expected Fisher to say, it wasn't that. Marco was shocked and realized that it must have shown on his face because Fisher said, "I can't quite believe it either. But that's what it's come to. I've got to knock it down before it hurts anyone else."

Marco leaned back in his chair.

"Then what the hell was all this for? You hire a guy like me 'cause you're so desperate to get rid of Aldryyd. Al kicks the bucket in the process of helping me, and now Maggie's life is pretty much ruined." He stood up. "I know I'm being insensitive at a shitty time for you, but I can't believe what I'm hearing!"

Fisher didn't reply, just gestured to the chair. Marco sat down again.

"A man wants to leave a legacy. Something that stays behind after he's gone," said Fisher.

"I've got no kids, and the wife left me long ago. All I have is that ruddy old building that's been in my family and the money that's wrapped up in it. I wanted it to mean something, but it didn't. It's just a box for a killer to operate out of."

"Fuck your legacy," said Marco. "That's where Al died, and in case you forgot, the kid is still trapped in there."

"Kid?" asked Fisher. "Oh, Harriet. Yes. That's unfortunate. I was hoping she'd have moved on."

Marco shook his head.

"She won't. Not alone." He knew it was true as soon as he'd heard his own words.

"I see you're not happy with my decision, so I'll say this," said Fisher. "Do what you will. If you decide to try again, I'll not stop you. I'll wish you luck. If ever there was a man who deserved to die twice, it's Aldryyd Morgan. But I plan to take the whole lot down by the end of the month."

With that, he got up and walked away from the table, leaving an unfinished bowl of chicken soup behind. As he neared the door, he heard Marco's faint voice. "You don't even know if knocking it down would stop him."

The door creaked open loudly, and Marco stood up and walked over to it when he heard the sound. He was just in time to see the bundled-up

Fisher plod slowly to his old yellow Volkswagen. The man looked older than ever, gray at the temples and dark pockets under his eyes that Marco could have sworn were not there the day before. As the car slowly sputtered out of the parking lot, Marco stood, unmoving, fingers tapping the envelope in his pocket unconsciously.

It was over.

He turned from the door and saw the girl at the cash register eyeing him. A finger was aimlessly twirling through her dark hair.

"Hey, kid," he said. "If you could go anywhere, where would you go? And don't say Times Square."

Catherine thought for a moment.

"Don't know. The beach, I suppose."

"Yeah," replied Marco. He started for the door, touched the latch, and let it go.

Catherine watched him as he stood silently, nodding to himself. Finally, he said, "A beach sounds good." He dug into his pocket and produced several papers. When he stepped forward and placed them on the counter, Catherine found herself looking at twenty-five, one hundred pound notes.

"Don't waste your time on Times Square," he said, "but The Grand Canyon is pretty cool."

He left. Catherine stood still as she heard the door creak open and bang closed, her eyes never leaving the pile of money in front of her. A quick movement caught her attention and she looked up to see a little Nuthatch speed by the doorway. Behind it, the big man was fading into the dark afternoon horizon.

Chapter Twenty-Five

Morgan's Mount Cemetery

The pouring rain was unbearable for most people that day, but the man in the brown jacket didn't care. He stood, head bowed in front of the gravestone he'd sought out. Hands in his pockets, he looked down at the stone and spoke.

"I know you're not in there, but I'm sure you're watching. I hope you can see me."

He looked up toward the castle and thought he saw movement on the second floor. Hopefully, his desired audience was in attendance.

"I wasn't invited to his funeral!" Marco shouted. "So, I came to yours instead!"

There was no response from the castle.

The cold rain was beginning to seep in, beneath his jacket and into his bones but it didn't matter. He wasn't finished here.

"I didn't see it coming," he said under his breath. It was a lie, and he knew it. The Trips had been straight with him as they always had been. They had shown him the painting and given him ample warning. There was no one to blame but himself for failing to protect Alan properly. No one, that was, but himself, and of course, Aldryyd.

"Watch this!" he shouted at the castle.

As the rain ran down his arm and sped along his sleeve, his hand reached to the dark grass below. He grabbed the object there and hefted it into the air. For one moment, the silhouette of a sledgehammer posed in front of the gray-clouded sky before swinging in a long arc down toward the ground, only to twist one foot above the earth and curve its momentum upward. As the gravestone was blasted into myriad pieces, Marco hoped the noise wouldn't be lost in the thunder. When he was finished, he set the hammer down and, breathing heavily, sat on the chunks of stone.

There was no way of knowing if anyone had borne witness to this event. It was, at least, symbolic. At most, he hoped it would be perceived as a threat, but as he sat, bedraggled and soaked, Marco started to feel foolish. He couldn't make any credible threats. He hadn't been effective against his opponent and had failed to save Alan even with advanced warning.

He sat outside the castle where his foe could not go, ashamed of his cowardice. Entering the castle again was a terrifying thought. An opponent that couldn't be stabbed and could inhabit peoples' bodies was unstoppable. The best he could do was to demonstrate his anger in a graveyard outside the building. The worst of it was not knowing what had become of Harriet, and thinking of the child alone and scared inside doubled his shame. He had failed her too. Fisher was right. He should go.

If he had seen her face staring down at him as he walked away, Marco might have stayed, but Harriet was not there to see. Instead, he looked at his work one last time and spit on Aldryyd Morgan's broken headstone. The rain picked up as he trudged slowly to the car and slipped inside. A quick word to Peter and the car was off.

Far above, in the west tower, Aldryyd watched angrily as the man drove away, leaving his busted gravestone in his wake.

Chapter Twenty-Six

The Fountain, Morgan's Mount, Wales

Water trickled through the pipe. This was not the pressured rush that forced great blasts of water high into the air when the lords and ladies had graced the castle lawn in their finery. Nothing in the Mount served such a purpose any longer. The body of the building was as dried out and worn as the rusted pipe that ran its way to the cistern of the once magnificent fountain. A rearing horse rose to the east while the form of a wild stag faced the land from the opposite side, each a representation of the once wild lands these had been before men and their machines. Not a large fountain but certainly a grand one in its time, now covered with a green creeping fungus that spread through the basin and cascaded to the cistern below, where small eyes peered out at the world.

He would come. Harriet was sure of it. Sometimes it took longer than others, but in the end, he always found her. Then she re-experienced the living suffering from so long ago. There were lulls, perhaps months at a time, in which he would leave her be—to play freely. But not even those times were truly free from fear because she always knew they were temporary. Eventually, his hunger for her pain would resurface, and he'd find her again. Hiding in the towers had been the worst decision she'd made in those times. Going to the basement had also been foolish. It became ever more difficult to find places where he would not locate her quickly, and she had only squeezed her way through the pipe to the cistern under the fountain due to Oliver.

As she ran, her legs shaking, eyes open wide, looking for someplace, anywhere, to escape from Aldryyd, the cat had perched on the pipe and screeched loudly until Harriet stopped to pay attention. At first, she had not understood. As she heard his booming voice drawing closer, she finally realized what Oliver had found. Compressing herself into the pipe was not a problem, she was noncorporeal. The pipe allowed her to leave the main building while not exposing herself to the outside world where she could not go. Still, she knew that he would come. Eventually, he always did.

The light rain stopped, and so did the trickle through the pipe. Harriet sat with her knees bunched up to her chin and tried to enjoy every moment of peacefully looking over the front lawn with its bushes, its elms, oaks, and yews before the fear began again.

Chapter Twenty-Seven

Ios, Greece

The color was draining from the day. This seemed almost funny to him since the days there were so full of whiteness. The box-like buildings stacked at the base of the hill were all of the brightest white and stampeded a portion of the way to the summit before giving in. Then there were the buildings with the small round-capped towers, and he didn't know what they were. In the evening light, with the line of orange spreading over the sea below, all that counted was the beauty of it all. Even the beach sand was light in color and soft on the feet to an almost unreal degree. Marco had been to Montauk. once as a boy and remembered the rough, gritty grains of sand under his toes. This place was different, otherworldly in its perfection. Not even the tour groups of yapping fools with their overly large sunglasses and zinced noses had been capable of ruining this for him.

Marco had never been much of a wine drinker but it hadn't taken long for Ios to make him into one. He drained his glass, placed it on the table, and decided to walk into town for a new bottle. He'd take the long route, down the winding hotel steps, and along the beach. In a place like this, shortcuts were unappealing. They didn't allow enough time to look around. The usual group of Eurotrash college kids was partying by their pool-level hotel rooms. One of the loud drunk ones shouted something in a language Marco couldn't identify. At the bottom of the steps, an old man in a turquoise shirt dragged a rope to a beached rowboat. Marco continued past the boat and walked directly to the ocean until he felt the hard pavement give way to the cushioning beach sand.

The store with his favorite red wine was far down the beach. He practiced what he'd say as he walked. "*Thelo kokino krasi.*"

A couple held one another while they leaned on a nearby seawall, and a gull floated along the breakage; otherwise, Marco felt he was alone. He stopped for a moment to catch the beam of an unseen lighthouse spreading its ray upon the shallows. The waves rolled in. The gull took flight as it occurred to Marco that this was the first time he'd truly been by himself since his arrival in Greece. Days of clubbing and bar-hopping through the night, restaurants among the finest in Greece, and the people he'd met along the way had kept him constantly occupied. Standing on that beach in paradise, lighthouse beam flashing away, allowed him no escape from the thought he'd unconsciously been trying to push from his mind. *Harriet is alone.*

It wasn't fair. Even a killer like him could understand that it wasn't right for a little kid to spend eternity alone. If she only had the guts to step out the door, maybe she would find her parents out there somewhere, waiting. Then, of course, there was the lesson he'd learned long ago: Some men deserve to die. The whole situation had turned out wrong. Now it was over, and he had to put it out of his mind. Marco focused on the incoming waves, their rolls, their crests, the arhythmic crashing on sand. After a moment, when his thoughts had cleared, he began walking again.

A breeze blew in from the west. He felt it blow his hair back, and his body registered the coolness through his thin shirt. A moment passed before he realized that he had felt the rushing breeze on every part of him except for his left hand. Curiously, he clenched his fingers, finding no feeling in his pinky, middle, or ring fingers. He had just enough time to think, *Shit. Not again*, before his entire body succumbed to numbness. As his knees buckled and his body collapsed, he was grateful for the fact that he was landing on sand. At other times the Trips had come at more inconvenient moments; when he was on a sidewalk or a stairway. After his vision, he'd awaken with new bruises and cuts from the fall. This time his head touched down lightly on the beach sand and he lay on his side, watching the waves come and go. A wave was on its way toward him when his mind raced away from his control.

***

The woman sitting across from him asked if he was ok and he assured her he was. After finding him lying still on the beach, she'd shaken him awake and brought him up for a drink.

"You ok? You seemed like you went away for a moment," she told him. "I said, why don't you take me up to…"

"Sorry, Theresa" interrupted Marco. He tried to pronounce her name with the proper accent and failed.

He stood. The wheels were spinning in his mind, and a thought long kept out of his grasp rapidly surfaced. As he looked out upon the blue waves below, he found his answer. It had been simple all along. Costly, but simple.

"Look," said Theresa. "I'm not going to sit here with you if you're going to act like an ass all…"

The look in his eyes stopped her this time. The vision he'd had on the beach ran through his mind once again, and he felt something click into place. Marco turned his wild eyes upon her and spoke softly, slowly. "Goodbye. Sorry, but I need to get to the airport."

Chapter Twenty-Eight

Morgan's Mount, Wales

Buildings have a way of drying up so that the most important pieces, the things that once gave them life, fall away. The bones of a house when its people have moved on. Foundations remaining after a collapse. These places lose their color and attitude. But some buildings hold on longer than others. Some hold on across centuries. Once in a while, a building persists because its inhabitant will not allow it to do otherwise.

What remained of the castle court was nothing more than a heap of rubble. Centuries of wear, hard Welsh rain, and the instability of being built near a massive drop had toppled the old stone towers that overlooked the forest long ago. As he surveyed the pile of gray moss-covered stones outside the window, Aldryyd remembered the days when he'd sat in the court enjoying a show and drinking ale with friends. Other than the greenhouse, the rear lawn of the Mount didn't include much of anything these days.

He looked away and caught a flicker of movement in the corridor. The cat. Once every so often, the mangy beast would slip by on its way to nab a mouse, and he would spook it purely out of spite.

It had eluded him since its arrival in the castle. Each time he gave chase, the dastardly feline managed to slip away in some unforeseen fashion. The chases were becoming tiresome and pointless. Aldryyd decided to let it go this time. He looked away and sank back into his memories.

Oliver had heard the sound of large paws, human paws, walking on the hard floor. It wasn't particularly loud, but he'd decided to investigate because he hadn't simply heard it, he'd felt it too. It was as if the sound was telling him that it was finally time to abandon his post near the pipe and check into this new occurrence. The cruel human, the one that chased his friend, was in a room nearby, but Oliver rushed past. It was important to find the source of this new noise as quickly as possible. There was no time for a chase.

He wound down the large steps and paused partway to poke his head between the railings and view the large room below. Oliver's keen eyes quickly spotted the figure by the doorway. The form was large and dark, standing still, and looking straight down at the floor. Oliver recognized him. It was the man that had followed him to the girl in the basement. The man was here to help his friend, Oliver was sure of it. This was more than enough reason for him to bound down the remaining steps and run to the man. He would offer his services as a guide one more time.

Marco spotted the cat speeding toward him across the floor of the great room. It surprised him to find himself cheered by this; strange to think he could feel any happiness at such a moment. Oliver leaped into his arms, and Marco let him perch there while petting him.

"How you been, buddy?"

Oliver replied by rubbing his head on Marco's neck.

"Good to see you again," Marco said. "We didn't know where you'd gone off to."

He allowed himself a few minutes of comfort and calm, petting Oliver and trying not to dwell on the next step in his mission. The cat seemed to be alright with that. They both knew the calm was temporary, and it was Oliver that acknowledged it first by withdrawing from the man's arms and climbing onto his shoulder.

"Yeah," said Marco. "Time to get on with it. Do you know where she is?"

Oliver leaped down from the impressive height and landed lightly on the floor. He didn't wait but dashed ahead toward the grand staircase. Marco decided to stay put. He'd had plenty of time to think about this and the acoustics of the great room were exactly what he needed. Harriet could come to him there.

As he stood, staring ahead at the stairs, hoping to see Oliver and Harriet coming down them any second, his right hand crept slowly down his hip. An unconscious action. His fingers had only just touched the object there when he heard something that distracted him.

"Hello," said Harriet.

Marco turned to see the girl floating openly in the room. He hadn't seen her enter.

"Hi," he said. "I see that Oliver found you."

"Yes," she said.

"Sorry I went away for so long."

"Tis no matter," said Harriet.

Oliver bounded back into the room and sat next to Harriet.

"Is Alan here? Did he stay behind with you?' asked Marco.

"I have seen no sign of him. I believe he went beyond the door."

Marco nodded, then reached down to his hip once more, but this time he gripped the butt of his Beretta and drew it. He stood facing Harriet, gun in full view, and asked a question. He couldn't help it.

"Does it hurt?"

Her misty face swirled and went out of focus for a second in a ghostly gesture of thought. When she finally replied, her voice sounded small, faded, and like it came to him from a faraway place.

"The hurting comes before," she began. "It ends quickly. Later comes the difficulty. Thou awakens as though on a vessel. Tilting and unstable. Colors are dull. Voices hollow."

"But it works, right? I can stay if I want to?" Marco asked in earnest.

Harriet continued as though he hadn't spoken. "To be alone. Then thou must move, and 'tis ever a struggle to step. Too light. A new world in which one lacks substance." She paused in thought. "Terrifying."

When she'd finished, they stood in silence, Harriet looking toward him but not at him. Marco thought about the beach in Ios and what he'd seen. His last vision: *I'm in the great room. It's dark. She's there with me, watching. I look around then I raise the gun. Click. Now I'm seeing an upward view of the room. The rafters begin to blur.*

"Stay with me?" he asked.

There was no answer, but she made no move to leave. Marco said, "Alright", put the barrel of the gun against his head, and took a deep breath. Maybe the Trips could be changed, but Marco now thought they showed the inevitable. He hoped that this last one had provided him the solution he needed and would be the key to freeing Harriet from the fear that separated her from her parents. Marco pulled the trigger. The rafters began to blur.

***

There was a tremendous cracking that echoed throughout the building and reached him easily on the second floor. He flew through the first wall he came to, then changed direction, heading to the center of the castle and picking up speed on his descent. Aldryyd had done his share of hunting and knew the sound of rifle fire well, but the report of the Beretta was a louder and sharper sound. Despite never having heard such a gun fired, he immediately knew the sound for what it was. Given the echo he'd heard, there was no question in his mind where the sound had come from. Someone was in the great room.

Harriet wasted no time. Whatever she chose to do would need to be done as quickly as possible. Aldryyd would have heard the gun and would be coming to investigate. Perhaps that had been the idea all along. She rushed to the first spot that came to mind and did what she could. Then she looked at her surroundings. Aldryyd wasn't there yet but it wouldn't take more than a moment for that to change. Harriet thought of the day she'd saved Maggie with her hobby horse and dug deep for that same courage. She would need all of it.

"Here!" she shouted. "I am here!"

Then she flew as quickly as she could down the corridor, turning here and there, floating through walls, and shouting all the while. She did not risk a glance behind her. It would do no good. The little ghost sped through the castle with darkness gaining ground behind her while trying once more to think of a hiding place she'd never used. Nothing came to mind.

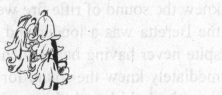

Chapter Twenty-Nine

Betws-y-Coed, Wales

The French Onion dip was behind the flowers. She brushed the bouquet aside and reached for the small bowl. The cracker she'd grabbed wound up being some strange tomato citrus flavor she didn't like, but Maggie knew what to do with it. Anything could taste good as long as it was dripping in French Onion dip. The glass of Pinot Noir in her hand would help as well.

"Hey there."

It was cousin…what was his name? They'd gone to the zoo together once as children. He'd been blonde. Now, she found herself looking at a balding office-type fellow with a considerable paunch. Maggie couldn't remember anything else about him. Sometimes having a large family was difficult.

"I just want to say that I'm sorry…"

She felt the next words coming and silently tried to stop them. *Don't say 'sorry for your loss'. Just don't say it.*

"…for your loss."

There was nothing to do but thank him as he began a story about a time he and Alan had gone fishing. Alan had hated fishing. The man was shaped like a tall gourd, and she only just managed to stop herself from saying so. She drank more wine. A short time later, she was rescued by Carrie, who came up from behind and put an arm around her shoulder, comforting and steadying simultaneously.

"Let's go sit," suggested Carrie.

It was a good idea. Maggie went along willingly enough, although her feet wouldn't step in the places she wanted them to. Carrie supported most of her weight as they made their way to the big couch in the next room. Maggie sank onto the cushions, and Carrie let go only when she was sure her friend wouldn't be tipping off of the couch. Carrie sat and motioned to a large man across from them. She caught his attention, then pointed to the bottle on the table near him. He nodded, picked it up, and was able to hand it to her without hardly getting out of his chair.

"Thanks," she said. To Maggie, "Cabernet?"

Maggie finished what would've normally been a few sips for her in one fell swoop. With her glass now empty, she was more than happy to accept Carrie's offer.

"You know how your head is gonna feel tomorrow morning, don't ya?" asked Carrie.

Maggie nodded, clearly not caring. Carrie poured. They clinked glasses and were each one sip into the Cabernet when they saw someone approaching. A tall woman wearing a patterned dress Maggie recognized...

"Hello, Maggie."

"Hello, aunt Charlotte," Maggie replied.

"How're you doing?" asked aunt Charlotte as she sat in a chair next to Maggie.

"I don't know," said Maggie. "It's all been such a rush. The funeral and now here."

"Yes, I'm sure it has. If you need anything, dear, let me know."

"Thanks."

"At least we can rest knowing that he's in a better place now," said aunt Charlotte.

A surge of anger rose inside of Maggie. She hadn't known it was there until this very moment.

"Better place? What the hell do you mean?"

Aunt Charlotte was visibly taken aback by her response. Her wrinkles betrayed her age beneath her caked-on makeup as her mouth dropped open. She leaned back in her chair and chose her next words carefully as she took in the expression on Maggie's face; the look of a woman daring any challenger to an argument.

"I just mean, dear. Well, he was such a wonderful man. He rests with the angels now."

Carrie saw the anger in her friend's eyes flaring up again, tried to stop it by offering more wine, and failed. There was something Maggie intended to say.

"Heaven?" said Maggie. "You're saying he's in heaven. How is that better than him being down here with me?" She leaned closer to aunt Charlotte, who leaned away in response.

"I just...my dear…" stammered aunt Charlotte.

Maggie stood on wobbly legs. Carrie steadied her.

"What proof do you have?" Maggie shouted. "Show me how you can be so sure he's in fucking heaven!"

As she looked down at her aunt, Maggie felt the tap on her back. She knew it was Carrie's way of telling her she was being crazy; a behavior Carrie had employed on many drunken nights in their university days. After taking in the aghast look on the older woman's face, Maggie allowed herself to be led from the room. A glass door swung open for her and she stepped out onto the deck. A light rain was falling. It felt good.

"You were a lot more fun to drink with back in Uni," said Carrie.

Maggie laughed. Carrie had always known how to make her do that.

"I'm sorry," Maggie said. "I'm just so sick of it. For the past week, it's been 'we're so sorry' and 'he's in a better place.'"

Carrie shrugged her shoulders. "It's what people say."

"Yeah, but it's wrong. That's my point. We have no idea where Alan is, do we?"

Carrie opened her mouth to speak, paused, and closed it again, having realized she had no idea how to respond. She waited to see where Maggie took the conversation.

"What if he's a ghost or spirit, and he's stuck somewhere? And he can't move on?"

"Do you think he is?" asked Carrie, looking genuinely curious.

Maggie leaned on the deck and turned her face up to the rain. She let it calm her before responding. Drop after drop, it brought her a bit of peace.

"I think it's possible," Maggie said, "but if that's the case, where would he be now? Not the castle. I certainly hope not there."

"His house?" suggested Carrie.

Maggie shook her head. Alan had no real connection to his family home and his apartment had never been more than a place to store his things. The only places he'd ever truly cared about were her apartment in Newport and that damned castle. Now, she wasn't sure if she could ever stand to live in that apartment again. There were too many memories of him there.

"No," said Maggie. "He's got to be some-where. But...I don't know. It's driving me crazy."

"Any word about the guy who did it?" asked Carrie.

Drunk as she was, Maggie just barely stopped herself from saying that she knew exactly who'd killed Alan. Carrie was a helpful friend, but she hadn't been there in the castle. She could never truly understand.

"No," said Maggie. She shook her head. Her anger had subsided for the time being but she found herself thinking of Marco and his strange questions. Whatever it was he'd had in mind, she hoped it would work. "I hope he kills him."

"What?" asked Carrie.

"Nothing," Maggie replied. "Let's go back in. I'll be a good girl if you get me some more of that dip."

Carrie nodded and slipped her arm under her friend's. They walked in the door closest to the kitchen. People kept talking as though there hadn't been any disturbance. Half an hour and two glasses of wine later, Maggie made her polite goodbyes to family and friends. A friend of her parents drove her back to her cottage to rest and recoup.

Chapter Thirty

Marco

Time is a stubborn thing. It will not reverse itself for anyone, and yet it will gladly drag a person screaming back into memories long forgotten: even those best forgotten. There's no way to beat it. Time will inflict suffering until it loosens its hold or crushes a person under its intensity. It doesn't care either way.

Marco was a child of indeterminate age. An oak tree...no. The oak tree. He'd seen it before. The branch came down after a winter storm putting his entire block out of power for a full week. The oak tree was still standing. He didn't understand how he could access a memory so old as this. He searched for his age, but it was denied to him. The house nearby was white with brown trim. His house.

Darkness. Then a new image arose.

Dripping. There was blood on his lip. It tasted warm. Welcoming. He stood up again, knuckles aching but ready for more action. The world went red. Jimmy Metcalf lay on the sidewalk bleeding and clutching an arm that was pointing at an impossible angle. The red vanished from his vision. He had done this and he felt fine.

Another leap, this one clearer.

The radiance wound around him like a blanket. Not a light at the end of any tunnel but the cheap bug-filled fluorescents of his mother's kitchen. She was baking while he was sitting. Her words were unintelligible but as warm as the muffins she was making.

The next jump in time was darker. The room fading into existence held little light. The bed was the center in a vignette of shadows. He knew that his car keys were resting on a shelf in the shadows to the left. That's where he always set them when he got home. The sound of an impossibly distant phone was ringing in the background. It would be a job offer, and it would require a certain kind of person. He would do well.

Life doesn't flash before your eyes in a near-death experience. It waits until you're dead to throw every memory you've ever had at you all at once. The sheer number of memories is overwhelming; most only register as feelings. The clearest memories are the ones that hold the most significance, even if a person doesn't understand why.

He felt like he could stay here, wherever, whenever this was, but something nagged at his mind, and he couldn't bring it into focus.

He had seen the face of a woman. The closest he ever came to love. She vanished and was instantly replaced by a series of fluctuations that brought happiness, confusion, and loss to them. Emotions changed from moment to moment, second to second. He couldn't even understand the associations of the feelings any longer. There were too many of them. The one thought began to grow.

It was different from the others. Unlike the barrage of memories and feelings rushing through him, this thought was about something he had not done. It was no memory. His mind raced through days of shopping, eating, walking, running errands, doing nothing of import. These memories came at him with little to no clarity at all and were gone as soon as they arrived. Detached from these mundane things, he was finally able to grasp what he'd been trying to figure out.

He couldn't stay here. He had a job to finish.

Letting go was like saying goodbye to a lover. He stepped away and came back repeatedly, knowing each time he had something important to attend to but not wanting to go. He did his best to clear his mind of all thoughts and memories. It was surprisingly simple. The rush of memory ceased for a moment and he latched on to a word that stood tall in his mind. The word made it easier to take the extra steps to walk away. He kept it in his mind until he felt himself fading from this where and when while hoping for a new one. The word was Purpose.

Chapter Thirty-One

Harriet's Chamber

The paint on the back was slightly chipped; white flakes fell on the counter. The mane was a narrow gold line twisting down under the horse's jaw, and the same paint ran along the tail. The statuette featured an ornate brown saddle, although the images it showed were now too faded to make out. Someone, long ago, had taken great care to craft the little horse into a child's dream toy. The artist had most likely been a horse lover, evidenced by the attention to detail. It was a sight to behold. *If only the damn thing would move.*

He flexed his fingers. Or thought he did. That was what kept coming back to him: the uncertainty of having done something or having only thought he'd done it. There had been one moment, almost immediately after he'd come to, when he'd lashed out at the door. The door held, but the swipe of his arm knocked a small pot to the floor, where it shattered into tiny pieces. It was possible to touch things, he knew that now.

It felt as though he were constantly in flux, a mass of contained energy, yet still unable to make a move without conscious effort. Once again, Marco reminded himself that he no longer had a body. He was a mental and spiritual being now. A quick look at his misty white hand was all it took for the initial shock to come back to him.

After overcoming a heavy daze that might have lasted any time from a few hours to a few days, Marco realized what Harriet had done. She had hidden him away as quickly as she could. Harriet had suddenly remembered the difficulty of the transition Marco was undergoing and had understood that he would need time. When he'd woken in the chamber, he'd been unsure of everything, unable to focus his vision or control his thoughts. It had taken this much time to learn to control his actions. Now he needed to graduate to interacting with things other than his floating form.

It occurred to him that he would've taken a deep breath before trying again, but now such a thing was impossible. There was strange humor to it and he felt himself grinning. He wasn't sure how he'd made the expression, only knowing it was the effect of his amusement, like the fallen pot had been the result of desperate vitriol he'd felt at not being able to touch the door. Perhaps emotion was the tool he required to focus his actions. He looked at the small statue once again and calmed himself before reaching out his hand. Like before, his fingers passed through to the other side of the statue unimpeded. He withdrew his hand.

The tattered pink curtains fluttered on a light breeze coming in through the window and caught his eye. He looked out at the forest far below. Harriet had been right; the colors seen from dead eyes were indeed dull, but outside the windows was a verdant canopy stretching miles into the distance. It looked to him like the world outside the castle was a brighter, more welcoming place. It relaxed him while awakening a yearning to be out there among the trees, smelling the leaves and the crisp air again. At once, a sad and hopeful feeling. He held that moment in his mind, turned to the statuette once more, and tapped it with his finger. It fell on its side.

He looked at the door. *Like taking off a Band-Aid. Do it fast.* Wrapping his present calm around him for protection, Marco floated at the door and rushed through it without a thought. It was easy, and the next moment found him on the second-floor landing with a view of the castle door below.

Now to find Harriet.

He looked around, wondering where she might have gone off to. Perhaps the greenhouse. It was the most likely place, so he started for the grand staircase only to stop a moment later. He didn't need to use the stairs any longer. Instead, he floated through the second-floor railing and down to the room. Marco was fully intent on heading to the back of the castle and straight to the greenhouse, but he didn't move. It was immobility for the simplest reason: he didn't want to move away from the door.

The castle door was a large wooden block of thick oak. A massive black deadbolt was engaged and did nothing to stop a sliver of sunlight, peeking through a crack underneath the door and into the great room. In the murky grayness of the castle, that light on the floor shone like a beacon calling him toward it, drawing him to all that awaited him on the opposite side of the door. He wanted to go to the sunlight and found that he had already floated a few feet toward the door.

Whatever was beyond the castle door was certainly better than being stuck in this old ruin. He was a lapsed Catholic and hadn't gone to church or thought much about the religion in years. There might be a heaven out there but he could just as easily consider other possibilities. Maybe it was some new world, or perhaps he'd have to relive his life in this one. Marco didn't know, but he remembered what he'd seen from the window. It was all so green out there, so filled with life. How could he bear to stay here when he could pass through the big door as easily as the other?

Harriet was afraid to leave, and because of that, she'd been trapped in the castle for centuries. Fear kept her a ghost, along with the futile hope of her parents' return. Aldryyd was different. He was unwilling to leave his home and delighted in shedding blood far too much to give it up. Staying was a choice; existing as a ghost a conscious decision not to venture out into the world after one's own death.

He floated without movement. Thoughts began to play in a twisted stream through his mind: Sixteen years old at his old house. The fight. Prison. Harris. The gun. The figure in the doorway. Pulling the trigger. It had all led him to this point.

Marco would never know what made him turn around. Speculation did nothing but wrap him in confusion. He didn't know what was beyond the door, however appealing it may feel. What he did know was that little girls didn't deserve Harriet's fate. He also knew how much he hated leaving a job unfinished. As he floated in place, Marco shook his hands, a habit he'd developed soon after holding Alan's bleeding body. He bid the front door a silent farewell and hoped to be returning to it soon as he dashed off down the main corridor.

***

The castle sat waiting. It had one place left to show this new inhabitant. It was here that the man would find his true end. The mount may have very well planned accordingly. As he sped to the greenhouse, finding no one there, moving on, Morgan's Mount whispered and willed Marco to find the narrow staircase. The silver-girded door was cracked open in invitation, although no being had left it so. Buildings of power have defense mechanisms and are not above snaring outside forces to assist them.

It would guide him, help him along with the flash of a torch, a pulse in the air, creaking of wooden beams. He would make his way to the proper place, and, if all went according to plan, he would remove the parasite. It would all end deep below where the only light shone through the cracks in the stone, and the torches had long been extinguished. Morgan's Mount prepared to host one final show.

Chapter Thirty-Two

The Theater

Shards of stained-glass windows covered rows of seats of tattered red cloth. Seat 3F, having once been graced by a king, was nothing more than a cushion with holes that spewed stuffing onto the damp ground. The high walls boasted fanciful murals that towered and curved toward the mighty stage, yet remained hidden in the dimness of it all. It was a cave of seats and stage and black.

Only a partial curtain remained, paled by time and shredded by rodents; it hung aslant across the stage. Dust hid its bright red color, but it wouldn't have shown to begin with in the gloom of the theater. It was here, beyond the curtain that Aldryyd waited, knowing the man would eventually find his way. The girl had given him nothing but gibberish when pressed for information. He had threatened to do worse than ever before, but still, she refused. The man had done something of significance but Aldryyd could not fathom what it might be. Either he would show up soon enough, and all would become clear or Aldryyd would think of a way to frighten the answers out of the girl. He'd always controlled her before. He would again. For now, he could only wait.

Her mind was nowhere in particular, but her eyes covered all, darting from the yellowed theater wall and panning down to the back rows of dim distant seats. Onward. Marco would come. When she'd left him, he'd been almost entirely unresponsive and lacking the weight of the living, easy to carry. She caught a glimmer of light that might not have truly existed as she trained her eyes on the far doorway. Two hundred years of daily fear had led Harriet to this moment when her actions against the only other of her kind would free her or bring about consequences she didn't dare to think on. The carpet on the floor used to be burgundy. She couldn't tell what color it was now. Harriet realized she had been mistaken. There was one more of her kind now. Marco had made it so. She would hold fast until his arrival. She remembered the last show she'd seen on the stage: *A Midsummer Night's Dream*. Marco would come.

A flash of light that was undeniably there shown in the doorway and hurled into the theater, whereupon it dropped to the ground behind the rows. Orange flames flickered briefly from its landing site, reaching for the nearest chair, before being snuffed out by the remnants of day-old rain trickling through the cracks in the wall. Such sudden movements were unheard of in the quiet of the castle and Aldryyd was startled.

"There you are," came a voice that carried easily with the acoustics of the space.

At first, he saw nothing more than a light blur by the entrance, but another moment showed the form of the speaker. The large smokey shape levitated above the chairs as it made its way across the room. The arms were clearly defined, while the bottom held mere suggestions of legs. It was the obsidian shade where the eyes belonged that assured Aldryyd of who he was seeing. Somehow, the man's eyes in death held the same stare as in life.

"Finding you was easy," said Marco. "I turned down a corridor I'd never been down and just kept getting pushed in this direction. At one point, part of the ceiling caved in and blocked my way. I realize that I could've gone through it. But, somehow, I knew that I had to turn back," He paused. "It was as if I couldn't go the wrong way."

Aldryyd, realizing he was still behind the curtain, slowly emerged, flowing out onto the stage. He was disturbed by what the man said and hoped it didn't show on his face.

The ghost of Marco stopped advancing and hovered above the fourth row of seats, glaring with his used-to-be eyes at the opposing being. His smoky face broke into a wide grin.

"We're both killers," Marco said, "but you kill kids and old men, you piece of shit. Chances are, anyone who ever saw my face deserved what I gave them."

Aldryyd crept slowly forward to the apron as he anticipated the man's next words.

"Now we'll see who's the better killer, won't we?" Marco's grin grew wider. "I wonder what will happen to you when it's over."

Unknowingly, Marco had touched upon a subject that had been on Aldryyd's mind for centuries. If this phantasmal existence is what followed life, then what came next if this were taken away? It was the reason he had never done more than torture the ghost girl, fearing that if he went too far, he would be forced to contend with the horrible answer to the question. He felt startled for the second time in the space of a minute. The thought struck him through with a fear he hadn't felt since his human days. For the first time in all of his existence, living and dead, he was facing a being that could bring about his demise.

"Hey, kid!" Marco shouted.

Harriet rushed out from her backstage hiding spot and flew into view. The sight of Marco filled her with momentary hope. He was a large ghost with steady energy circling him like a cloud shield. She felt the great theater vibrate for an instant as it recognized the magnitude of power it witnessed.

"You are here," she spoke.

"Yeah," replied Marco. "Hold on a little bit." He looked back at Aldryyd. "This shouldn't take me long."

Marco half flew half leaped over the remaining rows and touched down on the stage
apron, a mere foot in front of his opponent. Aldryyd sneered at him. As Marco advanced along
the stage, something turned in his mind; an unforeseen possibility that he couldn't identify was
now in play. There was a level to all of this he
had never considered, and as Morgan rushed him,
Marco wondered if he could truly fathom what he
had gotten himself into.

The shoulder came in low, driving Marco
upward and back off of the stage. In life, the shove
would've pushed all of the air out of his lungs, but
this only registered as damage. Damage without
pain. Synapses no longer fired in his brain to tell
him to feel, yet Aldryyd's attack hit with definite
impact. As they sped across the cavernous space,
arms entangled, Aldryyd pushing, Marco seeking
an effective handhold, the space around them twisted and turned upside down. He was too disoriented
to be prepared for his opponent's next move.

The girl's warning came a moment too late.
She screamed, "Look—" and he had just enough
time to wonder why she'd said it before understanding that she'd also spoken a second word
that he couldn't hear. Harriet shrieked this across
the theater, where it echoed along the walls at the
precise moment Aldryyd Morgan drove a broken
pole through Marco's shoulder.

Again, there was no pain, but the spinning
continued, and with it came a feeling close to

blacking out. Was this what happened to ghosts? A final blackout and then…Marco didn't want to find out. He struggled for mental purchase, searched for a way back to consciousness. Up became down once again. Angles shifted in his blurred vision.

This was no way for things to end: The girl trapped here for eternity. Maggie alone and mourning. Alan gone. His mind seized on that last thought. Alan. A good man if there's ever been one. In a life of killing, Marco had not known many people he could ascribe the label of Good Man to. It angered him that such a man would pass at the hands of this ghost—this bloodthirsty scum who'd spent the last few centuries eliminating anyone that entered his sanctum.

He forced his eyes open as wide as he could and ascertained that he had righted himself. Aldryyd was coming down from above and the long iron pipe still protruded from Marco's shoulder.

The girl looked on from far below. She shouted another unheard warning that was lost somewhere between the stage and the vastness of the room. Harriet was trying to help him again. Maggie had helped tremendously before leaving to mourn her fiancé. Even the cat had been invaluable in the whole mess. All of them, every one, had been on Marco's side from the beginning. He looked up into Aldryyd's glare and spoke.

"I don't need the Trips. I already know what I'm going to do to you."

When his opponent's fist struck, it was only a glancing blow. Marco had tilted right at enough of an angle to rob the hit of its main strength. It spun him and he went with it. Finding himself floating in the center of a great open space, with Aldryyd a short distance away, gave him enough time to snap the pole free from his shoulder and listen as it faintly clattered on the seats below. Morgan had made an about-face and would be coming at him again at any moment. Marco forced himself to remember the horse statue. He had forgotten that need to focus, the emotional aim that was necessary for him to act in this form.

As Aldryyd charged again, Marco drew in all thoughts of Alan's face, Maggie's voice, and Harriet above all. She would be free. *Even if it kills me.* He laughed at the thought.

A hand grasped at him, and he swiped it aside. Marco found himself outside of Aldryyd's reach and took advantage of the position by turning inward, toward his enemy. Grunting angry Welsh accompanied an arm that thrashed backward toward him but missed its mark. Marco was now behind Aldryyd. The latter made the fatal mistake of lowering his arm. As hands took hold of Aldryyd's chin and the nape of his neck, the old specter finally understood the reality of competing against a professional.

He'd never had a chance.

Ghosts do not have bones, and therefore, there is no snap, no sound at all when one breaks the neck of another. There is only the understanding of how it would've gone with living bodies and the realization that a line that makes one a spirit has now been crossed.

Aldryyd did not fall. Never yelled. He simply floated forward, head slumped, body slack, and had enough time to wonder. *What now?* Then he vanished.

While sinking downward back to the stage, Marco began to feel light in a sense that had nothing to do with corporeal weight. The job was done. His mind could finally be at ease. When the mark had been dispatched there was no more for him to do. That's how it had always been.

"Is he…?"

He looked up in time to see Harriet emerge from the near wall, the question still on her lips. Marco nodded his answer. Her head drooped. She looked tired far beyond her years.

They made their way slowly from the large red curtain to the path between the rows of seats. As they came upon the dark stairway leading back to the main castle floor, Marco realized he'd been mistaken. This job was different. His work wasn't over yet.

"Harriet," he said.

"Yes."

"The front door—" he began.

She cut him off.

"Yes, it is time. With you, I believe I can do it."

They floated into the great room, and Marco thought to assure her that she was safe and that no one would hurt her anymore. Before he could speak, he realized that he couldn't remember the name of the ghost he'd just fought.

"That's weird," he said. "I forgot his name."

"His cruel visage is still clear in my thoughts," said Harriet, "but yes, his name is gone to me."

They stopped. Marco wondered. Not only had the name of his recent opponent left him, but the more he searched his memories the less of his foe there seemed to be in them. Two fierce dark eyes burned deep into his thoughts and he felt as though he'd never forget the power of the hatred he'd seen in them, but he had no memory of the face that surrounded the glare.

"He was..." Harriet began. "Who was he?"

At that moment, Marco finally understood. What is a ghost if not a memory given form? The haunt of Morgan's Mount was now gone, and all thoughts and remembrances of him would vanish from the world. Such was death for a spirit; a world in which one wasn't ever remembered again.

"Heh," laughed Marco.

They were halfway across the floor, angled slightly to the front entrance. He looked around for a moment and took in the details of the castle. Gloom and broken things. Harriet had been here far too long. He reached down and took her hand. "Let's go together," he said. "It's time to find your mom and dad."

They went slowly, hand-in-hand, to the massive door. There was no talking along the way, and neither paused at all. Each was lost in their thoughts. They crossed the floor and found themselves in front of the large arching door frame. If Harriet had any apprehension about leaving the place she'd been trapped in for the past two centuries, it didn't show. She was not alone any longer. This man would be with her in The Land Beyond the Door, and they would meet it together. Man and girl passed through the door smoothly, each grasping the other's hand tightly, and moved on into the world outside of the castle.

Chapter Thirty-Three

Morgan's Mount, Wales

Men in hard hats had blocked off a hundred-foot area in front of the castle with yellow "Caution" tape. Workers milled around the fountain. The foreman stood by the entrance, reading from a clipboard. He'd planned to be underway by 2:00. Fisher checked his watch. It was 1:57.

It wasn't a bad day for this. The weather was warm without being wearisome for the crew; a constant wind was keeping them cool enough as they prepared. Clouds were forming but they weren't the threatening kind, more the type that promised continued sun.

"In a moment!" shouted the foreman.

Martin Fisher sat in a lawn chair on the far end of the castle's circular driveway, just outside of the yellow tape perimeter. He nodded to the foreman; an idiot of a man, but he was the cheapest available and Fisher didn't think it took much in the way of brains to blast a pile of ruins to bits. He reached over to the rock next to him and lifted the bottle there. One swig later, he saw something running across the grass.

"Hey!" he shouted. "Hold on!"

The foreman and his men looked at him with curious stares. He'd been so eager to get things going. Why was he stalling now?

A streak of orange ran toward him. Fisher walked over to it, then bent down and beckoned.

"Hey, kitty."

He scooped up the cat and carried it with him back to the car. When he was beyond the caution line once again, he gave the foreman a thumbs-up gesture. The crew went back to their preparations.

"You're Maggie's cat, aren't you?" Fisher asked as he stroked Oliver's back.

He couldn't remember the cat's name. He recalled a vague mention of it somewhere. As he sat back in the chair, he decided it would be nice to have a friend at this little ceremony. The foreman shouted, "All clear!" Fisher raised his bottle.

To the cat, he said, "And good riddance to it." He drank as the demolition crew began the blasting. The east tower collapsed first, unsurprising as the outer wall had broken away decades before. Then went the roof, and he imagined that the greenhouse had probably been crushed in the falling debris. To his surprise, he felt very little. By the time he was halfway through the bottle, the blasting had finished. The front and rear walls still stood. That part was up to the wrecking ball. It was over more quickly than he'd expected.

He walked on shaky legs down the hill with Oliver held in one arm. The only question left to him was what to do with the money he'd save by letting the castle die. He'd thought of a new house. Now he was considering items a cat owner might need. Pet food. Cat litter. Were scratching posts a necessity?

As the demolition crew began the next phase of their work, Martin Fisher took Oliver home. He didn't think for a second about his family line or their precious castle. Days ago, he'd come to a realization: Some things deserve to be ended. He'd ask Maggie about the cat tomorrow.

The river below the mount was built on past decades' sediment and contained everything from spilled oil and litter to wine and blood at various points in time. Now it held large chunks of broken stone that had dropped into it after a detonation far above. Like the other unwelcome substances that had invaded it in the past, the river pushed the blocks of stone away. Not far from the falling point of the rocks, the river widened considerably and picked up speed. There, the water would smash the rocks into bits and cast them aside.

Chapter Thirty-Four

Betws y Coed, Wales

The red light was on. Without thinking, Maggie made her way to the counter and lifted the coffee pot. It was the third time that morning she had filled the pot, but she was still intent on drinking it all. She didn't care. There were worse things to be hooked on, after all. When her mug was full, she pushed the button, and the red light went off.

Her tousled hair fell onto her face as she sat. When Maggie made to brush it away, she nearly spilled her newly poured coffee. However, hair, coffee, and woman managed to function together well enough to avoid catastrophe. After a quick sip, she determined it was too hot and placed it on the table, missing the coaster by an inch. She picked up a day-old paper and perused the front page: an economic crisis somewhere, a blurb about unemployment rates, and a celebrity she'd never heard of had done something that didn't matter to her. She dropped the paper and stared straight ahead at the vase of flowers set there.

There was a strange parity of death and flowers. It wasn't as strong as tea and biscuits or chocolate and vanilla but it was common. Since Alan's death, she had frequently been visited by well-wishing sympathizers. They always said a few kind words, then told her they were there for her, and most of them meant it. There's nothing like the death of a loved one to let you know who your real friends are. But whatever else they did, one thing was for sure; when she opened her door to them, they'd be holding flowers.

She sipped again. The coffee had cooled off. The Andersons had dropped by the night before and brought their shepherd's pie. It wasn't the best, Fiona Anderson always put in too much onion, but it was passable, and she thought it might be a decent lunch. Maggie got up and walked to the refrigerator. When she'd seen them, Mr. Anderson had been holding a small bouquet. Mostly lilies. She'd accepted them graciously, along with the heavy pan of food, and when they'd left, she'd placed the lilies in an enormous vase with most of the other flowers.

The shepherd's pie was heating, and she looked out the window while she waited. It was a bright day outside, and the forest nearby was filled with new growth. There would be plenty of flowers out there. Flowers had taken over a large portion of her life. Maggie had no true knowledge of flower identification but she'd recognized Pansies, Roses, Lilies, and Marigolds in the various bouquets people had given her. If they'd known her well enough, they would have understood that her favorites had always been the ones her mother called Bluebells. They were abundant pale blue flowers that grew near the coast and held memories of childhood day hikes in them. Alan would've known.

The microwave called. Back at the table, she poked at the food, toying with it in thought. There was a project a colleague had mentioned the week before. He'd suggested that the best thing for her might be to get back to work, and she thought he had a point. All of this time off was weighing on her. He'd said that his university needed a hand with some 16th-century artifacts they'd unearthed in Scotland. She tasted the shepherd's pie. Too much onion.

As she finished her last bite, Maggie decided to take a walk. It was the biggest decision she felt up to at the time. She lifted the plate and walked over to the sink. It would be fine if she just left it there for a while. She put on her sandals and made her way to the door.

Maggie stopped.

Something felt different. She turned around and looked back into the kitchen. The plate was still in the sink, still unwashed. Her coffee mug rested on the table where she'd left it. The newspaper was flopped open as before.

That's when she saw that a small spot of light blue shone among the myriad colors, the white Roses, yellow Marigolds, and various Daisies. Bluebells, a bunch of them, placed together in the center of the large bouquet. She was sure they hadn't been there before.

Maggie took a hesitant step closer and, upon inspection, saw a spot of dirt along the table, leading toward the vase. In the vase now rested many of her favorite flowers that she'd never been given by any of the funeral-goers and friends. And what to make of the dirt? It looked fresh.

A breeze blew by and tousled her hair. It was so sudden that she instinctively turned to see where it had come from. Nothing but the still house and things within. And the new Bluebells.

"Alan?" she asked aloud.

She stood, unmoving, as another breeze blew by. Outside the small house, the day went on, bright as ever. A dog rested on the lawn of a neighboring home, breathing heavily, wishing for the smallest bit of wind to cool him off.

The End

Barclay felt that for this internal development to take place, the country needed an open-door policy that will give the European access to the economy of Liberia. In his first inaugural address to the Liberian Legislature he expressed his opposition to the closed-door policy as seen in the Port of Entry Law of 1864:

> *"Liberia was purchase for us from its native inhabitants by the Europeans. The colony was founded by Europeans. Its expenses paid by the money of the European, until it declared its independence. They lavished their money on the establishment of schools, churches and other agencies for the elevation of successive Lodies of Negro colonists. It was a European, too, who made possible, the annexation of the State of Maryland in Liberia to the Republic...., but by an organic law, we shut him out from citizenship and denied him the rights of holding real estate in fee simple... The European having stood shoulder to shoulder with us in the organization and building up of this state naturally expected his reward. Shut out from privilege and property but one thing remained with which to compensate him for his services, that was commercial freedom... But our policy of commercial freedom to the European lasted but fifteen short years" (1850-1864)* (van der Kraaij, F.P.M., 1983).

He went on to say in this address: *"We can only save and develop our hinterland by the help of the European trader."* (van der Kraaiji, 1983). Because of his vehement opposition to the closed-door policy of the country, he could not galvanize support for his plan in parliament for the changes he had wanted during his eight years of administration.

Edwin J. Barclay (1930-1944)

He was the nephew of Arthur Barclay; the first African head along with Tubman to be entertained at the White House in

Washington DC by President Franklin D. Roosevelt in 1944 (Richardson, Nathanial R., 1959). He ruled Liberia for 14 years, more than three terms.

During his regime, Barclay was faced with the secessionist agitation among the Kru in Sinoe County, the global economic depression, international pressure to reduce Liberia to a protectorate, and the beginning of the Second World War. Besides the internal conflict with the tribal people, the economic depression made it impossible for Liberia to make payment on its 5 million dollars international debt. It is reported that by 1932 payment on the 1926 loan consumed nearly two-thirds of the government revenue (Pham, John-Peter, 2004).

In response to these pressures, Barclay ordered the adoption of the US dollar as legal tender in Liberia which indicates the Free Salves dependency on their former slave masters, though in the political arena it was considered the open door policy for capital investment. But the dilemma it puts the country in was that since the US dollar was not a property of the country, Liberia had to look up to the US with all its cronies and business practices to survive. Remember during the independence of Liberia, the US did not recognize Liberia as a sovereign nation when the Europeans did but at this point in history Barclay was entrusting our economy to the Americans by making their dollar a legal tender. In 1944 Liberia revenue and expenditures were controlled by the US. The presence of Firestone in Liberia dictated that control as the country economy solely depended on the Firestone Company, an American franchise. Firestone was the owner of the Bank of Monrovia by 1930 after the closure and withdrawal of the Bank of British West Africa.

I wish to mention <u>five hallmarks</u> of this regime and its effect on today's Liberia. The first is how he bravely handled the bleakest of the depression years. Edwin Barclay spoke and advocated for his country when the council of the League of Nations proposed to confine the republic of Liberia to forty miles from coast to inland wanting colonial administration over the other parts of the country. Barclay declared: "We shall never consent to those from the outside taking over control of the affairs of our government. If they do so it will have to be done by force" (Wilson, Charles Morrow, 1947). It was through his bravery and leadership that Liberia held its sovereignty in those tumultuous years of the 1930s.

The second is the **Lone Star**, a national song written by him:

> When freedom raised her glowing form
> On Montserrado's verdant height,
> She set within the dome of night,
> Midst lowering skies and thunder-storm,
> The star of Liberty!
>
> And seizing from the waking morn,
> Its burnished shield of golden flame,
> She lifted it in her proud name,
> And roused a nation long forlorn,
> To nobler destiny!
>
> *Refrain*
> *The lone star forever!*
> *The lone star forever!*
> *Unfurled in the currents of heaven's pure breeze,*
> *O long may it float o'er land and o'er seas*
> *Desert it? No! Never!*
> *Uphold it? Ay, ever!*
> *O shout for the lone-starred banner, hurrah!*

II
Then speeding in her course, along
The broad Atlantic's golden strand,
She woke reverb'rant through the land
A nation's loud triumphant song,
The song of liberty!
And o'er Liberia's altar fires
She wide the long-starred flag unfurled,
Proclaimed to an expectant world,
The birth for Africa's sons and sires,
The birth of Liberty!

III
Then forward, sons of freedom, March!
Defend the sacred heritage!
The nation's call from age to age
Where'er it sounds 'neath heaven's arch,
Wherever foes assail,
Be ever ready to obey
'Gainst treason and rebellion's front,
'Gainst foul aggression. In the brunt
Of battle lay the hero's way!
All hail, Lone Star, all hail!

This song would become a uniting foe and means to established national identity for the nation, and later year would be used to cultivate the spirit of freedom fighting in Africa. I still remember in grade school we sang this song with pride; it brought meaning and purpose to young and old.

The third is the handling of the 1931 Kru Revolt which had a great diplomatic impact on the protective image of the country. The brutal suppression and the kind of human rights abuse of the Liberia Frontier Force (Liberian Army) led the British to break off diplomatic relations with the Liberian government. This subsequently led to the army being put under American command.

The fourth is the policy implementation in terms of establishing a bilateral relationship with the Free Slaves' former master (America) with which American interests were paramount than the interest of the Liberian state. The turning over of the country's economy to the Americans and making the US dollar legal tender led to the underdevelopment of our country today. Rather than developing our country, the US dollar was exported from the country to develop the farms and infrastructures of their former master (America).

The last is the granting of explicit authority for America to lead the country's military in 1942 which subsequently led to the establishment of an American base and other installations like the VOA, etc. to police and spy on other African countries. Unknowing to Barclay this agreement would be to the advantage of the American and in the distant future, Liberia would be left to benefit nothing from it. This was vivid during our civil war. As we entered the heyday of our civil war, when Liberians were dying and calling on the world for support, America had no interest in our country so it was indicated to the Liberian people that America will not intervene in what was considered an internal conflict. Unlike Iraq Liberia had no oil at the time or could be used as a security threat to America, so we were not considered a priority on the American policy dashboard. The bilateral relationship was now archaic, VOA was obsolete, new technologies were being now used to police the African nations and so we were of no importance to American dominance in the world. Therefore, we were left to experience the carnage of seventeen years of rebel and insurgent brutality. More Liberians died and were displaced as refugees.

However, through these President Edwin J. Barclay deserve some credit based on the context of his presidency as Sawyer asserts:

> The forced resignation of the King's administration in the face of the contract labor scandal struck a blow to presidential authority. The League of Nations' attempt to establish a mandate, under which Liberia was to become a protectorate of European imperial power, created a grave crisis for the Liberian elite. Developing concomitantly with the pressure to reduce Liberia to a colonial protectorate were internal demands for secession, particularly along the Kru Coast. Faced with these internal and external pressures, President Edwin Barclay sought to reestablish presidential authority. For him, however, the establishment of presidential authority was not an end in itself; he sought to use that authority as an instrument to preserve the integrity of the state (Sawyer, Amos, 1997).

William VS Tubman (1944-1971)

He was born November 29, 1895, in Harper Maryland County, and is often referred to as the "Liberian Politician." He was the 19th president and succeeded Edwin J. Barclay and is the longest-serving president of Liberia. He was a Methodist lay preacher and was also regarded as the "father of modern Liberia" because his regime was marked by the influx of foreign investors and the modernization of the country. Under him, Liberia gained considerable economic and social stability. His regime has some similitude with that of Biblical Solomon. Although biblical Solomon had a god-experience through which he asked God for wisdom and led Israel for a length of time marked with peace and stability; Tubman had political wisdom and was smart. During his tenure, the country experienced a period of prosperity and some stability and peace. He championed the policy of national unity to reduce the social and political gap or divide between his fellow Free Slaves and the indigenous people. He was known in the Senate as the "Convivial Cannibal from Downcoast Hinterlands," (Richardson, Nathaniel R., 1959) a scheme under which he fought for constitutional rights for the Liberian majority, the indigenes.

In fact, during his regime there was a steady acceleration of the elevation of indigenes into the honorable class or elites but was done to cope with the vast economic changes and the creation of the diplomatic post in various parts of the globe which has placed a marked strain upon the limited post of talent available among the Free Slaves and from the list of the top fifteen or twenty elites families. The demands for skilled manpower meant that the number in the upper levels of the economy and governmental bureaucracy was expanding relatively to those who were the guardians of the Whig hegemony. Couple with the complexity of society as well as government commitment to technology and the new industrial enterprise pressurized him to vision that the indigenes and aliens at the time as indispensible to the continual operation of the Liberian society (Liebenow, J. Gus, 1987). However, as he went into years of leading, his way of governing became more than Arthur Barclay's "indirect rule" to dictatorial leadership.

At one point before becoming president, Tubman, as the associate justice of the supreme court of Liberia represented Liberia before the League of Nation on charges of the country leadership slave trade under C.D.B. King.

The milestone of this president included but was not limited to the following: First, the *National Unification policy* under which he tried to reconcile the interest of the indigenous people to that of the Free Slave elite. It is reported that under his unification policy, he encouraged the participation of "country people" from the Liberian interior in politics and extended suffrage to indigenes. It was during this time that the constitution was amended (1945) giving women the right to vote in Liberia (Pham, John-Peter, 2004). In other reports, voting rights were extended to the indigenes during his regime providing in theory for universal suffrage, but a restrictive property clause was maintained. It was during this time that the hinterland provinces were changed to county status with some improvements to their administration. However, it must be noted here that despite these political reforms, there was a representational parity between the 30,000 Free Slaves and one million indigenes. The historical economic ascendency of the Free Slaves and the absolute political power of the presidency remained in place (Dunn, D. Elwood, Beyan, Ammos J. & Burrowes, Carl Patrick, 2001).

But the indigenes love and respected him. He was their president because he had some sense of empathy for their plight under the governance of the Free Slaves. Despite the corruption that marks his administration the indigenes loved him. No one dare say anything ugly about this president in front of my grandmother in our home if you wanted to have dinner at her table. To my grand mother this man was the epitome of leadership in Africa; he was moral and loved by people, even Queen Elizabeth of Great Britain. In fact, the indigenes took years to mourn President Tubman after he died. To them, he was not just Solomon, a man of wits but their biblical Moses.

56

The second, was the success of his *"Porte Ouvert"* (Open Door) policy. He was aware that Liberia never benefited from the colonization therefore as a remedy to this unbenefited scheme of colonization he set into motion the *porte ouvert* which attracted foreign businesses, especially Lebanese into the country. It is reported that between 1950 and 1960 Liberia experienced an average growth in the economy of 11.5% (Richardson, Nathanial R., 1959). His economic success helped to modernize Liberia, paving the streets in Monrovia, created a sanitation system, hospitals were built and the literacy program was launched and the port of Monrovia was transformed into a free port. Under this policy, the country saw the retirement of the Firestone loan in 1951, the introduction of iron mining by Liberia-American-Swedish Mining Company (LAMCO) in 1953, and the 1948 maritime Code enactment which brought registration of foreign-owned ships to fly the Liberian flag, enjoy tax and other benefits but also generated revenues for the Country (Pham, John-Peter, 2004).

The third thing is the *severing of the relationship with Germany*. It was under his regime that Liberia finally made the difficult decision to relinquish its tie with Nazi Germany. Liberia finally signed the declaration of the United Nation declaring war on Germany and Japan. Remember Germany was one of the country's allies in its economic maneuvering; she was Liberia's major trading partner; most of the medical doctors at the time in Liberia were from Germany. Because of this Liberia had to expel all Germans from the country and declared the full might of the Liberian economy against Nazi Germany and the Axis.

Fourth, *the degeneration of the political system to autocratic rule*. Based on the success of his economic policy, Tubman felt that he and the True Whig Party should remain in office for the rest of his life which he did. To keep himself in power

Tubman had the PRO (People Relation Office[r]) system in place, where he had informer to eavesdrop on his enemies and subsequently get them to disappear. It appeared that everything was about him. One journalist described him in the following excerpts:

> He was the president of Liberia for twenty-eight years, and belonged to what is today a rare category of political boss who rules his country like a squire his manor: they know everyone, decide everything... Tubman received around sixty people daily. He made appointments to all official positions in the country himself, decided who should receive a concession, which missionaries were to be allowed in. He sent his own people everywhere, and his private police reported to him everything that was happening in this village, or in that one. Not much happened... Now and then, a group passed before the gates to the government palace carrying a large banner reading "A gigantic manifestation of gratitude for the progress that has taken place in the country thanks to the incomparable Administration of the President of Liberia—Dr. W.V.S. Tubman." (Kapuscinki, Ryszard, 2001)

There are lengthy legends about his rule of self-gratification including infidelity with and even against some of his cabinet members. Those cabinet members dare to complain as they would lose their positions or would never be heard of anymore (disappeared).

To keep himself in power, he used his influence to repeal Barclay's one-term limit law on the incumbent, returning to the previous system of unlimited four-year-terms and disqualified new political party supported by indigenes, making him run unopposed in 1951 (Pham, John-Peter, 2004), and by 1953 he had banned registration of other political party making Liberia a one-party state under the True Whig Party.

With that Tubman concocted a complex network of security services, including a criminal investigation division (CID) of the national police force, a Special Security Services (SSS), a National Bureau of Investigation (NBI), and Executive Action Bureau (EAB), and a National Intelligent and Security Services (NIASS) (Pham, John-Peter, 2004). These agencies were used to spread fear among the populace especially after the killing of Daniel Coleman in 1955, son of former President Coleman and chairman of Independent True Whig Party (ITWP) that was already banned in 1953.

Fifth, *the prioritization of education to some extent.* He created the needed environment and incentives that expanded Liberia College to the University of Liberia. It is reported that Tubman realizing the need for cadre in civil service, used his newfound wealth to increase the educational budget of the country from 83,000 to 2 million in 1959 as well as sent lots of students to school abroad and incorporating them in his administration upon their return to the country (Melady, Thomas Patrick, 1961). To meet the needs in the schools, Teacher training schools were established throughout the country to train the desperately needed instructors for primary and secondary schools. It is reported that a domestic arts school and a commercial school were started during this time. Other training facilities, especially in agriculture, were established with the purpose to educate the people on the new methods for raising crops and livestock. Technical and vocational schools were opened to empower its citizenry in the mine industries since Liberia was exporting iron ore and other minerals. Liebenow reports that the Tubman and Tolbert regimes have greater per capita exposure to higher education than most of the country's leadership in the history of the nation and the newer African states. Between 1960 to

1980 majority of the Liberian cabinet and subcabinet rank holds at least one college degree and most of them had some graduate education abroad (Liebenow, J. Gus, 1987). And this was due to Tubman's policy on education.

President William V.S. Tubman was an African leader and a typology of biblical Solomon; at his death, the country mourned for months. It appeared as if the earth stopped its rotation; he was missed and loved. The leading American scholars of Tubman's time asserts shortly before Tubman's death:

> For all his authority, however, Tubman is not a dictator. He has served rather as the managing director of an experiment in a controlled charger, and he has not been able at any partic-ular moment to stray away from the interest of the Americo-Liberian group that constitutes his main base of political power. Nevertheless, to the possible detriment of his own program of long-range reform, he has become the Indispensable Man. Tribal challenges have not lingered long on the scene, and few Americo-Liberians have been able to build substantial bases of support among the tribal people... The frequency of Tubman's extended health leaves and his age compels the leadership of the Liberian state to ask the long-avoided questions: "after Tubman, what?" (Liebenow, J. Gus, 1969).

Samuel Kanyon Doe (1980-1990)

He was the first indigene to rule, the twentieth President, and the first President of the Second Republic. Samuel K. Doe was probably born on May 6, 1951, in Tuzon, a small town in Grand Gedeh County, in the Southeastern part of Liberia. It is reported that his parents were uneducated and poor and belongs to the Krahn ethnic group (Ojo, Emmanuel Olatunde, 2012). He accomplished primary education when he became a career soldier which was then an opportunity to be gainfully employed since there was a lack of other job opportunities. He was promoted in October 1979 to Master Sergeant in the Liberian Army. At said time Doe was in night school to complete his GED or high school. It was during these nights of High school that Doe along with a group of soldiers planned their strategy to usurp the power of the Tolbert's Government. On April 12, 1980 this group of soldiers seized power, assassinated President William R. Tolbert, Jr., and established, for the first time in Liberia's history, military rule over the country. For them the seizure of power was to end governmental mismanagement characterized by "rampant corruption, misuse of public office, and violation of human rights" (Dunn, D. Elwood, Beyan, Ammos J. & Burrowes, Carl Patrick, 2001). Doe as the high-ranking militant in this group became the chairman and ushered in the People's Redemption Council (PRC).

I chose Samuel Doe in this panoramic historical analysis to point out highlights of his administration but also to critically reflect on the relationship and effect of his administration on the future decision-making of Liberians about the trajectory of where the country is headed.

In highlighting his regime, let us first recognize him as the First President of the Second Republic. Doe ushered in the Second Republic, a republic that the indigenes saw as hope and liberation from the generation of Free Slaves. Doe came to power after staging a coup d'état in 1980. He ruled the first five years with military dictatorship, and having been pressured for political reform, his military junta agreed to a program of democratization which culminated in him being elected, as the first president of the new republic (Kufour, K., 1994). Doe masterfully used the military as Arthur Barclay used it but for Doe, it was to show power and maintain control, unlike Arthur who used it to suppress and tax the indigenes. This military take-over was a bloody one, labeled as 'revolution' (Ojo, Emmanuel Olatunde, 2012) slaughtered an entire Cabinet of the Tolbert's administration, having put them on trial without a lawyer and no right to appeal against the verdict. It appeared to be vengeful as they were publicly executed on a beach near Monrovia. By the end of the first five years of this regime, Doe's administration had executed 80 persons for political reasons and detained over 600 without trial, usually in connection with one alleged coup plot or another. In fact in August 1984, by the order of President Doe, the AFL matched on the student protesters at the University of Liberia, leaving several dead, many raped and over 100 injured (Dunn, D. Elwood, Beyan, Ammos J. & Burrowes, Carl Patrick, 2001).

Though President Doe professed commitment to constitutionalism and the rule of law, his regime was marked by human rights violations. Not very long he settled in office then he embarked on the elimination of all forms of opposition, whether real or perceived. One writer indicates that the seventeen of those who had staged the coup in 1980, including himself, Thomas Wey Syen, Thomas Quiwonkpa, Abraham Kollie, Nicholas Podier, Fallah Vanney, Jeffery Gbatu, Larry Bortey, Harrison Pennoh, Robert Sumo, Harrie Johnson, Harry Zuo, Jacob Swen, Albert Toe, Nelson Toe, William Gould, and Kolonsh Gonyon (Omonijo, B., 2003); by 1990, Doe had eliminated sixteen. Within a decade of his presidency, life in Liberia had become unsafe and all the popular politicians joined forces calling on Doe to quit (Ojione, Ojieh Chukwuemeka, 2008). These human rights abuses, coupled with a growing economic crisis, precipitated the outbreak of the civil conflict.

Next is the appointment of the Constitutional Commission. A year after the military coup d'état, on April 12, 1981, which was the first anniversary of the PRC, Doe announced the creation of a 25-member constitution commission under the leadership of Dr. Amos Sawyer, which was then seen as a gesture to pave the road to genuine democracy. A new constitution was crafted, and one of the clauses of this new constitution stipulated that the new president of the country was to be at least 35 years of age. President Doe having read this clause changed his birth date to meet this criterion. So rather than being born May 6, 1951 it was changed to 1950. Givens in a subtitle summed it up: 'The man, who changed the course of Liberia's history three weeks before the age of 29, celebrates his 30th birthday' (Givens, Willie A.(ed.), 1986). Unfortunately the dream to constitutionality was unrealized. His love for power sabotaged his vision for the country returning to constitutionality. He surrounded himself with members of his Krahn tribe and excluded the Free Slaves from power, failing to realize that these Free Slaves were the ones that had built this franchise and had international alliances.

The third thing about this administration is the silence of the US to the political abuse of power of Doe and its support of this regime. Ojo indicates that the US was greatly relieved when Doe maintained the country's pro-Western stance and he was invited to the White House by Ronald Ragan. This regime received more political and military assistance from the US in the decade of Doe's rule than the country had ever received, despite the increasing deterioration of the political climate and human rights record (Ojo, Emmanuel O., 2012). In another report, Dunn et al indicated that American aid which has never exceeded $20 million per annum prior to 1980, topped $91 million in 1985, with military aid increasing from $1.4 million to $14 million annually (Dunn, D. Elwood, Beyan, Ammos J.

& Burrowes, Carl Patrick, 2001). The US State Department seemed to have been pleased after Doe was declared winner of the controversial election of 1985 and sworn in as the 20th President and First President of the Second Republic in January of the following year. The issue here is not solely Doe's election fraud or abuse of political power but rather the interest of the US. From the First Republic to now, the Second Republic, America who is the ally of Liberia, had always sought what it gets from the relationship; as long as the US interest is served, she is willing to blind herself to other indignities of the relationship. Therefore Doe's regime brought to vivid light this characteristic of the ally.

The fourth mark of this administration was the creation and implementation of the Liberian Dollars. Throughout the First Republic, the country has used US dollars as legal tender. In the effort to continue developmental projects in Liberia, President Doe's vision of having a legal tender for the country was beneficial to the people; the money could not be taken out of the country as has been with the US dollars. In fact, during this time many road projects were started including the Du-port Road and the Rehab roads. The country enjoyed brief period of economic come back; local businesses became to realize their investment; real estate bloomed for a period in Liberia. The economy made strides.

Last his death was the most humiliating death of a President on the continent. On September 9, 1990, President Samuel Doe was captured by Prince Y. Johnson in Monrovia while in route to visit ECOMOG-headquarters. Doe was tortured, mutilated, and finally brutally killed by Johnson and his men. Ojo asserts:

> Ironically, Samuel Doe died in the hands of a mentally defective Liberian, like his predecessor who had also succumbed in the

hands of a mentally unstable person. Doe's repressive military dictatorship and his transformation from a shy, thin, soft-spoken Master Sergeant into a corpulent, well-fed and well-clad Commander-In-Chief earned him a place next to other notorious heads of state like Idi Amin (Uganda), Jean Bedel Bokassa (Central Africa), and Baby' Doc (Haiti). The greed for power, the corruption, nepotism and the abuse of human rights which Doe had reproached Tolbert had become a trademark of his regime (Ojo, Emmanuel O., 2012).

The love for power and insecurity sabotaged this first indigenous rule, making many ask the same question Nathaniel asked in scripture, "Can anything good come out of Nazareth?" especially seeing what is going on now in the country.

Culture

Culture as shared patterns of behaviors and interactions, cognitive constructs and understanding that are learned by socialization, is typical of the Liberian peoples' group. Thus, for this argument, it is considered as the growth of a group identity fostered by social patterns unique to the group. Culture for us here is the knowledge and characteristics of the Liberian groups of people, as defined by their language, religion, cuisine, social habits, music, and arts.

The word "culture" holds its root in a French term, which in turn derives from the Latin "*colere*," which means to tend to the earth and grow, or cultivation and nurture. Cristina De Rossi, an anthropologist at Barnet and Southgate College indicates that culture shares its etymology with several other words related to actively fostering growth (Zimmermann, Kim Ann, 2016).

The Liberian culture like any other culture continues to go through metamorphosis although some elements within the culture remain resilient to the changes. It is no longer fixed if it ever was. Culture is essentially fluid and constantly in motion. This makes it so that it is difficult to define any culture in only one way as the Liberian culture. It is the key to any people interconnected world which is made up of so many ethnically diverse societies but also riddled by conflicts associated with religion, ethnicity, ethical beliefs, and essentially the elements which make up culture (Zimmermann, Kim Ann, 2016).

The Liberian culture has two distinct roots, the Southern American heritage of the Freed Slaves or Americo-Liberians and the ancient African descendants of the indigenous peoples or tribes. Most of the Free Slaves or former Americans belonged to the Masonic Order of Liberia, which was outlawed by 1980 when President Samuel Doe came to power. However, it originally played an influencing role in the nation's politics. Being a member of the Masonic order had its privileges as well as social stratification and identity. It also advocated setting social behavior and norm among the Free Slaves thus making them distinctive. It was also considered a secret society since most of its gatherings were held at night or behind closed doors. However, its members were loyal to each other as well as helpful in assisting each other in terms of needs or climbing the social ladder at the time. There were few Baptist, Methodist, and Presbyterian churches that one could not hold a leadership position in or even become their head pastor if one was not a member of this elitist group of Masonic order.

Other things about the culture of the Free Slaves were one, their skills of embroidery and quilting; it became firmly embedded in the national culture (Liberia—History and Culture, 2016).

Next was the haunting slave music and songs of the American South which had ancient African rhythms and harmonies. It blended well with the indigenous musical traditions of the region. The third is their creole and English language. These had an Ebonic tone as they annunciated their words which made it quite different from Western and British English. And lastly is their religion. The Free Slaves considered themselves as Christians; often they would see the indigenes as barbarian or heathens failing to be aware that their god is repressive and oppressive. They often boasted about their religion as the true one which of course was the religion of their former slave masters. Some of them considered themselves as missionaries or evangelists to the dark continent of African to Christianized and civilized the indigenes.

The indigenous people which consist of sixteen ethnolinguistic groups, and are characterized as tribes, have never constituted unified, historically continuous political entities. However, they contribute to another form of culture in how they live their lives and how they related to the Free Slaves. Unique to their culture was their belief system. The Indigenes believe in a supernatural world of ancestral and spirits that depicted their relation to one another to a larger extent and that impacted their daily lives. This belief includes the conviction that there are deep and hidden things about an individual that only diviners, priests, and other qualified persons can unravel (Olukoju, Ayodeji, 2006). It also presupposes that whatever occurs or exists in the physical realm has already occurred or existed in the spirit world. It is this belief system that enlivens their communal life as people. Several feasts are celebrated to appease whatever form of ancestral or spiritual entity. Most of the Indigenes groups participate in the traditional religious practices of the Poro and Sande secret societies, except the Krahn and Grebo ethnic groups. These secret societies are also used to educate the younger generation about being able body men and domestic women for the culture. In the initiation, the girls are taught to be home makers and mangers of the homes; while the boys are taught hunting, blacksmith, and other skills to be the breadwinner for the families and the clans.

Next is their ethnic relation. In Liberian northwestern, Mande-speaking groups formed multiethnic chiefdoms and confederacies that coordinated trade and warfare, especially during the period of the slave trade. Although there were no pre-colonial states, the northwestern peoples were united in two pan-ethnic secret societies: Poro (for men) and Sande (for women). This link to the Poro and Sande lodges became a mobilizing instrument for the entire population under the authority of elders for farming and warfare (Advameg, Inc, 2016). The tribes represented more than a group of people and chief but it meant group work, group play, community housing and defense. The tribe became the basis of the social establishment. Every man, woman, and child alike was obliged to work for their community without pay (Wilson, Charles Morrow, 1947). This ethnic relation was extended to how the indigenous or tribe cares for their orphans and their aged populations. It is their pride to take care of their old folks and was considered as attracting the blessing of the gods and ancestral spirits. Wilson alludes to this pride of the indigenes when says the indigenes pitied the Free Slaves who have been robbed of all the heritages and advantages of being African tribesmen.

The third is the Indigenous graphic arts. Today Liberia is known as the home of the "classical" African mask. The artistic ability of indigenous woodcarvers is unprecedented and recognized. Many of the masks are commissioned by the Poro and Sande societies for use in initiation rituals; some powerfully charged masks may be seen only by initiates, while others are used in public masquerades. The range of forms produced by indigenous carvers is impressive as is the continuity of some styles over time. Other indigenous art forms include murals painted on the exterior walls of buildings, pottery, weaving, music, and dance (Advameg, Inc, 2016).

Family

To understand the context of human society, it is expedient to understand family. A family is a group of people related either by consanguinity, affinity, or co-residence or some combination of the above. The purpose of the family is to maintain the well-being of its members and society. Ideally, families would offer predictability, structure, and safety as members mature and participate in the community (Collins, Donald, Jordan, Catheleen & Coleman, Heather, 2010). In most societies, it is within the family that children acquire socialization for life outside the family. The family serves as the basic unit for meeting the essential needs of its members, it provides a sense of boundaries for performing tasks in a safe environment, builds a person into a functional adult, transmits culture, and ensures continuity of humankind with precedents of knowledge.

Family in the Liberian culture is important, on which the survival of the culture depends. Southall relates the strength of the Liberian family ties in the African urban population to types of urban administration (Southall, Aiden (ed.), 1961). The administration of communion policy and stability of any Liberian community solely depended on their family relationship. And family here is a large entity that included extended family members. One important thing about the family was the rule that establish recognition of the existence of the family. It was done through marriage. And in Liberia there are two types of marriage contracts: the civilized which was done in church or by the justice of the peace, and the tribal which was supported by tribal customary law. These two types are considered legal contracts in Liberia today. The civilized contract was mainly practiced by the Free Slaves while the tribal was by the indigenes and documented in the Internal Affairs Ministry if it is reported by the party involved. These rites or rituals served as the basis for the recognition and establishment of the family so as to hold each other accountable within the community. It's worth saying here that in the indigenous African societies the institution of marriage stood at the intersection of gender roles and family life. For the male, marraige is a sign of maturity but also an emblem of citizenship in the local community. The indigenes had an understanding and practice of rights and obligations of members of the marriage relationship which specified gender roles. On the other hand, marrage is not just a bond between the couple but includes their in-laws and kinsfolk. As Olujuko puts it marriage in the patrilineal society involves the transfer and exchange of individual and property rights. The male's family is entitled to the woman's domestic and other conjugal services, her assets, and the product of the union whereas the woman's family is entitled to the bride price or wealth in cash or kind by the groom and his family (Olukoju, Ayodeji, 2006).

The significance of the family and its ties is seen in its social, political and economic power as was lived in Liberia amongst the people's groups. Among the indigenous people, the building block of their ethnic society was the nuclear family which consisted of a man and his wives—polygamy being the ideal and norm, and his offsprings. The greater size of a man's retinue, the greater his prestige in the community. Liberia like other African countries patrilineal system of reckoning social obligaion was and is practiced. Liebenow indicates that the family is the most significant social unit for the indegenous for birth into patrilineal kinship which gives one legitimacy, support in times of crisis, and companionship (Licbenow, J. Gus, 1987). On the other hand, polygamy establishes an expanding number of marital ties with women of otherkin groups as well as other indigenous or ethnic groups. Therefore this form of marriage became the mechanism to resolve conflicts even in those political units without a formal structure of government.

The family structure in many instances was the most important economic unit among the indigenous people. For example the growing and processing of rice, cassava, and other farm produce have been family enterprise. The more wives and children a man has the bigger his farm because he has the number of people to work in it.

Family as seen among the Free Slaves has great importance to individual bilateral ties at birth, the one acquired in marriage and even the marriage of siblings and children. Licbenow indicated that within the said group there was an understanding in its community to adhere to endogamy, or marriage within a larger settler group (Licbenow, J. Gus, 1987). Therefore birth and marriage made one a member of a series of family groups that imposed obligations and also provided political allies in times of crisis as well as in need to advance one's career and standing in the community. It is reported that family ties within the Free Slave community, provided information regarding changes in political climate and access to the spoils available to the True Whig Party Leadership then. The Free Slaves' knowledge of his ties and the family ties of others is a *sine qua non* for social and political survival as an ambitious person (Licbenow, J. Gus, 1987).

Consequently birth and marriage among the Free Slaves were political, social, and economic events which established broader bonds than those between two or more persons. The Free Slaves view themselves and their personalities as representatives of family groupings. This was clear in where they chose to settle in Liberia and how they maintain their leadership in government, church and the mason. For example if you were to go to Fordsville, Grand Bassa, you will meet the Flemings, the Reeves; in Buchanan, the Morgans and the Hammons. Or if you were to go to Brewerville, you will see the Walkers, the Richards or the Capeharts; in Bentol the Tolberts, the Rouhlacs; in Sinoe the Grigbys; in Monrovia, the Barclays, the Grimes, and the Kings; in Harper, the Tubmans and the Gibsons, in Cape Mount, the Shermans and Freemans and most of these families intermarried to maintain their echelon. Based on this family system among the Free Slaves, one would choose who his affiliations were, cultivated his friendship as well as avoided which company to not affiliate with.

Although romantic love is a factor in marriage among the Free Slaves but within the honorable class marriage was made possible by other factors like one's affiliation in school, church and social status or class identification and family loyalty within the community. Notwithstanding, there were certain permissiveness and consideration across the class line for the political advancement of an ambitious man. That permissiveness came in the 1960s for premarital and extramarital situations which were meant to provide formal political alliance.

Chapter Four
Education in Liberia

L iberia like any other country or society has had an educational system that purposes to transmit the cultural
heritage, development of the younger minds, and building
a responsible citizenry. In the ACS charter of establishment
of the new colony, there were key objectives which included:
1. To rescue the free colored people of the United States from
political and social disadvantages; 2. To place them in a country where they may enjoy the benefits of free government,
with all the blessings which it brings in its train; 3. To spread
civilization, sound morals and true religion throughout the
continent of Africa; 4. To arrest and destroy the slave trade;
and 5. To afford slave owners who wish and are willing to
liberate their slaves an asylum for their reception (Lanier,
R. O'Hara, Summer, 1961). Education became one of the
strategies from social disadvantages as well as spreading what
they would consider morals, civilization, and religion.

However, amongst the indigenes, education was a form of life
and was done through the Poro and Sande societies which
are considered informal but dear to the heart of most of the
indigenous group besides the Grebo. The Poro and Sande were
exclusive to members only.

Jones attests to this exclusivity of this informal education and societies. She indicates that no other person, other than their members could enter the bush schools. Most importantly, peace within the country was to be maintained once the bush schools were in session. Tribal war could not be waged or other hostility during the session of Poro and Sande schools. Entering a bush school as a non-participant meant being banished or killed (Jones, Sammer Saleh, 2016).

Educational Development

The development of former education in Liberia can be traced to the arrival of the Free Slaves called settlers. But this form of education went through phases and experienced impediments as to its progress. Such education is often referred to as western education. The western form of education was introduced by the Free Slaves, missions and later the government but was aimed at civilizing and Christianizing (Lymas-Reeves, Ruth, 1995). Educational laws were enacted to give support to this endeavor. To promote such a form of education, compulsory education was enshrined into the philosophy of education giving equal opportunity to all at age 6-16 to education (Caine, Augustus F., 1986).

For the Free Slaves, education had an individualized meaning and for many of them, it serves different agendas in different societies. For those who witnessed the direct uplift and empowerment of themselves and their communities, education meant liberty and freedom. As former residents of the antebellum South, education offers the promise of hope. Seeing the advantages of advancement through 'book knowledge,' the Free Slaves wanted education to be cultural norms in this new colony. Remember that in the antebellum South some laws and customs forbid blacks or these slaves from learning to read and write. To the White man education was the key to power, influence, and wealth; therefore, forbidding the blacks from it would keep the whites in control. It was this idea to keep blacks from being educated and that created yarning in a young slave like Booker T. Washington to view the mysteries of reading and writing from a distance whenever he escorted his slave master's son to the schoolhouse he was forbidden to enter. It excited his curiosity and when his mother explained to him that the whites considered reading too dangerous for black people, it made him more anxious to acquire this skill (Litwack, Leon F., 1998).

It was this desire to uplift themselves, build influence and power that encouraged many of the Free Slaves to journey to Liberia. In the context of this new colony, education for the emigrants, as well as for the young and natives, who were considered "heathens," was crucial to the development and sustaining of the new nation.

Moreover, besides nation-building, many including the ACS and philanthropic organizations saw education as a means of Christianizing Liberia. Jones writes:

> During the first decade after arrival, the purpose of education in the colony was geared towards a missionary agenda. What better way to bring the 'dark' continent out of darkness? Educating its people with the Christian values and doctrine offered some form of control over the way in which they lived. In order to accomplish this, the recruitment and leadership efforts of the ACS during the first decade was selective and partial to those they considered to be of 'good character' (Jones, Sammer Saleh, 2016).

Despite the above, this form of education experienced impediment as to its progression as a result of the background of its would-be founder, the Free Slaves. Frankel writes about this group as: "... most, but not all, were illiterate and unfamiliar with any form of employment other than plantation labor. The remainder had at least some experience of life as free men—4,000 have been born free—and they include individuals of some education and several artisans(carpenters, mason, bricklayers, etc.), although as an unfranchised section of the population they had no experience at all of the participation in government." (Frankel, M, 1964). This contributed to the poor education which has eroded our civilization over the years. Even Kitchen in the 60s was critical about the form of education that went on and he wrote: "Liberia thus labors under several handicaps. The ruling group... has limited education background itself and, therefore, has not been very critical in its approach to education." (Kitchen, H. A., 1962).

Before this former education or western education, there was in existence non-formal education among the indigenes. Ruth Reeves talked about this form in this way: "Liberia like most West African societies had, and in a way still has an educational system the purpose of which to transmit the cultural heritage. The system has been modified to relate the existing conditions and many ethnic groups achieved this goal through the institutions of the Poro and Sande secret societies." (Lymas-Reeves, Ruth, 1986).

Purpose of Education

In each of the forms of education in Liberia, there were rationale for their existence and perpetuation. In this light, Mary Antoinette Brown argues that the Poro called the bush school aim has always been the transformation of the immature individual into an adult member of his society. The oath-taking ceremony climaxes this transformation of boy to man to which the entire period of training has to be geared. The boy must gain the physical, intellectual, and moral development necessary for being at home in his world and recognizing his social obligations. Specifically, the school aimed to train him in those ideas, attitudes, skill which his culture valued in a male, adult, such as, respect for the elders, pride in the traditions of his tribe, sharpness in wit, and ability to work for the support of his family and the discharge of his kinship obligations (Brown Mary Antoinette, 1969).

The Sande School, like that of the Poro, was conducted in secrecy and considered bush school. It usually begins after the Poro School closes. Entrance into the Sande society was a rite of passage for any native lady who wanted to be respected. Girls were generally admitted between the ages of four and twelve and would typically stay in session from a few months to seven years. On entry, girls were taken into the forest for a rite of passage that included female circumcision. The Sande society aims at providing education that would transform a girl into an adult female with the cultural values, attitudes, and skills required for serving as a responsible woman, good wife, and mother. She was also taught about sexual relations. The focal point of her training was family life and domestication; however, she was taught some dancing and singing (Jones, Sammer Saleh, 2016).

As western or formal education was introduced by the Free Slaves, mission, and later government, it aimed at civilizing and Christianizing. Greater emphasis was placed on literacy education (i.e. mere book learning) while very little thought was given to vocational education and training as the Free

Slaves tried desperately to transplant the system that existed in America (Lymas-Reeves, Ruth, 1986).

Tension

Base on the assertion of Lymas-Reeves, the control of education seemed to slip out of the hands of the Free Slaves' government thus becoming a franchise of the missionaries. This also created tension within the society. For example, De La Rue observed:

> When the government assigned its school funds, they believed the mission schools could take over the education of their children; there were plenty of mission schools and there was plenty of money from America to maintain them. The mission school believing in Liberia complex took over the work (De La Rue, S., 1930).

De La Rue and others had to protest against the government consent to substitute mission school for the public, having assessed the mission schools in this except:

> The mission schools were systematized and equipped not for training of salesmen, administrators, government clerks, stenographers, mechanics, and agriculturist which the nation must have if it is to strive—they were specialized for the purpose of training ministers of the gospel and "natural workers" to aid in missionary work. Their substitution for the public schools and colleges put them a burden for which they had never been intended (De La Rue, S., 1930).

Let it be known here that one of the purposes of education was to Christianize the people, especially the indigenes who the

Free Slaves thought of as heathen. It was the mission schools' purpose to achieve this goal and to control the people. But the government entrusting the education of the general public with the mission schools did not go well with others in their rank since others saw it as another antebellum South coming to the West Coast of Africa.

With this, the government came to its senses and on January 25, 1900 approved a resolution providing for the appointment of General Superintendent of Public Instruction and Common Schools plus a Bureau of Education. This was done by the Liberian Legislature (Payway, Paul T., 2001). It was in this light that the government again began to exert its control over the educational system of the nation. This reinforces the obligation of any democratic government to its citizenry in terms of national development.

Consequently, the Liberian Government adopted some principles which are clearly expressed in the pronouncements of political and educational leaders of that day while others are implied through educational practices. Moreover, at such time education came to be considered an instrument of national development and stability. In this light Azango asserts:

> The philosophy of education as an instrument of national development was emphasized in the message of the National Consultative Conference on education Policy in 1974 by President Tolbert:

> ...Our country's promise of equal opportunity can be best realized by education geared to the needs of people through diversification of educational programs and adequate learning facilities (Azango, Bertha Baker, 1968).

The Liberia government began to provide the opportunity for its citizenry including both female and male to education. Education became the gateway to equal opportunity. Caine attest to this ideal when he writes:

> Education is recognized as a gateway to equal opportunity; therefore, we must ensure that equal opportunity is available to all that can benefit it. In 1971 Conference on Development Objectives and strategies urged Government to adopt "regional equalization of educational opportunities" as a goal and that the nation, in its socio-economic development plan for 1976 – 1980 committed itself to provide "universal, basic education" to help the masses improve their lives and to ensure "equitable geographic distribution of education opportunities". These policies prescriptions were clearly aimed at harnessing education to national goals, such as the drive for greater equity in economic life to enable the people to know their rights so as to take a more meaningful part in the process of political decision-making (Caine, Augustus F.).

With that, access to education became an intentional goal for the country. Earlier the Legislature had passed the compulsory school attendance laws in 1921 for all children up to age 16.

Azango further stated that this enactment:

> Every parent, guidance or other person having control of any child between the ages 6-16 shall cause such child to attend some recognized public or private school regularly for the entire time during which school is in session; provided, however, that this provision shall not apply to any child whose physical or mental conditions render his attendance impracticable; or to any child who shall have completed the school course. For every willful neglect of such duty as prescribe above, the offender shall be fined the sum of ten dollars recoverable before a court of complete jurisdiction (Azango, Bertha Baker, 1986).

The provision was updated in 1937 increasing the fines from $10.00 to $25.00.

Another thing that was a subtle mark regarding education was discrepancies in terms of the opportunity given to both sexes. Though there were laws on the book that compelled parents to send their children to school, the culture seemed to promote education for the boys than the girls as seen per the statistics in both elementary and secondary school attendance in the country. From the onset, the Liberian government advocated for female education by the mere fact of the opportunity it provided for its citizenry. There were other organizations within the country especially the missionaries that were advocates for female education. Reeves (1995) asserted:

> Besides the efforts of individual immigrants like Lott Carey, several ladies in the United States organized societies to promote education in Liberia. Ladies Benevolent societies, as they were formed in several major cities in the United States. The aim of these societies was to promote education of the female in Liberia. The Ladies Society of Richmond, for example employed a colored female to teach an orphan school in Monrovia. She taught 32 girls between the ages of 4 and 14 reading, writing, arithmetic, geography, plain sewing, and baking (Lymas-Reeves, Ruth, 1995).

The Catholics are known for the champion of girls' education as they open more convent schools, like St. Theresa, St, Mary and others. However, these schools became schools of the elite and middle-class families. The majority of the descendants of the Free Slaves found opportunity in these catholic convent schools because they could afford it unlike the children of most indigenous people. Moreover, gender imbalance in the educational system remains a foe to reckon with. In 1980 the Ministry of Education reported the following about girls' enrolment:

> Female students constituted a smaller proportion at all levels. At the elementary level, they amounted for 36%, at junior high level 30%, and in high school 28% (Payway, Paul T., 2001).

The tension remains as to how and what can be incentives to parents and their girl children to motivate for school attendance. On the other hand, among the indigenes, there is a high attendance rate in the Sande society for their girls. It is something every family looks toward; even sometimes girls are taken out of the formal western education for a semester or two to go to the Sande.

Another tension is the issue of accessibility. Education is pivotal to decreasing poverty in any country. In Liberia education can even mitigate the fragility of the country. Unfortunately, the country has a longer road to universalizing its educational system after these years of civic conflict. During the war, almost an entire generation of Liberians had no education whatsoever except for those in the diaspora. This has left a gap in knowledge and increase the illiteracy rate in the country.

One author asserts that Liberia education system has been devastated by the war: schools have been destroyed, trained staff lost and governmental infrastructure decimated. Of the estimate population of 2.5 million of which 55% of school-going age, 45% have no access to education. This is especially true of the rural area for young indigenous children and girls (Reynolds, Barbara G., 2015). Roads have been destroyed, making children journey to school more arduous and schools have been destroyed increasing the distance children have to travel on foot to attend school. Some children have to travel between five to seven miles to school. This remains a significant national challenge to be addressed.

Couple to accessibility is the issue of quality in education which has resulted in poverty, unemployment and hopelessness. If this is not addressed timely and appropriately by the political leadership, the propensity to drive the younger and uneducated Liberians to forceful recruiting agents for armed militia in Africa is high since it is the new form of business in Africa. We saw this in Sierra Leone, Baukinafaso, and the Central African Republic where child soldiers and young people are trained and contracted for mercenary expeditions to destabilize other African countries. Given the recent history of Liberia, the need for quality education is an important area to reassess. The civil war has left the educational system with more challenges regarding both access and quality of education.

In terms of quality, it is reported that around 70% of schools in Liberia was destroyed during the war (International Development of Law Organization (IDLO), 2010). Therefore children had to travel great distances creating attendance challenges due to fatigue and security. On the other hand, huge numbers of trained teachers had either left the profession, gone into the diaspora for security, or died; leaving unqualified and profit-seekers to managed and operate school systems. This can be seen by the emergent of newly operated private schools sprouting out around the country without being thoroughly assessed by the Ministry of Education (MOE). It appears that the purpose of education as enshrined in the philosophy of education of Liberia has been secondary to profit-making by these sprouting schools.

The civil war has greatly imparted and exacerbated the tension crippling the educational system. It has deemed Liberia as a 'fragile state' in the international development discourse. As a 'fragile state', Liberia lacks the political will power, and capacity to provide the basic functions needed to reduce poverty, to develop, and safe-guard the security and human rights of its population (Reynolds, Barbara G., 2015).

Notwithstanding, visionary leadership and love for the nation can mitigate some of the tensions. For example, the renewed efforts of the Ellen Johnson Sirleaf's government saw education as pivotal and sought partnership with the international community to revitalize the educational system. The Ellen Johnson Sirleaf's government promoted school enrollment which resulted in 24% for girls and 18% for boys in public primary school between 2006 and 2007 (Tsimpo, Clarence & Wodon, Quentin, 2012). Education and health services became one of the government's pillars in the reduction of poverty strategy. This government sought to ensure that more children had access to schools as well as more people in need of care receive it. During this time assessment of the system was done. In said assessment, the following was found about the educational system of the country.

One it was discovered that school enrollment in both elementary and secondary schools in rural areas was lower as compared to urban areas; and they were much lower among poorer household (Tsimpo, Clarence & Wodon, Quentin, 2012). The rural areas are where the indigenes live to emphasize.

Next, it was discovered that government or public school remains the primary service provider for rural students as well as for the poor in the country. However, the reasons for the lower enrollment were due to the cost to attend and distance from the homes of the students (Tsimpo, Clarence & Wodon, Quentin, 2012). In as much as the government operated these schools in rural areas, the price tag to attend those schools was high that the poor family could not afford to send their children. This involved registration fees, books, toiletries, test fees, etc. The public school seemed to be like a private school for the poorer or rural communities. The distance to school is a factor to preventing children to continue their education. As indicated earlier, because of the distance, the journey to school for the children in rural communities has become arduous and even dangerous.

Chapter Five
The Liberian Spirituality

To understand the spirituality of the Liberian peoples group, it is good to evaluate the dimensions of religious beliefs and worldviews across space and time. Both Free Slaves and the indigenes have some specific beliefs but also overlapping beliefs and worldview. Among the indigenous, we term their beliefs as typical of African Traditional Religion (ATR) and have some values and practices in common with other religions. Said religion proposes a relationship between the supernatural or the invisible world and the physical world. That is to say, indigenes like any other African relate all dimensions of human life and especially their struggles for freedom and empowerment to a transhistorical source of power and meaning. They believe that humanity is surrounded by a realm of invisible, powerful beings comprising sub-divinities and ancestral spirits governed by one supreme God (Mbiti, Jolm S., 1980). Therefore, whatever happens in the physical is sanctioned by the gods or had already occurred in the supernatural invisible world. As a matter of fact, indigenes cannot conceive of life apart from its relationship to the realm of invisible spirits. As one scholar asserts,

> Africans believe that neither humanity nor nature is alone in the universe but, rather, is surrounded by and dependent upon the superior power of the supreme God, numerous

sub-divinities and ancestral spirits. Thus, for them, the realms of nature, humanity and spirit comprise a cosmological whole and, hence, it is unthinkable for them to think of humanity apart from its connectedness with that larger world perspective (Paris, Peter J., 1993).

So, to appease the spiritual world, they pray and make sacrifices including libation, and putting on acts of honor for their ancestral spirits. The indigenous spirituality simply acknowledges that beliefs and practices touch on and inform every facet of human life, and therefore indigenous religion cannot be separated from the everyday or mundane. The second thing about indigenous spirituality is the belief that the supreme God is the Creator. Peter Paris asserts,

> The widespread traditional African belief that the Supreme God is Creator and Preserver of all reality, may be the single most important commonality that exists among the vast diversity of African peoples (Paris, Peter J., 1993).

In indigenous theological thought, the supreme God is here with the indigenes (Africans) and was never brought to the African continent by missionaries nor by the Free Slaves, rather it is this supreme God who brought both the missionaries and the Free Slaves to the land of the indigenes.

In this light, it is worth noting that the term "religion" has always become problematic for many indigenes because it suggests that religion is separate from the other aspects of one's culture, society, or environment. But for many indigenes or Africans, religion can never be separated from all these. It is a way of life, and it can never be separated from the public sphere. As one author puts it, "Religion informs everything in traditional African society, including political

art, marriage, health, diet, dress, economics, and death."
(Chiorazzi, Anthony, 2015).

Unlike the indigenous, the Free Slaves as the architect of
Christianity and freemason, religion seems to be part of their
life but does not inform it as seen in how they related to the
indigenes. Though they had a mind to evangelize the indigenes and so made several missionary endeavors among the
indigenous—opening schools, hospitals and literacy centers
and translating the Bible into indigenous languages so that
the indigenous would read, understand and worship the
Christian gods in their language and understanding, yet they
dealt with the indigenes in ways that were in contradiction
to their Christian book, the Bible. The key to their religious
practices was control—having political, economic, social, and
environmental prowess in the Gold Coast.

The Foundation of beliefs

Stephen Ellis, an anthropologist, once said that belief that all
power has its origin in the invisible world, where God and
spirits dwell, is a constant of Liberian history. As we investigate
the various beliefs and worldview among the Liberian peoples,
one thing that was discovered is the accommodation in religious practices that continue to dominate the trend among the
Liberian people's groups. Another issue is how the dilemma of
irreconcilable religious differences is resolved on the altar of
expediency. As one writer puts it, "It is possible to generalize
that in a spirit of their difference in religious convictions and
outlook, most Liberians assign a leading, if not fundamental,
importance to spiritual forces and powers to their daily lives
and fortunes." (Olukoji, Ayodeji, 2006). In Liberia it is apparent that everyone believes in life after death, as seen in the

practice of ancestral veneration when prayers and sacrifices are done at graves. Such practice is based on the belief and conviction that ancestors intercede on behalf of the people (offspring) to avert calamity and to protect and have a positive end. Most Liberians believe in the propitiation of sacrifice to negotiate human relationship with the spiritual world.

Despite the popular belief that Liberia is a Christian state because of the dominance of the Free Slaves and their transplanting of Christendom on this West African soil, it must be noted here that said perception is misleading. According to research, Liberia is a conglomeration of religions that have been synchronized to reflect the spirituality of its people although the power to be seemed to determine the religion of the country as seen here. In the case of Liberia, Christianity was transplanted but it did not replace the African Traditional Religions but rather African Traditional Religions absorbed Christianity into themselves thus transforming both religions.

History also reminds us that the Free Slaves did not just bring Christianity to Liberia but also brought the western practice of freemasonry (a secret society) which became one of the pillars of the True Whig Party that dominated the government and public life until the 1980 coup. Freemasonry was one of the stools on which the nation rested during the first republic.

On the other hand, the indigenes had their belief (ATR) which in some term had some common practices with Islam, a religion associated with the Mandingo, Vai, Gola and Gbandi peoples group. It was reported in the 2002 census that the religious affiliation of the Liberian people was at 40 percent African Traditionalist, 40 percent Christianity and 20 percent Muslims.

However, despite the religious affiliation of the Liberian people groups, there is a common thread about the supernatural and the keeping of secrets. Secrecy has been one of the hallmarks of Liberian religious culture and it is ingrained in its beliefs in the intervention of the mysterious forces in human affairs. It's worth noting that regardless of religious affiliation, Liberians believe in the power of evil in human affairs. Indigenes like any other Africans believe in God, they strongly believed that spirits (good and bad) inhabit the world. For the indigenes, evil spirits were the creators of sickness and death. Therefore, in their thought, there is an association between medicine and religion. That is why the indigenous priest or the medicine doctor practiced sorcery and witchcraft, although he had many valuable remedies (Dale, Gilbert R., 1947).

This belief seems engrained in the culture that even it was exhibited in the leadership of the country. For example, President Tolbert (1971-80) was said to have had a phobia about sleeping in the Executive Mansion, the president's official residence; therefore, he commuted from Bentol his residence about 72 miles to work every day. Unfortunately, the day he slept in the Executive Mansion was the day he was assassinated (April 12, 1980). The report was that Tolbert had a fear about the ritual of the freemasonry done in the Executive Mansion by his predecessor, William V.S. Tubman, a Methodist Minister. The point is that both elite and nonelite Liberians usually attribute events of the activities to secret powers and forces (Olukoju, Ayodeji, 2006).

The same is said of President Samuel Doe (1980-90), the indigenous president who was believed to have been endowed with great supernatural powers to the point that he proclaimed that the gun that would kill him was not yet manufactured especially after the Quiowonpka's failed coup of 1986. Even at his capture, his capturer could not give him chance to be left alone because they believe he would disappear.

This is to say that fundamental to Liberian belief in the supernatural is illustrated by the fact that President Doe, like a good number of his compatriots of all religions persuasions, fortified himself with various charms in open and intimate parts of the body which was discovered by his captors. He went through a gruesome death experience because of the vengeance and belief of his enemies that he was potent with charms that could make him disappear at any time when given an opportunity and space to be alone.

Belief in spirits had been fundamental to Liberian life, world-view as well as religious life. The indigenes confidently believe in the existence of various spirits which include water spirits, ancestral spirits, bush spirits, genies and spirits of their association like that of the Poro, Sande and even the Clan. In essence, the unseen spirits represented the source of power and therefore the indigenes have medium through which to communicate with and appease such spiritual power. In their world, consulting and praying to and against these spirits was what made their life meaningful but also provides them the wisdom and capacity to live with their neighbors, even the one they did not like—including the Free Slaves.

Another caveat to the belief of spirit among the indigenes is the concern about the continuity of the human spirit after death. This is given expression in the following ways: 1) the return of the ancestral spirit through masquerades and incarnation into the family line. For that dreams and prayer were means to determine whether that spirit of an ancestor was coming back or being masqueraded among them. 2) The practice of eating the heart of the dead man especially the heart of brave men with the hope of ensuring the continuity of their life and spirit. This became more prominent during the Liberian civil war when valor men's heart were eaten by their enemies with the hope to be possessed by the brevity and power of such man to do exploit in war (Olukoju, Ayodeji, 2006).

Besides these, indigenes also believe in the multiplicity of spirits. Though the concept of monotheism is not in their vocabulary there is a concept of the supreme God. For example, the Bassa people see *Glapue* as the supreme God so do the other group of indigenes and have names for such god. There is also the belief in good and evil. The supreme God is that of the good and powerful god and evil is attributed to Satan and the devil.

Most importantly the tenets of indigenous religion (ATR) are preserved through rituals, songs, parables, narrative theology and stories, myths and education as practiced in the Sande and Poro societies. The indigenous religion and belief are historically and culturally passed down to generation; the Poro and the Sande are the entities through which these systems are propagated and preserved. Those that are unable to go to the Poro and Sande like me had the time of indoctrination through the narrative theology and stories as propagated by the elders. The grandparents in the context of the indigenous family are the narrators and teachers of religion; they give incidences of their life that pointed to the supreme God as well as to the evil at work in their world. They made simple the parables and maxims as they gather kids around the village fire heart and taught using stories. I can record my maternal grandmother doing this in *Kpa-vah* Town, Rivercess County where I grew up with her and grandfather. Notwithstanding there are the priests and priestesses that filled that role for the community and clans.

Christianity in Liberia

Christianity was brought to the shores of Liberia by the Free Slaves in the 1800s. It is reported that among the slaves that arrived on the coast of Liberia were Methodist, Baptist, African Methodist Episcopalian, and others. Olukoju reports that the Methodist church was the first to be planted on the soil of Liberia on January 7, 1822 (Olukoju, Ayodeji, 2006). Prominent leaders of the country, like Joseph J. Roberts who became the first President of Liberia, and William V.S. Tubman, the longest-serving presidents were all Methodists. Perhaps later the Baptist, the Episcopal, the Presbyterian, and the Catholic enterprises were established as seen on the map of what was then the Dukor that became Monrovia. In the vicinity of Ashmum, Michelin, and Johnson Streets are these churches.

As time went on this first group of Free Slaves using their contacts and influence were able to galvanize support for the need for missionary adventure as others later follow them. By the twentieth century there were other denominations including Seventh-Day Adventist, Catholic, Pentecostal, Lutheran, the Aladura which was meanly African in context, and the spiritual movement of the famous Prophet William Wade Harris, an indigene of the Grebo people's group.

Prophet Harris led the West African revival from 1913-1915 using Ivory Coast and Southwestern Ghana as his base of operation (Groves, C.P., 1964) though he started in Liberia. His prophetic message of liberation and break with traditional African religion including freemasonry did not' go well with the Free Slaves' government of Liberia leaving him with no alternative but to travel the West African coast for this spiritual awakening. It is estimated that during this time Prophet Harris won between 60,000 to 100,000 people to Christ and baptizing them

(Omulokoli, William A.O., 2002). Other report shows that the number of people baptized by Prophet Harris was 120,000 adults "in just over a year" (Barrette, David (ed.), 1971).

It seems clear that the ACS plan to Christianize Africans was being realized as various mission groups spread among the indigenes. The Lutheran mission was intentional as it moved away from Monrovia, the Free Slaves' center to the hinterland. The Lutheran plan was to evangelize and Christianize the Loma and Kpelle of central and north-western Liberia. Olukoju reports that the Lutheran Mission introduced formal or western education and in an effort established literacy programs to serve this group of people. It emphasized evangelization and literacy in the indigenous language and later provided translations of the bible into Loma and Kpelle so the people could worship God in their tongue (Olukoju, Ayodeji, 2006).

The dominant protestant group in Liberia has been the Methodist though the Baptists were one of the key founders of the Nation. It is written on the cornerstone at Providence Baptist Church where the declaration of Independence was signed on July 26, 1822. The Providence Baptist Church bears the symbol of Nation independence of which the Baptists are proud. However, over the years the Baptists dwindled in political maneuvering and freemasonry that they seem to lose the original focus to Christianize the indigenes as was planned.

Consequently, other Protestants especially the Methodist saw it as a calling to evangelize the indigenes.

On the other hand, Christianization as seen in the context of the ACS is a scheme of imperialism for West Africa. As it is often said whenever the missionaries Christianized the Africans, they made them sing the song "I have decided to follow Jesus, no turning back. You can have the whole world but give me Jesus, no turning back, no turning back." While giving Jesus to the Africans, westerners were taking away their minerals and natural resources for the west and exploiting the Africans. Liberia was no exception to this plan. Africans were baptized; their names were changed to western or biblical names thus giving them a new identity. But the Lutherans broke away from such a scheme in Liberia. They did not change the people name but translated the Bible into their language for them to be able to read for themselves and by 1965 they have trained more indigenous pastors to manage their churches under the supervision of the first indigenous Bishop.

In effect the plan to Christianize Liberia seems to have taken off; churches are springing out in every city and village of the country. But this growth was mostly precipitated by the establishment of educational institutions and literacy centers by the mission.

As Jones indicates, "The need for education and schools were relevant for the purpose of imparting Christian-based knowledge and wisdom to the younger generation. The need for a Christian-based settlement was pushed by those in authority to make decisions for the newly formed colony." (Jones, Sammer Saleh, 2016).

As many of the indigenes get formal or western education, they seemed to gravitate toward Christianity, embracing this newfound faith. However, most of them still held on to some of the African traditional beliefs. Many aspects of Christianity were synchronized into the African form of life to some extent that its rituals and observances found a home in the African culture.

The mission of the church had created educational institutions, hospitals, media institutions and using them as means to an end. The need to evangelize is still paramount in Liberia today as more churches being planted. Consequently, the emergence of independent churches seems to indicate a break away from the Western form of Christianity. Today in Liberia there are more than 200 independent churches; it seems that every Dick and Tom is having visions like the Prophet Harris. But unlike Harris who did not establish institutions, these Dicks and Toms have become bishops over these people, most often exploiting them with feel-good messages. Buchanan city, the home of the Bassa people group has always carried the title of the Bible belt in Liberia. It is said that in every ten block in that city is a church, whether it is Methodist, Aladura, Baptist, or Independent. The people of Bassa can be compared to the people of Texas for the love of their faith though they do not carry guns. But it appears that this group of indigenous seemed to gravitate toward Christianity than to any other religion. One of the reasons is that this group of people are interested in education for the male child; so as the church established educational centers the Bassa took advantage of it; most of them were willing to change their identity, to serve the Free Slaves just to be able to read and write or speak the pidgin English that the Free Slaves spoke. The Bassa people begin to name their children among many western names: David-gar, Sunday-ma, Obadiah, etc. My dad named all of us besides my eldest sister, western and biblical names (Jeremiah, Emmanuel, Oretha, Paul, Samuel, Daniel & George) because of the new-found faith on Christianity. That is the effect of the church's mission.

During the reign of the Free Slaves for the century, especially the 1930s Christianity was understood as a religion of the elite. The socially mobile elite group of Free Slaves combined business and politic along with the profession of Christianity with freemasonry and indigenous belief to create a synchronistic religion. As its leadership participated in freemasonry and indigenous practices, it created an era of spiritual sycophancy.

It is reported that President Charles D.B. King (1920-30) was the first President to be associated with both the Poro and Alligator society as well as a practicing Christian. William V.S. Tubman (1930-1972), the King Solomon of Liberia because of his success, was reported to have also joined the Poro and became head of the Poro though he was a Methodist Minister and a freemason. Even President William R. Tolbert, a Baptist Minister and president of the Baptist World Alliance was said to have joined the Poro becoming one of the zos (Olukoju, Ayodeji, 2006). To be a zo, one should have had gone through series of rituals and the ranks of the secret societies; one should have pledged allegiance and endowed oneself with the charms of the underworld. And here were ministers and leaders of the church being involved in such practice. It is like King Saul going to a psyche to talk with the dead.

That was the form of Christianity that existed for centuries in Liberia. Many Liberian Christians, like their West African counterparts, except the Pentecostal, think nothing of concurrent adherence to diverse beliefs. What Liberians did was to conform to a general pattern in Africa where practices associated with indigenous religion, such as spirit possession and soothsaying have been appropriated into Christian liturgy and practices (Olukoju, Ayodeji, 2006).

But let it also be known that there were others like the poor and indigenous that received this new faith and appropriated it according to the Bible. There were prophets and prophetesses in the annals of history who proclaimed the engrafted world with boldness and had the power to break the yoke and hold captive every defile spirit that came as a result of practicing in the underworld. There are still people like that in today's Liberia that would prefer not to synchronize their Christian belief into other beliefs and practices.

Challenge for Christianity in Liberia

The challenge of Liberian religiosity can be extracted from prevailing theology and praxis. When I say theology, I mean the lenses through which the various people's group articulates their perception of who God is. And for praxis, I mean how each of these groups lived their articulation of who this God is, has been and will be. But let me be clearer here, as a member of the indigenous group or native Liberian, we bring to the theological discourse both oral and symbolic theological streams (Mbiti, John S, 1998) that are deemed important and meaning making for us and must be held in regard as westerner and the Free Slaves seek the Christianization of all of Liberia. That is to say we indigenous people must be allowed to interpret and apply the biblical text to our context to develop or come up with a theological construct. The "incompetence" of Christianity or western theology is its failure to engage African or indigenous context, therefore indigenous or African theologians including myself resolved to 'own' our theological reflection, rather than to borrow it from a context that has so unfairly denigrated our African or indigenous heritage. Given this Akinsulire asserts,

> The African context must therefore "reprocess" or reconstruct Christian theology in order to engage African questions which often are ignored by orthodox works on Christian theology (Akinsulire, Dotun, 2007).

The challenge for Christianity in Africa has been the idea of inculturation. After Vatican II (November 21, 1964) (Kurgat, Sussy G., December 2011) the term was accepted and made popular challenging Christendom to rethink its method and thought of Christianizing the world. The concept is defined as an incarnation of the Christian message in a particular cultural context, in such a way that this experience not only finds expression through elements proper to the culture in question but becomes a principle that animates, directs, and unifies the church and remaking it so as to bring a new creation (Akinsulire, Dotun, 2007). Until Christianity can let go of its control of power and imposition on indigenous, I fear that it will lose its influence in the life of Liberia. One of the signs of this in Liberia is the rapid growth of independent churches in the country. These churches have grasped the concept of inculturation as compared to the denominational churches establish by the Free Slaves. Today Liberia has over 200 or more independent churches and independent churches are forming their conventions and fellowships. In fact, some pastors have breakaway from fundamental denomination to form a more perfect union and freedom of contextualizing the gospel for the people.

The next challenge is in the field of indigenous Liberation thought. Indigenous Liberation thought is a critical reflection of the obnoxious plight of indigenes and the African state as evidenced in the exploitation, poverty, oppression, conflicts, and wars that beleaguer it, being the creation of its systems and leadership and the desire borne out of this experience to evolve a more equitable and humane society (Akinsulire, Dotun, 2007). If Christianity is to be the religion of influence in Liberia, it must be able to critically reflect on the exploitation, oppression, and the poverty its system has created in the nation and be able to evolve to a more equitable and humane society from such experience.

For the indigenous theology cannot be separated from their history as a people. Their history is marked with inhumane treatment—they were strapped to trees and beaten for failure to pay hut tax under President Arthur Barclay; forced to labor for elite Free Slaves and some taken to Fernando Po Island to work for both British and Spanish, while payments were given to the Liberian government. This indigenous liberation thought must engage their life but also narrate how the expression of the indigenes pains was mainly through songs, bodily rhythms, functional crafts, anecdotal stories, humor, mimicry, parody and code language. This cannot be forgotten—it cannot be erased or eradicated from the lives of the people. However, it should be means through which a more equitable society and humane community can be built. The Prophet Micah aware of this cautioned his people in Micah 6:7-8:

> "Will the Lord be pleased with thousands of rams, with ten thousands of rivers of oil? He[God] has shown you, O man[Liberia] what is good; and what does the Lord require of you but to do justice, and to love kindness, and to walk humbly with your God?" (The Bible: The Revised Standard Version, 1980).

Another challenge for Christianity in Liberia is to engage what I would term Indigenous African liberation. Liberian history has not been pleasant when it comes to how the indigenes fare. They were treated like the slaves in the antebellum South where most of the Free Slaves, the birther of the new liberty and boaster of Christianity came from. However, if Christianity is to continue its progression it must be able to engage what it means to be free for indigenes. Christianity must explore and highlight the themes of struggle, oppression and inequality exemplified in the Free Slaves' system of government and seeks the theological dimensions of these issues. The issue of theology or the study of God or who God is—is to see God as incarnational which is an African thought. In such thought God, the divine *logos* becomes incarnate, taking on humanity for the purpose to impart and impact humanity. When the gospel of John says in its first chapter "The Word *(logos)* became flesh and dwell among us" is the incarnation of the Bassa people's *Gla-pua* (God) for each generation to be relevant to the life and lots of every Liberian. This is the indigenous reflection of God that provides an appropriate hermeneutical framework for Christianity and the church in Liberia, to effectively engage its 'own' people with the Gospel.

My father, the Rev. Gardea Payway was fully acquainted with this hermeneutical framework. As a little boy, several times, I listened to him preached and he related this God to the indigenous plight of his time. My father felt for the gospel to be powerful and relevant for indigenes the gospel needed to engage his own story as a slave boy of the Liberian Government in Fernando Po Island. He said there were days when he would read Luke 4:18-19:

> "The Spirit of the Lord is on me, because he has anointed me to proclaim good news to the poor. He has sent me to proclaim freedom for the prisoners and recovery of sight for the blind, to set the oppressed free, to proclaim the year of the Lord's favor." (The Bible: Revised Standard Version, 1970)

For him, this is the God that comes to not just dwell with him but impact his life and the life of people he was leading. This was the God that moved the League of Nation in the 1930s about his plight and other indigenes to set them free from

Fernando Po Island. This God was also interested in their struggle to break away from the Free Slaves AME church that didn't see them as people God died for or redeemed. For him this God was not just God of the elites or free Slaves but God of the margined indigenous—the poor and the disadvantaged, the prostitutes, the societal deviants, and the tax collectors. This is the God that had come to set them free from personal sins, societal and generational enslavement and give them a life that was full and abundance.

The last challenge for Christianity is to de-institutionalize God. The Christian system in Liberia over the decade has institutionalized, politicized God, and made God a power-grasping demagogic. This god has consistently justified its rampant discrimination against indigenous people and women calling it western civilization. Indigenous Africans are no longer tolerant to gather and worship a god that does not see them as human imbued with the capacity to run their own life or determine their destination. A theology that makes god civilized and of the bigots has no place in the indigenous public square. Therefore the challenge for Christianity is to be able to engage such thought of removing God from the institution. God cannot be confined in the sanctuary of the church; he must be able to interact and respond to the plight of the people. The church should be the first to speak against the evil of the society, and of the power that does not govern appropriately. What is the church saying in Liberia these days when only .5 percent of the population has accumulated all the riches in the country and 95 percent lives in abject poverty. Or when the pastors/bishops of the institutional church are riding Bentley and BMWs and their church members cannot afford a day's meal, yet they are asking them to bring their tithes and offerings to the church. Such institutional god has no relevance in where we go from here as Liberians. We need the God that pursues its people, that sees the tears of its people, and act on their behalf to bring about a more just society that is quite equitable and empowering.

Chapter Six

Whre Do We Go From Here?

L iberia as a state with a record of independent statehood surpasses any other country in West Africa by 110 years, should at the same time have a reputation as one of the most thorough neo-colonial states in Africa. Such seemed paradoxical on the basis that in the mere passage of time since its independence Liberia has shown no enhanced assertion of independence either in economic, political and social management or in foreign policy (Clapham, Christopher, 1994). Throughout its history, Liberia seemed to be handicapped by its context as well as poor management. My intention is to critically maintain a level head as we reflect on this land of Liberty for which many has died, imprisoned and others have made their wealth. Liberia is one of the remarkable lands and its people are more resilient than any people on this globe today. Lanier asserts

If there ever was a story of survival, Liberia is the grand example. Without either the benefit or questionable desirability of pure colonialism, and saved in the final analysis by "dollar diplomacy", and a corps of self and home-made "Liberian" diplomats, who without Oxford, Harvard, or Heidelberg degrees, maneuvered themselves into position between the Scylla of the League of Nations and Charybdis of colonial powers, by clever statesmanship, although the European foreign powers at that time had no intention of encouraging a free and independent country anywhere in Africa, she managed to maintain her sovereignty (Lanier, R. O'Hara, Summer, 1961).

Truly Liberia is a survival story as evident in her birth, her struggle with imperial power of the West, her self-destruction, her miraculous survival amid coup, war, and pestilence; her struggling economy and her struggle with corruption today.

In order to know where we go from here, let us reason what brought us here and how we the Liberian people can survive and maintain the tapestry we are made out of. History has become the parameter through which we can assess our capital and behavior, and thus forecast our future. As one writer puts it, Liberia has become a laboratory for democracy in one of the frontiers of the earth. It stood the test of each century of her existence.

In the wake of western imposition, Arthur Barclay cautioned its people in the following: "We shall never consent to those from the outside taking over control of the affairs of our government. If they do so it will have to be done by force" (van der Kraaij, F.P.M., 1983). This galvanized a united front, creating a resisting foe that made the country and its people resilient against colonial power to protect its sovereignty during the first republic.

Consequently, to look ahead we must all understand how we got here; what have we brought thus far; what do we need to go ahead; and how do we get there.

Our history tells us how we got here. Ignoring our history makes us fools to repeat the mistakes of the past. Let us be reminded that the 1800s brought the free slaves to our seashores as an aspiration of their freedom though there were 16 other major indigenous groups, each possessing its tradition, customs, religions, philosophy and languages and dialects. After the declaration of Independence by these Free Slaves, they adopted a form of government based on the American model. Liberia became the only country in Africa with which the US has had historical affiliation, and the Free Slaves regarded the US as a friend, ally, and relative. English became the national language, US colors except for the one star became the national emblem, and the US dollar became the national currency. History reminds us that a professor of Harvard drew up its constitution on the American model in 1836, and professors from Cornell codified its laws in the 1950s (Dalton, George, 1965). This constitution delineated sharply between the Free Slaves and the indigenes. The indigenes were ineligible for election and voting, something the Free Slaves experienced with their white masters in the Americas. This lay the foundation for entrenched alienation between the different ethnic groups in the nation, and between these groups and the Free Slaves who were the upper class.

From 1870 after the True Whig Party was established, and for the next 110 years Liberia was that de facto one-party state for the benefit of the Free Slaves (Boas, M., 2009). Under the TWP, a small elite of Free Slaves and their successor—never more than 3-5 percent dominated and ruled the political, economic and religious life to their benefit and survival as elites during the first republic. Such a system had the support of other powerful aliases including the US.

Another thing that makes our history unique in itself is the institution of military force in the construction of the Free Slave hegemony (Boas, M., 2009). The military was used to establish administrative boundaries but also used to keep the construct of insider and outsider as it came to the relations of the Free Slaves and the indigenes. The indigenes became the outsider in this construct. They had no rights in their native land as the Native Americans in the US were treated. Arthur Barclay used the military to subject the indigenes to a centralized authority.

Next is the philosophy of indirect rule as was practiced in British colonies. The Free Slaves used this system to rule indigenes through district commissioners who in turn ruled through local chiefs. As a result, such a system of indirect rule contributed to the sharpening differences among the many ethnic groups of Liberia. Before the establishment of this system, the ethnic structure of Liberia had by and large, a flexible and inclusionary character (Schroder, G. & Siebel, D., 1974).

As we grew together as a nation, the line between us indigenes and the Free Slaves narrow but could not merge because of the uncomfortableness and insecurity among the power to be. The change could not be easily embraced or meaningfully cultivated; the fear that the other would revenge and retaliate lingers in the minds and spirit of the power to be. Each leadership during the first republic had its way of dealing with change—how much of it should be allowed in terms of the freedom and opportunity given to indigenes. For example, during the Tubman era, a man vastly loved by the indigenes; his regime brought about economic growth but had institutional arrangements that reduced the wage rate. One-fourth of the wage-earning labor force was supplied involuntarily—labor recruitment was the euphemism for forced labor and the unions were kept ineffective by his government (Dalton, George, 1965). It is reported that in 1960 65% of the Liberian workforce engaged in subsistence agriculture; about 30% of that were wage-earner, most of whom were unskilled indigenous on rubber farm who earned 75 cents a day by 1962 (Dalton, George, 1965) under the government and Firestone franchise. Despite the rapid growth in primary commodities for export produce by foreign firms during the Tubman regime, which meant a higher wage bill and higher taxes paid in government covers to induce significant output expansion in production lines undertaken by Liberians but the latter did not happen which remains a question to economists as to why it didn't happen. The saying goes if you are not at the table of the power, then you are bound to be on the table (menu), so it was with the indigenes. President Tubman created an illusion that made the indigenes think he loved and care for them but in reality, and policy implemented they were not benefited only the elite Free Slaves. The indigenes remain the outsider in the construct thus the system is designed to work against them no matter what they do. Said system finds its origin in America where the Free Slaves fought for their rights and later disposed to the Gold Coast. They were using a similar system to rule native Africans.

Notwithstanding, as each leadership struggles with this balance according to the context given them, some braved the storm and decided progress though unpopular. For example, during the Tolbert administration, many indigenous young men and women were exposed to higher education, some obtained scholarships to the West to have an experience that the Free Slaves so pride themselves with, while others remain subservient to the culture and society because of the system in place. It was true of the Tolbert administration that free speech was being allowed as part of the civil discourse on campuses allowing students to engage one another about political, socio-economic issues of their day. Liberians began vocal about their rights and the rights of other Africans. Liberia at the time became the home of freedom fighters from South

Africa. There were students and secret movements that champion the cause for black South Africans making Liberia once again the beacon of hope in Africa as we navigated through the 20th century. Can we reclaim that zest for the 21st century? In doing so we need to look at six guiding principles as seen in the acronym: **LEADER:** Leadership, Education, Accountability, Development, Economy and Renewal/Reawakening.

Leadership

As we look forward to where we go from here, the principle of leadership is needed. We need leaders to have our crossover, as Moses and Joshua did with the Red Sea and Jordan episodes. In like manner Liberia needs leadership. But let us make it clearer here that every leadership is given a context—without context the function of leadership remains oblivion. The Liberian tapestry gives us the context for each of the leadership practiced in both the first and second republic. However, it is expedient to unpack the term leadership.

Recent research on leadership indicates that 60% of the leadership studies conducted between 1910 and 1990 had no clearly stated definition of leadership and that researchers simply tended to assume that others shared their concept of leadership. One researcher argues that having a myriad of definitions for leadership is useful in that "defining leadership in many different ways can help you to understand leadership as a phenomenon" (Okpokwu, Theresa, 2017). However, the major critique about the theories of leadership comes in light of its limitedness by certain biases that are influenced by Western, industrialized, and patriarchal perspectives. Steady also points out the gender bias within leadership theories in terms of the "great man theory". She argues that said theory credits highly influential men (not women) and heroes who possess outstanding intellect and charisma with the making of history (Steady, Filomina C., 2011). Therefore it is expedient to be aware of the biases as we unpack this phenomenon of leadership since it is not just men that lead. It was under the Leadership of Ellen Johnson-Sirleaf that sanity, democracy, and peace including development was restored to war-torn Liberia. It was not a man's thing.

Ebegbulem, an African scholar sees leadership as "an individual appointed to a job with authority and accountability to accomplish the goals and objectives of the society" (Ebegbulem, C., 2012). A leader must be able to manage the availability of resources for the general good of all. He or she must possess the ability to create in the followers the necessary enthusiasm and motivation for selfless service by example. With that said he or she becomes assessable to his or her followers.

On the other hand, Clawson sees leadership as managing one's energy first and then the energy of those who are being led. He suggests that when walking into an institution, it is possible to quickly identify what the energy level is and, as a result, what the quality of the leadership is in that institution. If the institutional energy level is low, the leadership is likely to be weak (Clawson, J., 2006). What I want us to thoughtfully desire or reflect on here is the idea of self-management. One cannot lead well when he or she cannot manage self. It entails self-discipline, self-awareness, and Self-motivation. Proverb 30:27 puts it well allegorically,

> "The locusts have no king, yet all of them march in rank." (The Bible: Revised Standard Version, 1970)

The locusts are destructive creatures, yet they all move in packs without leadership but because they have mastery of self, and they move in ranks or an orderly manner. Each knows the position it plays in the pack and is motivated to move along. Therefore, it is important to note here that leadership starts with self; one should be able to accept responsibility for the choices he or she makes, be responsible for the mistakes he or she makes and not scapegoat others, and overall be self-controlled. Can we be certain of such quality in whomever we call to lead this nation, our dear country? This also goes to every entity and institution in the country including the church.

With that said, leadership is essential to the growth and development of any institution or organization. And on the other hand, the prevailing condition of a country is majorly determined by the type of leadership in governance. Those of us who live in the west, have seen it in the last four years with the American leadership. Leadership that has divided the nation in race relationship, pivoted citizen against immigrants, wealthy against poor, religious against non-religious, and powerful against the less fortunate. Leadership can influence and produce positive action through vision thereby bringing about a positive change or it can lead to discouragement in followers resulting in inaction and chaos. To grasp the phenomenon of leadership, the concept of management is interwoven. How does one who has been called to leadership in an institution or governance manage all at his/her disposal; how does he/she relate to those who follow him/her. And lastly, how does he/she manage self—ethically and psychologically. The issue of self-management is essential in leadership. If a man cannot come to grip with his shadow, leadership becomes a rod to beat others with.

Ebegbulem asserts that "All over the world, leadership is the most important number one factor that determines whether a nation can develop." He further states "a leadership that is free, brave, patriotic, people-oriented, destination-bound; the leadership that understands the psychology of leading and applies it to the development of the people must be at the affairs of men" (Ebegbulem, C., 2012). The issue about Liberia is how can the phenomenon of leadership that is destination-bound, people-oriented, and patriotic apply to our context. It takes brave men and women who are willing to make the decisions that are countercultural to the utopian and corrupt context we have sculpt over the century. Such men or women make clear the vision to ignite enthusiasm in people.

What stands up in leadership can be summarized in three concepts: people, influence, and goals. In recent times one of the scholars asserts that leadership is the ability to influence people to attain goals, but most importantly leadership is reciprocal and is a people activity (Draft, R.L., 2010). It is a characteristic of leadership to see that the follower has a clear goal to be achieved collectively. The leader must be able to influence his people in a way that they can rarefy their self-interest to adopt the goals of the group as their own; it is about building cohesive and goal-oriented teams or institutions. For example, during the Ellen Johnson-Sirleaf regime, one of the goals we saw was her goal on education; it was seen in the budget, policy, and reconstruction plan. We saw rapid development for the University of Liberia in a short period as compared to other leadership besides the Tubman regime. It was under her leadership that most public colleges in the counties were opened and operated, while during previous leadership the access to university education for young people in rural areas was limited.

One of the landmarks of leadership is to uplift the human spirit. Noonan asserts that leadership lifts the human spirit, ensures the survival of human communities, and promotes the adaptation of people to their environment. Leadership facilitates change and develops potential; it is about service and a visionary process-oriented to achieve positive results; it is neither greedy, immoral, unethical nor diminishing but is rather active, caring, constructive, creative, playful, and courageous (Noonan, S., 2003). To go from where we have been as a nation, there's a need for reeducation or indoctrination of the concept of leadership in a developing democratic society like ours. Who are the people in leadership in our society today—the government, the church, the family, and indigenous societies? What do they need to relearn for the betterment of the institution they lead? I must admit here that leadership can be learned. Some may be gifted in the art of leadership but leadership is a craft that can be taught and learned.

Next is cultivating a list for leadership in preparation to take on the mantle. Each leader should be prepared to invest in others so when the time comes for a transition to the other there can be a continuity of vision from previous leadership. For example, the Tolbert administration was mindful and intentional about its cadet program though a majority of people accepted in that program were descendants of Free Slaves. This program became a model around the country. LAMCO adapted the program in Yekepa and Buchanan, giving high school students the opportunity for three months each year. CEMENCO and LPRC in Monrovia had a similar program. These programs were means to mentor future leaders of the country and provided a career pathway for many young Liberians.

At the same time, the Tolbert administration had visions that were scribed into its developmental plan. Doe attempted to continue that plan: the GSA and Du-port Road construction plan, the Stadium though most were done haphazardly. But Doe attempted despite there was not a prepared and proper transition because of the context through which he came to power. The issue is preparing the next generation for leadership. If the leadership is prepared, it is trained to carry out vision in terms of development. How can the appointed cabinet ministers, judges, superintendents of counties, the church leadership—leadership of the various conventions, diocesan, and mission board use their leadership to mentor the next generation to continue the vision. It is a challenge in Africa to mentor others for leadership because we have created a culture that promotes one should stay in leadership until he or she dies. Thank goodness that it is now an issue of constitutionality that the president of Liberia has two six years terms which are still humongous. But it is better to start from somewhere.

I hope that Liberians will learn from our collective history and thus become responsible for self and others in ways we cast vote and make choices for leadership for this country. Let's put aside personal affiliation and evaluate critically our political leadership—what have they done in the counties in terms of socio-political wellbeing of our people before we reelect them for another term.

Education

Where do we go from here educationally Liberia? It is a salient question we must face with critical thinking. Education is critical to any developing nation. Remember the Free Salves consider education as for the civilized and a way to freedom and self-sufficiency. I would also argue that education is the means through which any society releases the capabilities of its citizenry regardless of gender, class, and social status. My dad always said to us that education was the sustaining wealth he could ever give us, and I can say Amen to that today. For any democratic society and government to make strides or be sustained, it needs to make education one of its primary goals for the citizenry.

The great philosopher and scholar, John Dewey's conception of education and democracy were in parallel with each other. He saw them as coexisting in a reciprocal relationship (Dewey, J., 1916). With that Boone in agreement with Dewey, argues that democracy thrives on social order, ". . . in which interests are mutually interpenetrating, and where progress, or read-justment, is an important consideration," democratic com-munities should be more concerned with a "deliberate and systematic education" than other types of societies. To make it clearer here about the relationship between democracy and education is that "a government resting on popular suffrage cannot be successful unless those who elect and obey their governors are educated." (Boone, Mike, 2008) At present lit-eracy rate in Liberia is 48.3%; among women, it is 34% (Liberia - Literacy rate, 2019) as compared to other countries especially in Africa. The rate of out of schoolboys in Liberia is at 82.3% and for girls is 77.2% (UNESCO Institute of Statistics, 2020). Such a report is glaring that education is a critical endeavor and is a high stake in Liberian governance. The years of war contributed to this critical need. Therefore, in the recovery state, we need to prioritize education.

Consequently, it is important that Liberians review their edu-cational laws and policies, make progressive changes that fit the 21st century. The essence of any democratic government is the imposition of socio-welfare programs including creat-ing educational entities and opportunities for its people. I am aware that democracy by its very nature rejects imposition. However, alternatives can be found through developing its citizenry, creating habits and dispositions as required for a democracy to survive. John Dewey was keen about this when he argued that such habits and dispositions are created only by education (Dewey, J., 1916).

Education as Dewey argued is essentially a social process, through which individuals are taught to live into a particular democratic ideal. The relevant criteria for judging the level of democracy in any society are first "the extent to which the interests of a group are shared by all members" (Dewey, J., 1916) and, second the degree of freedom in which each group in the society interacts with other groups. To emphasize here, in an "undesirable society" internal and external barriers are set up to the sharing of group experience and group interaction.

However, as Dewey argues "A society which makes provisions for participation in its good of all its members on equal terms and which secures flexible readjustment of its institutions through interaction of the different forms of associated life is in so far democratic" (Dewey, J., 1916). If Liberian is to remain a democratic society it should be able to provide equal opportunity for its citizenry to participate in its educational franchise by all means.

The Liberian compulsory educational law was enshrined into the philosophy of education to give equal opportunity to all at age 6-16 to education. However, the government has been lacking in creating opportunities for the haves not or the public. Once the government updated this law but increase its fines from $10 to $25. In the 1971 Conference on Development Objectives and strategies, the government was encouraged to adopt "regional equalization of educational opportunities" as a goal and that the nation, in its socio-economic development plan for 1976 – 1980 committed itself to provide "universal, basic education" to help the masses improve their lives and to ensure "equitable geographic distribution of educational opportunities" (Cainé, Augustus F., 1986). This was one of the hallmarks of the Tolbert administration. With this the focus was shifted to the rural areas where the majority of the indigenes reside, public schools were built, teacher education was encouraged. I remember the early 80s when young Stevenson Seidi and others who have just come from Teacher College, were sent to Yekepa and became my Language Arts instructor. It was one of the catalysts that encouraged my 7th-grade class to aim high for college. The opportunity was there and nurtured. Can this be done on a higher scale for the 21st century? I want to believe that it can happen, but we need leaders to initiate and implement them. The government needs to put in place incentives to encourage families to send their kids to school. It also needs incentives for students to attend colleges in the country. Can we make public rural colleges affordable or free?

Liberia means Liberty. Liberty involves two aspects: knowledge and the ability to put one's ideas into practice. If there is not the opportunity to acquire the knowledge the liberty, we pride ourselves as Liberian is utopian. I believe that no man can be both ignorant and free. I concur with Dewey that man is a slave as long as he cannot act upon his ideas. In other words, a free man is the master of his private life and has a say in the affairs of the state.

The scholar Cimpean argues that the purpose of schooling or education is to promote a democratic state. He writes, "For Dewey, democracy is the ultimate ethical ideal for man. To

Dewey, democracy is the political system in which man's ethical ideals of liberty, equality, and fraternity can best be realized." (Cimpean, Claudiu, 2008) It is the business of the school or educational system that provides the purified medium for liberty and action. Throughout the history of educational philosophy, scholars have propounded that the relationship between democracy and education is centered on the conviction that school or education is the instruments of social change. The educational system became an instrument for change. This was the major reason the slaves in the antebellum South, were not allowed to attend school because their white masters knew it would strike social change. Boone writes,

> In his "pedagogic creed," Dewey stated forthrightly that "education is the fundamental method of social progress and reform." Dewey considered any social reforms that rested only on law or civil sanctions to be transitory. True reform depended instead on the use of education as a "regulation of the process of coming to share in the social consciousness, and . . . the adjustment of individual activity on the basis of this social consciousness as the only sure method of social reconstruction" (Boone, Mike, 2008).

When a society becomes more enlightened, the realization is that it becomes responsible as to what it transmits and conserves as achievements and what to make for a better future society. The school is its chief agency for the accomplishment of this end (Dahn, Kadiker, 2008).

To conclude let us reflect on the notion of quality in the education we intend to provide to the Liberian society. I must admit that often when we talk about quality; it is seen through the lenses of measured years of schooling which often has become the focus of policymakers and academic debate. While increasing access to education in Liberia is important, the actual goal of providing schooling is to teach skills and critical thinking and transfer knowledge to students in the classroom. This entry focuses on the outcomes of schooling – the quality of education. Therefore, there should be put in place a measuring mechanism for the said outcome.

At least there is some good empirical data on access to education in Liberia as I review educational journals, but we know much less about the quality of education. Unfortunately, there is no data on the skills and knowledge of students in modern Liberia. This is in part due to the difficulty and cost of creating and implementing standardized assessments that can be compared across borders and time. We need a system to measure the quality of our education in Liberia. In time past the WAEC test was one of the mechanisms including the University assessment test/entrance examination. However, no one can now vouch for these tests to be used to measure quality base on the easy accessibility of said test to the students before it is taken.

Quality is often measured by outcomes. Efforts to measure these outcomes are geographically difficult thereby making it less known about students' performance concerning the outcomes of education in the country over some time. The Liberian government needs to put in place assessment tools to measure learning outcomes, which in terms helps policymakers and educational practitioners to plan and implement strategically where we go from here as a nation of learned people—free and participants of its democracy. For example, a case in point is Ellen Johnson-Sirleaf's Partnership Schools for Liberia (PSL) program. This program transferred the management of 93 randomly selected public primary schools to private school organizations, and providing them with additional resources for the 2016-2017 school year. In as much as the program was criticized making it controversial, it gained media coverage to a place of prominence for school policy. At the end of the year, the report shows that the program increased test scores by 60% (.19 σ), teacher attendance by 50%, and satisfaction of both students and parents by about 10% (Romero, M., Sandefur, J., & Sandholtz, W., 2017). Quality always drives satisfaction. When there is a mechanism in place to measure what we do and the outcome in our educational system, quality becomes the benchmark.

Finally, the assessment tools should be able to measure the following three dimensions: Reading and language proficiency, Mathematics and numeracy proficiency, and Scientific knowledge and understanding. By the time a Liberian student gets out of high school, there should be a higher degree of proficiency in these areas. When this happens, we can be sure that we have the quality like other African nations

Accountability

As we sojourn in the 21st century, Liberia needs accountability. Whenever we talk about accountability, the issues of corruption and anti-corruption laws or endeavors are brought to the forefront. The term itself is inclusive of holding one's feet to the fire—it involves policy-making, behavioral assessment, and linking progress with funding. But let me unpack the term. In the socio-political arena accountability is a relationship between two parties in which one is accountable to the other. A said relationship may either be lacking in accountability or be highly accountable. It is a relationship between two key actors: the targets of accountability include the parties that are obliged to account for their actions and to face sanctions, that is, the duty bearers. Most often the targets of accountability groups are institutions of public authority and public officials. The next actors are the seekers of accountability which include parties entitled to explanations or to impose punishments as rights-holders. These are the citizenry (Friis-Hansen, E., & Ravnkilde, S., 2013).

In the academic arena, each field of study (humanities, sociologies, theologies, economies, etc.) has its concept to describe the accountability relationship. For example agents that are held accountable are characterized as supply-side (economies), stewards (theologies), accountees (sociologies), or duty-bearers (humanities), on the other hand, agents asking for answers and enforcing sanctions are characterized as demand-side (economists), The Divine (Theologians), accounters (sociologist) or rights-holders (humanities) (Friis-Hansen, E., & Ravnkilde, S., 2013). In these conceptions, the notion is that accountability relationships are brokered by agents with fixed roles acting within formal accountability mechanisms. In this definition, it is expedient for us to be aware of the de jure accountability, meaning who our institutions or governance is accountable to according to the law, and the de facto accountability also meaning who our institutions or entities are accountable to due to relationships of power or the practical power to impose a sanction (e.g. projects/church as accountable to donors). As a theologian, I would be quick to say that my sole accountability is to God. God holds me responsible for how I manage the wealth entrusted to me, the family, the church and even the state which means public office. However, I am also under the jurisdiction of the law, and the state has the power to punish or deter any form of misappropriation of the church funds/property or the abuse of human capital that I have been given an opportunity to manage. In this light, both the de jure and de facto accountability parallel each other.

Moreover, accountability also involves a dimension of power in terms of the capacity to require someone to engage in giving reasons to justify their behavior and the capacity to impose a penalty for poor performance (Goetz, Anne M. & Jenkins, Rob, 2005); that is, a means of restraining power (Joshi, A. & Houtzger, P., 2012).

It is the means whereby ordinary citizens, the media, and civil-society actors attempt to enforce standards of performance by public officials and service providers. In this definition, periodic free and fair elections are the classic form of vertical accountability (Goetz, Anne M. & Jenkins, Rob, 2005). Most often political theory refers to political accountability, which is viewed as a key component of a democratic system. Political accountability is when elected leaders are answerable to the public for their actions and decisions, thus providing checks and balances over the power of elected leaders. Elections are, however, limited to a certain number of actors, and are not able to ensure access to services for the poor.

In order to hold our government accountable, we need a public awareness campaign that helps build a political will for the citizenry to deter every form of corruption in society. Robert Rotberg once said that political will is the single most critical variable in any effective campaign against corruption (Rotberg, Robert, 2017). The citizenry need to be aware of the implicit power at their disposition to require their public official to justify their behavior and spending as well as restrain them from unwarranted and amoral behaviors.

To increase governmental accountability and transparency as well as enhance public participation in decision making, strengthen the public sector and civil society institutions and greater adherence to the rule of law will not only improve governance but will help counter corruption (Lawal, Gbenga, 2007). The citizenry is key to all the above. The argument has been anti-corruption efforts succeed only when local civil society is strong—when citizens "are able to build inter-group coordination mechanisms" and foster "elite accountability" sufficient to swell social trust and inhibit the corrupt behavior of persons in political and economic power (Friis-Hansen, E., & Ravnkilde, S., 2013). I would agree but I think it needs to go further and what I mean is that civil society like Liberia, needs to hold itself accountable; avoid enabling the corrupt schemes of the public office. That means, for example, refraining to bribe public officials for your passports, National ID, from paying the taxes owed to the government or paying the police officer for not having a driver's license. As a citizen of Liberia, it is your right to have a passport if you pay the required fees to process it and one does not need to pay any extra to get it. If we all abide by this intrinsic rule, we make a mark in strengthening our resolve as a community against corruption.

The entire society, not its various parts, must be transformed if ethical universalism and a norm of non-corruption are to replace the many kinds of compromises that we permit or facilitate the corrupt default impulse to take hold or to remain embedded in today's Liberia. It sounds hard to do but I think we can do it. Other countries had tried and doing well with it; Liberia is not an abnormality. Liberia battle against corruption can be successful when the collective consciousness eschews corrupt behavior—when from societal point of view episodes of graft and extortion become shameful and amoral rather than commonplace.

Moreover, the Liberian society needs committed and credible leaders to maintain the status of accountability. That means each of our leaders in the public domain must strive to maintain an appropriately chaste behavior. As Robert I. Rotberg asserts,

> The more completely a ruler and a regime have allowed themselves to be seduced by the wages of corruption, the harder it is to retrieve integrity for public servants or to regain a national moral high ground. A full embrace of corruption by ruling elites, no matter if nominally democratic or not, greatly alters governmental priorities across the board for the worse and accentuates a society's sense of spiritual decay. That is why it takes gargantuan efforts on the part of leaders, preferably with the backing of an aroused civil society and an observant media, to beat back the powerful forces of entropy—in this case representing those who are profiting well from corruption—and to start afresh (Rotberg, Robert, 2017).

With this we need leadership that can be transparent and accountable to its society and people. Most importantly we need leadership that has the spine to hold its corps of leadership team accountable for their behavior. Such emboldened leadership requires all instruments, institutions, and sanctions available, and abundant courage and determination. It also needs a vision of a better and more prosperous future around which it can forge a constituent consensus against continued corruption.

Unfortunately, we saw the contrary in the Ellen Johnson-Sirleaf 2nd term when a corruption watchdog, Global Witness, found that 20 of the country's largest logging contracts had been awarded illegally and that the process had been marred by graft (Lee-Jones, Krista, 2019). And this was mainly orchestrated by the former head of Johnson-Sirleaf's political party, Varney Sherman who was then a lawyer representing the Sable

Mining, a British company. It was reported that Sherman was tried for allegedly paying more than US$950,000 in bribes on behalf of her Sable Mining, to secure an iron ore concession (Clark, P., & Azango, M., 2017). However, Sherman was acquitted on 30 July 2019 along with other co-accused, former Speaker Alex Tyler, Chris Onanuga and Executives of Sable Mining (Davis, A., 2019).

Finally accountability in the 21st century Liberia is having a system in which it is incumbent on all public and private leadership to be held responsible for their actions and behavior as well as their spending of funds entrusted to them and to face sanctions for the unbecoming behaviors and actions. But for this to be successful, it needs societal consensus against corruption and bribery within the public domain.

Development

The fact remains that Liberia despite its size and the endowment of mineral resources has remained an extreme example of underdevelopment due to exploitation by the West, its political leadership, and mismanagement. At such a critical point, especially after a civil war, Liberia needs a vision for the development of all facets of its being. But let us reflect on what I mean by development. When I talk about development as applied to Liberia, it means having a standard of living as well as the level of industrial production that makes it possible with financial and technical enablement. The term itself has been deemed ambiguous in social sciences but it continues to generate debate among scholars. Schumpeter indicates:

> Development in human society is not a one-sided process but rather a multi-sided issue. Individuals perceive development as

increase in the skill and ability; they view it as maximum freedom, the ability to create responsibility and so on (Schumpeter,
J.A., 1934).

On the other hand, Dudley Seer (1977) asserts that development means not only capital accumulation and economic
growth but also the condition in which people in a country
have adequate food and job and the income inequality among
them is greatly reduced. He sees it as a process of bringing
about fundamental and sustainable changes in society (Lawal,
O.O. & Tobi, A.A., 2001). It entails growth, embraces such
aspects of the quality of life as social justice, equality of opportunity for all citizens, equitable distribution of income, and the
democratization of the development process.

Development for an underdeveloped society is all about the
capacity building for its membership with the intended goal
for self-actualization by participating actively in the social
engineering of their life and destiny. As Nnavozie argues, that
development "entails the ability of the individuals to influence and manipulate the forces of nature for their betterment
and that of humanity" (Nnavozie, O.U., 1990). Liberia like
any nation has been blessed with all it can use to bring about
growth in any form, be it economic, education, and physical
and environmental.

Rodney in the early 70s argues further beyond the individual
or people's perception of development. He conceived development whether economic, political, or social to imply both
increase in output and changes in the technical and institutional arrangement by which it is produced. In other words
and more importantly, development is a multi-dimensional
concept and despite the various conceptions, development is
basically about the process of changes which lies around the

spheres of societal life (Walter, Rodney, 1972). Development as capacity building requires a system that efficiently manages the resources with the purpose to improve the welfare of the citizenry and it is part of good governance. Unlike other African countries, Liberia lacks the capacity to manage its resources effectively and efficiently to improve the quality of life of the Liberian people because of the threat of corruption. This threat has posted impediments to development. One writer argues, "There is no reason to believe that Liberia will be appreciably more developed in 1970 than it was in 1960." Reason being as he indicates that from 1950 to 1962 Liberia had a high growth rate due to heavy foreign investment in iron ore and rubber, but it remains largely undeveloped otherwise (Dalton, George, 1965). And the problem mainly was due to its leadership and management. Liberia has become elephant meat where the able men come to feast leaving the unable to hunger and die.

If we are to become part of the developing world, we need the spirit of patriotism as well as technocrats to guide us in crafting developmental projects and programs. We also need managers to ensure that we achieve these developmental aspirations. We need our road networks to be developed; healthcare, and water and sanitation. These are basic to human welfare.

Economy

As we ponder on where we go from here, we must consider our economy. The economy of any nation is the driving engine for development, trade, and progress. The economy also features developments in the areas of production and investment, government finance, banking, and international trade. It provides the avenue to configure our relationship with globalization.

Liberia's economy from its inception had made strides and still needs to be innovated in the 21st century. Qureshi et al assert that Liberia experienced economic progress in the early 50s and the first years of the decade. They attribute this progress to the increase in the domestic product which was two and half times during 1950-62; increase in exports from 28 million to 67 million in 1952 and the increase in government revenue from 3.8 million to almost ten times of that amount. Additionally, the use of the American dollar as legal tender in the country and the government's strong commitment to liberal trade and foreign investment policies provided the environment to maintain the economic growth the country experienced (Qureshi, M., Mizoe, Y., & Francis d'A, Collings, 1964). At such time the economy was driven by the export of rubber and later iron ore. Though the Liberian economy experienced a boom, critics indicated that wage-earning for the Liberian people remain at 75 cents per day and the majority of the earners were indigenes.

Liberian economy continues to undergo processes of adjustment over the years. It was and is exploited by neo-colonialism. When I talk about neo-colonialism, I borrow it in context from Kwame Nkrumah's when he asserts that:

> Neo-colonialism is...the worst form of imperialism. For those who practice it, it means power without responsibility, and for those who suffer from it, it means exploitation without redress. In the days of old-fashioned colonialism, the imperial power had at least to explain and justify at home the actions it was taking abroad. In the colony, those who served the ruling imperial power could at least look to its protection against any violent move by their opponents. With neo-colonialism, neither is the case (Nkrumah, Kwame, 1965).

Liberia has been nominally independent and sovereign in her right because she has all the outward trappings of international sovereignty. However, in reality, its economic system and political policy were being directed from the outside mainly by America. It is clear in the Firestone, LAMCO and Maritime orchestration. Davidson puts it clearly when he argues that though African states gained independence from imperialist powers, they however, found themselves enveloped in another web of servitude tied to a whole system of economic control and conditions (Davison, Basil, 1992). The imperialist powers use these economic controls and conditions as integral parts of the broad array of modes of interactions within the global political economy to subjugate and transform peripheral states into neo-colonies (Kleh, George Klay, March 2021) and Liberian is no exception. Throughout the First, Second and the Third Republic led by George M. Weah, the economy of the country continues to be exploited by those who serve the imperialist power and this includes Liberian leaders.

A key example is the Taylor era, the worst time in the history of the country. The economy was exploited during the Taylor-led war era by both warlords and foreign investors and firms. As Johnston argues when he places the political economy of Liberian timber in the context of the theory of state failure in which he saw the Investment of foreign timber firms in Liberia to reinforce an informal, clandestine economy that thrived and took primacy after the collapse of Liberia's formal economy. Johnston saw that the relationship Charles Taylor and his associates had with these investors profited them, leaving ordinary Liberians alienated by the exigencies of collapsed political and economic institutions (Johnson, Patrick, 2013). In fact, Johnston was critical of the international community especially that of the United Nation for its complacency and long-time refusal to place a sanction on Liberian Timber.

During the war, the Liberian Timber became the resource for war-torn Liberia though none of its proceeds went into covers of the government or benefited the larger community.

The Liberian economy of the 1990s attracted shady firms whose interests included the extraction of primary commodities and the wartime economy of weapons trade (Johnson, Patrick, 2013). Western consensus encouraged such commercial activities in the name of the economy. Moreover, Taylor forced the Strategic Commodities Act through the Liberian Congress in late 1999 which granted him 'the sole power to execute, negotiate, and conclude all commercial contracts or agreements with any foreign or domestic investors for the exploitation of the strategic commodities of the Republic of Liberia' (Global Witness, 2001).

In the NGO report of said time, it is estimated that Liberia's timber industry was worth at least US$187 million in 2000, whereas the government reported revenues of US$6.7 million (Global Witness, 2001). At this time Liberia's GDP was significantly less than South Africa's or Nigeria's, however, Liberian investments in Swiss bank accounts were more than those from its wealthier African countries (Global Witness, 2001).

Such economic policy illustrated the weakness and lack of autonomy of Liberian state institutions and it perpetuated the failure, weakness, and instability of the Liberian state but also the neo-colonialism phenomenon.

I believe this must be the lesson we can learn as we go forward. As Liberians, we need to realize the reality of neo-colonialism that has created this web of control and confinement of the African state. It seems to be a phenomenon that is here to stay since Africans unlike Nkrumah had failed to address or expose it. Therefore, it calls for leadership that is farsighted, and patriotic; for the essence of governance is to seek the welfare of its constituents. The government provides the environment and incentives for Liberians to invest, earn and make living and this depends on the economy.

Because of this, Liberia needs to reassess its capital for economic innovation. In doing so, let's look at three areas: maritime, mineral resources, and infrastructure.

Since the inauguration of the Liberian Maritime Program in 1948, it has experienced growth but at a stagnation as of date. The most significant growth in its Registry occurred between 1965 and 1975, and the highest registered tonnage occurred in 1978. Liberia has become the "home" of more than 509 foreign petroleum tankers, making it the second-largest maritime nation on earth. At one time, Liberia's shipping registry accounted for 30 to 70 percent of the county's revenue. Liberia became a founding member of the Flag of Convenience (FOC) having established a partnership with the New York-based Stettinius Associates. Said partnership was established for the purpose of economic development in Liberia. It activities were to be conducted through a Liberian Company, with 65 percent of the profits remitted to the parent corporation, 25 percent to the Liberian government and 10 percent to the Liberia Foundation (Sharife, Khadija, Winter, 2010/2011).

Since then, tonnage has declined by about 36 percent. The reasons for the decline, I submit three arguments: one, the way the contract or partnership with Stettinius Associates was orchestrated. The western nation's agenda of imperialism often depicts the contracts with African countries that purposes to exploit and control. And this is what Stettinius Associates did. It exploited the Liberian Rubber Plantation and Iron ore since it was in control of shipping these goods. Another example is Liberia's Maritime code drafted in late July 1948 by Klein and Stettinius Associates member James Mackey which was purposely done to establish an offshore registry in the US. Said code had been largely cut and paste of relevant sections of the US maritime code which was later supported by the US State Department under the pretense that "its policy to encourage the economic development of underdeveloped countries through private American capital." Sharife asserts that during this period, under the stewardship of the American-owned Firestone Company, Liberia's economy became heavily structured around the exploitation of rubber, producing over 80 million pounds annually by the late 1950s (Sharife, Khadija, Winter, 2010/2011). Here what Francis Truslow Adams, the president of the Rubber Development Corporation of the time and a believer of the "American Century" and descendent of John Quincy Adams said, "We must finance increased productivity in the rest of the world or we cannot continue the trend in our export trade which we have enjoyed for the last fifty years."

Therefore, as we navigate through the 21st century, let's be critical enough about the kind of deal we make with Western nations especially with the discovery of crude oil on the coast of Liberia. My second argument is the corruption in most of our African dealings. It is apparent that Africans in power tend to look out for themselves than the welfare of their constituency. Political positions are now been used to enrich our leaders. For example, at one time an ally of President Taylor, a prominent business associate, and proprietor of Liberia's Hotel Africa, was listed as a beneficiary on the books of FOC registry International Trust Company. Liberia being an FOC haven is brisk business, and the flow of cash is of certainty. It is also reported that the Liberian shipping registry, the LISCR, was managed by an American attorney and lobbyist Lester Hyman, another friend and an intermediary on behalf of President Taylor (Sharife, Khadija, Winter, 2010/2011). Monies that should have gone into the covers of Liberia for development purposes were being pocketed by one man. Though Taylor is gone but the LISCR - the same structure created by Taylor continues to market Liberia's offshore registry in fulfillment of the country's original promise from the creation of its FOC system. (Sharife, Khadija, Winter, 2010/2011). This is the struggle for us Liberians today as we go forward. Liberian needs a guard in place over our Maritime that can evaluate its program and registry with the purpose to generate trade income for the development of the nation, but also job creation for Liberian seamen. Liberia needs protection in place to avoid shady business practices that benefit just one person or a few groups of bureaucrats.

Lastly, is the natural resources we have as a country. Though research has shown that dependency on natural resources deepens poverty, leads to economic stagnation, increase corruption, and makes arm conflict more probable (Ross, Michael, 2003), Liberia can be a case study in which its natural resources can be used in the rebuilding of the country economy with the necessary guard rail in place. I believe Liberians are war-weary and the probability of arm conflict is far probable. If you do not believe it, ask the women of Liberia as to what they did when they wanted the warlords at the peace table. This can be a lesson learned from the war.

The war was precipitated by the country's history of oppression and exclusion that was linked to controlling the land and natural resources (Reno, William, 1998). Beevers argues the unfairness of land ownership and tenure rights devised by the

Free Slaves in the 1800s which gave a small minority of the population the right to own land, while the indigenous population was largely made a tenant on government land (Beevers, Michael D., 2016). The war destroyed and incapacitated the potential of the country's natural resource industry besides the rubber. Notwithstanding, the conviction, that though Liberia may be knocked down she is not knocked out. Out of the ashes she can rise because it is part of her DNA.

Consequently, what we need now is to reassess our natural resources and their marketization as a way to promote economic recovery, attract investors and generate employment that form the basis of growth and development.

Finally, for the economy to become once again the engine for the country, we need to reassess our infrastructure. The war has damaged key institutions and infrastructures. It is time to rebuild and it is time to put men back to work. The government needs a bill for infrastructural development in which it can target road networks and bridges, public counties hospitals, public schools, and universities. It is time we asked our partner the IMF to give us grants for these endeavors. Notwithstanding we also need to have a watchdog in place to monitor how we use the funds for these projects. The moment the government creates the opportunity for Liberians to work, the more money they will have to spend and that helps boost the economy.

Reawakening and Renewal

As we go from 173 years of history of suppression, civil war, corruption at a higher degree and lack of leadership recently, I am obliged to call on Liberians, both in the country and in the diaspora to be part of the nation building; work together to transform self and the nation. And this requires a sense of reawakening and renewal for the betterment of every man in the country. The Bassa people have a proverb that goes like this "Life becomes worthless when nothing matters to us." In other words meaningfulness of life comes when we speak out and take action on things that of great importance to us as people. Liberia is a country that should matter to all of us, whether descendants of Free Slaves or indigenes. I want to speak out now why I have this life—the affairs of Liberia matter to me. It is one of the reasons I took on this project, wanting to contribute to the historicity but also push the envelope in motivating the civil society to hold its leadership and themselves accountable.

Liberia is where our ancestors struggled, lived, cherished, and died; it is where most of our umbilical cords were buried we would say it in Africa. So, in an African Traditional belief, we all have a connection to this piece of land called Liberia, our home. It behooves us to be part of the nation building.

The idea that nation-building should include cutting down the size of its governance seems to be an absurd proposal that needs to be fully analyzed in the affairs of Liberia. I say this because it is the dominant trend in world politics for the past generation to critique the notion of "big government" thus wanting to move the activities of governance to private markets sometimes refers to as a civil society. Some proponents want our water and sanitation, health and welfare, and the electrical grid to be run by private companies. And the reasons among them include doing away with bureaucracy that plague most of our government, for their efficiency and maintenance but failed to thoughtfully analyze the profitability for the private companies, and the removal of the buffer that supports the system when there is a stressor to the system. For example, is what happened in Texas in early 2021 when there was a snowstorm and every electrical grid was down plunging the state into total darkness and freeze warning. In less than two days, the cost of electricity went up 120% because the system was privatized and there was no buffer in place to absorb the shock the system was going through. When such a thing happens the common people bear the brunt of it. Having gone through 17 years of war couple with Ebola, the Liberian people are not ready to take on another burden to make the private company profitable. Their government should be the sole provider of basic services like water and sanitation, electricity and social welfare.

The fact remains that in the developing world, the weak, incompetent or non-existing government is a source of many problems. Could you imagine what it could have been if the Liberian government had been weak and incompetent during the Ebola crisis, the streets would have been chaotic. A government that is invisible and cannot meet the basic needs of its people invites mercenary activities in its domain and possible forceful removal of that government especially in Africa. Therefore, in Africa, we need a strong, competent and accessible government that can be trusted by the people. Strong and competent government is a government that responds to the plight of its people with urgency especially when there is calamity and emergency.

Though many Liberians died during the Ebola crisis its mitigation was a result of an active and strong government, government that was willing to put into action processes and resolution. Effective treatment of the disease at the time required a strong public health structure, public education, and knowledge about the epidemiology of the disease. Because of the stronger public health structure, the government was able to galvanize help from international communities and gather resources about the knowledge of epidemiology as it did public education. The government response team to the Ebola crisis is lauded around the world today as compared to the great America response team to the COVID crisis. So the idea of nation-building should not include cutting down the size of its governance in an underdeveloped country like Liberia rather it should improve the efficiency of governance.

Nation-building is an act of patriotism but goes further where one loyalty is to the country, its development, its defense and the idea that we make it better than when we met it. Let the generation that comes after us have better Liberia. My father, an indigene, was sold by the Liberian government and worked two years in Fernando Po Island. My father dares to have such Liberia when his children were born. He championed the cause for the indigenes and made sure that they break away from the AME church of Liberia because the system in the church was similar to the Liberian government that sold him into slavery. The indigenes were put on the margin in the church. Whenever they went for conferences, the church made the indigenes sleep on the floor in the sanctuary while the Free Slaves slept in homes and hotels; they made the indigenes be the last to eat or there was not enough food for them if they did not bring their food though they were all charged the same conference fees. Such a system of oppression and suppression could not go unnoticed by my father and other indigenous leaders. My father and others couldn't stand to see their children being treated like that because they were native Africans. For my father it was an issue of justice—and it was an issue that matters for him at that time. In as much as my Father loved the Episcopalian doctrine, he did not want us, his children to be treated the same way when he has gone off the

WHRE DO WE GO FROM HERE?

stage. As a result of this experience, my father along with his colleagues broke away forming the St. Mark AME church of Liberia, a version for the indigenes. There were Sundays, I saw him preach Luke 4:18-20. He had a personal experience with this passage as he related it to his Fernando Po experience. He was never bitter but always saw it as an experience God allowed him to go through like Joseph so he would advocate for his people, the Bassa indigenes in the AME church. At one point in each of our lives, we need to have a reawakening moment to stir us toward what matters or what would be our calling in this country; something we can do to make Liberia better before our Maker calls us from this world.

I wish our individual experiences and collective experiences as Liberians can reawaken us to those things that matter. Let's have a cause to drive us to a meaningful life—a cause to make Liberia better than the way we met it. This reawakening comes from our collective resolve and renewal in terms of pledging to do everything possibly good for the country and for one another.

That is if you are a politician, it becomes your calling to champion the cause for the people's welfare and act justly, seek the development of the country and the people, not to steal from them. If you are an ordinary citizen, participate in the political decision-making by voting and vote for people who can show results, people that can be trusted, not because they are related to you or in the same political party. If you are a preacher like me, never allow the king to morsel you. Speak the oracle of God and the oracle of God is often in contrast with the power to be or earthly powers. This is the reawakening we all need in this country.

Reawakening also means forgiving ourselves for past mistakes and sins and recommitting to a cause for the wellbeing of our society. Sharon Salzberg, a New York Times bestselling author and teacher of Buddhist meditation practices, cautions in similar view when she asserts,

> "If we fall, we don't need self-recrimination or blame or anger—we need a reawakening of our intention and a willingness to recommit, to be whole-hearted once again."

The issue is our willingness to recommit with a whole heart to the cause of Liberia. Can we recommit to say by the time we leave this stage Liberia will be better than we met it; can we be proud of the kind of Liberia we leave to our grandchildren if we were to look in the mirror.

Reawakening is an art of revival and transformation. It is not something easy to do; it takes guts and will. Victoria Erikson, an idealist and poet, once said,

> "Transformation isn't sweet and bright. It is a dark and murky painful pushing. An unraveling of the untruths you've carried in your body. A practice in facing your own created demons. A complete uprooting before becoming."

Next we must be willing to face the demons in us as a nation. When I say demons, I mean those issues that continue to drag us down. Liberia is one of the oldest republics but least developed; Liberian has mineral resources but its people remain poor and unemployed, and sadly has one of the highest illiteracy rates in Africa. For example let's face the fact of corruption in both the government and the church and let's bring it up in the open, let's ask God to redeem us from that stronghold of the demon, and let's begin to chart a new course. Reawakening require renewal of minds, will and being. Let us not be trapped in our history but let our history as a nation serves as a catalyst to spring us to higher goals as well as better living.

Finally, it is time for us, Liberians to rise from our degradation and put an end to the suffering of our people. We do this practically by making a conscious decision in breaking the chain of corruption and making every political decision paramount in our lives. It also means, as we look forward in the next two years, we must prayerfully and engagingly decide who is worth leading us as a nation. To the church, let's walk worthy of the vocation wherewith we have been called. And to us, in the diaspora, let's seek the peace and welfare of the country. Can we use our connections here for the development of the nation? I am encouraged to see Liberians go back home with businesses contributing to sociological, educational and developmental needs of the nation. Let's make Liberia belter than we met it. We can do it.

Biography

Dr. Paul Tarr Payway is an indigenous Liberian, a graduate of the Liberia Baptist Theological Seminary, Liberia, The Southern Methodist University, Dallas, TX and Texas Woman's University, Denton, TX. Dr. Payway is a former Pastor of Du-port Road Baptist Church, Paynesville, Liberia, Principal, Messiah Baptist High School, Paynesville, Liberia and Outreach Director of the Liberia Baptist Sunday School Convention. He is the fifth born of eight children and the first to earn a college degree. Over the years he has served as Pastor, educator and pastoral care counselor. He is endorsed by the General Baptist Convention of Texas as a Spiritual Health Practitioner, USA. Presently Dr. Payway serves as chaplain in an acute hospital, having served the State of Texas largest Mental Hospital (North Texas State Hospital) in Wichita Falls, TX for almost five years. His habits include reading, running and watching movies. His passion includes walking with others at the most difficult time of their life and sorting out key performance indicators. He strongly believes before one can lead, he or she must learn to serve.

Bibliography

Advameg, Inc. (2016). *Liberia.* Retrieved December 30, 2016, from Countries and their Cultures: http://www.everyculture.com/Ja-Ma/Liberia.html#ixzz4USlAujHh

Akinsulire, Dotun. (2007). *The Problem of African Christian Theology.* Ikorodu, Nigeria: Life Theological Seminary.

Azango, Bertha Baker. (1968). *Educational Laws of the Republic of Liberia.* Monrovia.

Barrette, David (ed.). (1971). Who's Who's of african Independent Church Leaders. *Risk Vol.1 No.3,* p. 27.

Beevers, Michael D. (2016). Forest for Peace and Development in Postconflict Liberia. *African Conflict and Peacebuilding Review Vol.6, No.1,* 1-24.

Berlin Ira. (1974). In *Slaves without Master: The Free Negro in the Antebellum South* (p. 135). New York: The New Press.

(1974). In I. Berlin, *Slaves without Masters: The Free Negro in the Antebellun South* (pp. 15-50). New York: Pantheon.

Berlin, Ira. (1974). In *Slaves without Masters: The Free Negro in the Antebellum South* (pp. 15-50). New York: Pantheon.

Boas, M. (2009). Making Plans for Liberia--A Trusteeship Aproach to Good Governance? *Third world Quarterly,* 1329-1341.

Boone, Mike. (2008). A Democratic Education: Three Interpretations. *Journal of Philosophy and History of Eudcation Vol. 58.*

Brown Mary Antoinette. (1969). *Education and National Development in Liberia 1800-1900.* PhD diss. Cornell University.

Caine, Augustus F. (1986). Access to Education. *The Liberian Educational Review Vol.2 No.242*, 36-46.

Chiorazzi, Anthony. (2015, October 15). *The Sprituality of Africans.* Retrieved April 4, 2019, from Harvard Gazette: https://news. harvard.edu/gazette/story/2015/10/the-spirituality-of-africa/

Ciment, James. (2013). *Another America: The Story of Liberia and the Former Slaves Who Ruled it.* New York: Hill and Wang.

Cimpean, Claudiu. (2008). Work or Love?: A Christian Evaluation of John Dewey's View on the Purpose of Schooling. *Journal of Philosophy and History of Education Vol.58*, 23-31.

Clapham, Christopher. (1994). Liberia. *The Political Economy of Foreign Policy in ECOWAS International Political Economy Series*, 66-85.

Clark, P., & Azango, M. (2017). *The Tearing Down of Ellen Johnson Sirleaf.* Monrovia: Foreign Policy.

Clawson, J. (2006). *Level Three Leadership: Getting Below the Surface (3rd ed.).* Upper Saddle River, NJ: Pearson Practice Hall.

Clover, R. W. (1966). In *Growth without Development: An Economic Survey of Liberia* (pp. 296-298). Evanston, IL: Northwestern University Press.

Clover, Robert W., Delton, George, Harwitz, Mitchell & Walters, A.A. (1966). In *Growth without Development: An Economic Survey of Liberia* (pp. 296-298). Evanston, Illonois: Northwestern University Press.

Collins, Donald, Jordan, Catheleen & Coleman, Heather. (2010). In *An Introduction to Family Social work* (pp. 28-29). USA: Brooks/Cole Cengage Learning.

Dahn, Kadiker. (2008). Sex and Brabery for Better Grades: Academic Dishonesty in Liberia. *Journal of Philosophy and History of Education Vol.58*, 46-50.

Dale, Gilbert R. (1947). *History of Education in Liberia PhD diss.* University of Missouri.

Dale, Gilbert R. (1970). *History of Education in Liberia PhD diss.* University of Missouri.

Dalton, George. (1965). History, Politics, and Economic Development in Liberia. *The journal of economic History, 25 (4)*, 569-591.

Davis, A. (2019). *Sherman, Tyler, Others Acquitted in Alleged Bribery Case.* Monrovia: Liberian Daily Obserber.

Davison, Basil. (1992). *The Black Men's Burden: Africa ans the Curse of the Nation-State.* London: James Currey.

d'Azevedo, W. L. (1962). Some Historical Problem in the Delineation of a Central West Atlantic Region. *Annals of New York Academy of Sciences 96*, 512-538.

De La Rue, S. (1930). In *Land of the Pepperbird: Liberia* (pp. 232-233). New York: G.P. Putman's Son.

Degler, Carl N. (1974). In *The Other South: Southern Dissenters in the Nineteenth Centruy* (pp. 41-46). Michigan: Harper & Row.

Dewey, J. (1916). *Democracy and Education: An Introduction to the Philosophy of Education.* New York: The Free Press.

Draft, R.L. (2010). *Management (9th ed.).* Mason, OH: South-Western Cengage Learning.

Dunn, D. E. (1988). In *Liberia: A National Polity in Transition* (pp. 126-127). New Jersey: Scarecrow Press.

Dunn, D. Elwood & Tarr, Byron. (1988). In *A National Polity in Transition* (pp. 126-127). New Jersey: Scarecrow Press.

Dunn, D. Elwood & Tarr, Byron S. (1988). In *A National Polity in Transition* (p. 57). New Jersey: Scarecrow Press.

Dunn, D. Elwood, Beyan, Ammos J. & Burrowes, Carl Patrick. (2001). *Historical Dictionary of Liberia 2nd Edition.* Lanham, Maryland & London: The Scarecrow Press Inc.

Dunn, Elwood D & Tarr, S. Byron. (1988). In *Liberia: A National polity in Transition* (p. 55). London: The Scarecrow Press Inc.

Ebegbulem, C. (2012). Corruption and Leadership in Africa: Nigeria in Focus. *International Journal of Business and Social Science, 222.*

(1970). In M. Faenkel, *Tribes and Classes in Monrovia* (pp. 197-201). Accra: Oxford University Press.

Fraenkel, Merran. (1970). *Tribes and Classes in Monrovia.* Accra: Oxford University Press.

Frankel, M. (1964). In *Tribe and Class in Monrovia* (pp. 5-6). London: Oxford university Press.

Friis-Hansen, E., & Ravnkilde, S. (2013). *Social Accountability Mechanisms and Access to Public Service delivery in Rural Africa*. Retrieved December 26, 2020, from Danish Institute for International Studies(pp. 19-31): http://www.jstor.org. proxy2.libraries.smu.edu/stable/resrep15646.5

Gifford, Paul. (1993). *Christianity and Politics in Doe's Liberia*. Great Britain: Cambridge University Press.

Givens, Willie A.(ed.). (1986). In *The Road to Democracy Under the Leadership of Samuel Kanyon Doe--The Policies and Public Statement of Dr. Samuel K. Doe* (p. 98). England: Bucks.

Global Witness. (2001, September). *Taylor Made: The Pivotal Role of Liberia's Forest and Flag of Convenience in Regional Conflict.* Retrieved from http://www.globalwitness.org/reports/show. php/en.00021.html.

Goetz, Anne M. & Jenkins, Rob. (2005). *Reinventing Accountability: Making Democracy Work for Human Development.* London: Palgrave Macmillan.

Gohn-manan, Syrulwa Somah Nyanyan. (2003). In *History, Immigration and Government of the Bassa* (p. 189). USA: CSB Publishing.

Groves, C.P. (1964). In *The planting of Christianity in Africa, Vol. 4, 1914/15* (p. 46). London: Lutterworth Press.

International Development of Law Organization (IDLO). (2010). *Liberia Country Report: Strangthening the legal protection framework for girls in India, Bangladesh, Kenya and Libeia.* Liberia: Women's NGO Secretariat of Liberia(WONGOSOL).

Johnson, C. S. (1987). In *Bitter Canaan: The story of the Negro Republic* (p. 44). USA: tranaction Publishers.

Johnson, C. S. (1987). In *Bitter Canaan: The Story of the Negro Republic* (p. 10). USA: Tranction Publishers.

Johnson, C. S. (1987). In *Bitter Canaan: The Story of the Negro Republic* (p. 15). USA: Transaction Publishers.

Johnson, C. S. (1987). In *Bitter Canaan: The Story of the Negro Republic* (p. 16). USA: Transaction Publishers.

Johnson, C.S. (1987). In *Bitter Canaan: The Story of the Negro Republic* (p. 24). USA: Transaction Publishers.

Johnson, C.S. (1987). In *Bitter Canaan: The Story of the Negro Republic* (p. 10). USA: Transaction Publisher.

Johnson, C.S. (1987). In *Bitter Canaan: The Story of the Negro Republic* (p. 15). USA: Transaction Publishers.

Johnson, C.S. (1987). In *Bitter Canaan: The story of the Negro Republic* (p. 16). USA: Tansaction Publishers.

Johnson, C.S. (1987). In *Bitter Canaan: The Story of the Negro Republic* (p. 44). USA: Transaction Publisher.

Johnson, Patrick. (2013). Timber Booms, State Busts: The Political Economy of Liberian Timber. In R. (. Abrahamsen, *Conflict and Security in Africa* (pp. 25-40). Woobridge, Suffolk: Rochester, NY: Boyddell & Brewer.

Jones, Sammer Saleh. (2016). *The Sweet Sweet Sound of Liberty: Black Settlers and their earlier Education Initiative in Liberia 1820-1860.* Champaign: PhD diss. University of Urbana-Champaign.

Jones, Sammer Saleh. (2016). *The Sweet Sweet Sound of Liberty: Black Settlers and their early Education Initiatives in Liberia 1820-1860.* PhD diss. University of Urbana-Champaign.

Jordan, Winthrop D. (1977). *White over Black: American Attitudes toward the Negro, 1550-1812.* New York & London: Norton.

Jordon, Winthrop D. (1977). In *White over Black: American Attitudes toward the Negro, 1550-1812* (p. 381). New York: Norton.

Joshi, A. & Houtzger, P. (2012). Widgets or Watchdogs? *Public Management Review Vol. 14 Issue 2*, 145-162.

Kapuscinki, Ryszard. (2001). The Shadow of Sun trans.Klara Glowczewska. New York/Toranto: Alfred A. Knopf.

Kerr, M.E. (2019, October 25). *One Family's Story: A Primer on Bowen Theory.* Retrieved from The Bowen Center for the Study of Family: http://www.thebowencenter.org

Kitchen, H. (1962). In *The Educated African: A Country by Country Survey of Educational Development in Africa* (p. 349). New York: Praeger.

Kitchen, H. A. (1962). In *The Educated African: a Country by Country Survey of Educational Development in Africa* (p. 349). New York: Praeger.

Kitchen, H. A. (1962). In *The Educated African: A Country by Country Survey of Educational Development in Africa* (p. 349). New York: Praeger.

Kleh, George Klay. (March 2021). Neo-Colonilaism: American Foreign Policy and First Liberian Civil War. *The Journal of Pan African Studies Vol.5, No.1*, 164-184.

Kufour, K. (1994). Starvation as a Means of Warfare in the Liberian Conflict. *Netherlands International Law Review 41(3)*, 313-331.

Kurgat, Sussy G. (December 2011). The Theology of Inculturation and the African Church. *Greener Journal of Social Sciences Vol. 1(1)*, 1-24.

Lanier, R. O'Hara. (Summer, 1961). The Problem of Mass Education. *The Journal of Negro Education Vol.30, No.3*, 251-260.

Lawal, Gbenga. (2007). Corruption and Development in Africa: Challenges doe Political and Economic Change. *Humanity & Sciences Journal 2 (1)*, 1-7.

Lawal, O.O. & Tobi, A.A. (2001). Bureaucratic Corruption, Good Governance and Development: The Challenges and Prospects of Institutional Building in Nigeria. Abujah, Nigeria: IPSA RC4 Mid-term International Conference.

Lee-Jones, Krista. (2019). *Liberia: Overview of Corruption and anti-corruption.* London: Transparency international.

Liberia — History and Culture. (2016). Retrieved December 29, 2016, from iExplore: http://www.iexplore.com/articles/travel-guides%2Fafrica%2Fliberia%2Fhistory-and-culture

Liberia - Literacy rate. (2019, December 19). Retrieved from Index Mundi.

Liberty, C. (1977). In *"Growth of the Liberian State: An analysis of its Historiography" Ph.D thesis* (pp. 885-86). New York: Stanford University.

Licbenow, J. Gus. (1987). In *Liberia: The Quest for a Democracy* (p. 19). Bloomington, Indiana: Indiana University Press.

Liebenow, J. Gus. (1969). In *The Eevolution of Privilege* (p. 219). Ithaca, New York: Cornell University Press.

Little, Kenneth L. (1966). *The Mende of Sierra Leone: A West African People in Transition.* New York: Routledge & Kegan Paul.

Litwack, Leon F. (1998). *Trouble in Mind: Black Southerners in the Age of Jim Crow.* New York: Alfred A. Knopf Inc.

Litwack, Leon F. (1998). *Trouble in Mind: Black Southerners in the Age of Jim Crow.* New York: Alfred A. Knopf.

Lymas-Reeves, Ruth. (1986, March). A Recommendation Strategy for Dealing with Liberia's Education Problem. *The Liberia Education Review Vol. 2 No. 2*, p. 23.

Lymas-Reeves, Ruth. (1995). In *A Short History of Education 1800-1900* (p. 23). London: David Beach Printing Press.

Lymas-Reeves, Ruth. (1995). In *A Short History of Education 1800-1990* (p. 15). London: David Beach Printing Press.

Mbiti, John S. (1998). *African Theology.* Maimela & Konig.

Mbiti, Jolm S. (1980). Encounter of Christian faith and African Religion. *Christianity Today 91 (27 Aug.-3 Sept.)*, 817.

McMaster, John Bach. (1914). In *A History of the People of the United States: From the Revolution to the Civil War* (pp. 556-57). New York: Appleton.

Melady, Thomas Patrick. (1961). In *Profile of african Leaders* (p. 105). Ithaca, New york: Mcmillan.

Nkrumah, Kwame. (1965). *Neo-colonialism: The Stage of Imperialism.* London: Thomas Nelson and Sons.

Nnavozie, O.U. (1990). The Bureaucracy and National Development: The Case of Nigeria. In S. Tyoden, *Constitutionalism and National Development in Nigeria: Proceedings of the 17th Annual Conference of the NSPA.* Jos: University of Jos.

Noonan, S. (2003). *The Elements of Leadership: What you should know.* Lanham, MD: Scarecrow Press.

Ojione, Ojieh Chukwuemeka. (2008). Public Opinon and Foreign Policy: analysing Nigerian Reactions to the Assylum Offered Former President Charles Taylor of Liberia. *African Journal of International Affairs, Vol. 11, No.1,* 71-97.

Ojo, Emmanuel Olatunde. (2012). An Exploration of the Historical and the Political Backgrounds of Liberia. *AFRREV International Journal of Arts and Humanities Vol.1 (3),* 187-199.

Okpokwu, Theresa. (2017). Leadership and Corruption in Governance: A Case Study of Liberia. *Capstone collection 2897.*

Olukoji, Ayodeji. (2006). *Culture and Customs of Liberia.* Westport, Connecticut: Greenwood Publishing Group.

Olukoju, Ayodeji. (2006). *Cultures and Customs of Liberia.* London: Greenwood Press.

Omonijo, B. (2003, August 17). From Doe to Taylor: The Dawn of Liberian War. *Vanguard,* 17.

Omulokoli, William A.O. (2002). William Wade Harris: Premier African Evangelist. *African Journal of evangelical Theology Vol. 21.1,* 3-24.

Paris, Peter J. (1993). The Spiriutality of African Peoples. *Dalhouse Review,* 294-307.

Payway, Paul T. (2001). *Facotrs Associated with Low enrolment of Female Students in the Secondary Schools in Liberia. Master of Science in Education Theisis.* Monrovia: University of Liberia.

.Pham, John-Peter. (2004). In *A Portrait of a Failed State* (p. 54). New York: Reed Press.

Pham, John-Peter. (2004). *Liberia: Portrait of a Failed State.* New York: Reed Press.

Qureshi, M., Mizoe, Y., & Francis d'A, Collings. (1964). The Liberia Economy (L'economie liberienne (La economia de Liberia). *Staff Papers (International Monetary Fund), 11(2),* 285-326.

Reilly Timothy F. (Autumn 1998). The Conscience of a Colonizationist: Parson Clapp and the Slavery Dilemma. *Lousiana History: Journal of Louisiana Historical Association,* 411-441.

Reilly, T. F. (Autumn, 1998). The Conscience of a Colonizationist: Parson Clapp and Slavery Dileman. *Louisiana History: The Journal of Lousiana Historical Association Vol. 39 No.4*, 411-441.

Reno, William. (1998). *Warlord Politics and African States*. Boulder: Lynne Rienner Publishers.

Reynolds, Barbara G. (2015). Liberia: Conflict and post-Conflict Trends. In E. Takyi, *Education in West Africa: a Region Overview* (pp. 16-24). New York: Boombury Academic.

Richardson, Nathanial R. (1959). *Liberia Past and Present*. London: Diplomatic Press and Publishing Company.

Richardson, Nathaniel R. (1959). In *Liberia's Past and Present* (p. 137). Lodon: The Deplomatic Press and Publishing Company.

Richardson,Nathaniel R. (1956). In *Liberia's Past and Present* (p. 106). London: Diplomatic Press and Publishing Company.

Romero, M., Sandefur, J., & Sandholtz, W. (2017). Outsourcing Service Delivery in a Fragile state: Experimental Evidence from Liberia.

Ross, Michael. (2003). The Natural Resources Curse: How Wealth Can Make You Poor. In I. &. Bannon, *Nature Resources and Violent Conflict* (pp. 17-42). Wahington D.C.: World Bank.

Rotberg, Robert. (2017). Curing Corruption: Lessons, Methods, and Best Practices. In *The Corruption Cure: How Citizens and Leaders Can Combat Graft* (pp. 290-309). Princeton: Princeton university Press.

Sale, Maggie Montesinos. (1997). In *The slubering volcano: american slave ship revolts and the production of rebellious masculinity* (p. 265). Durham: Duke University Press.

Sawyer, A. (2005). *Beyond Plunder:Toward Democratic Governance in Liberia*. Boulder, London: Lynne Rienner Publishers.

Sawyer, Amos. (1997). In *The Emergence of Autocracy: Tragedy and Challenge* (p. 15). San Francisco: Institute of Contempory Studies.

Sawyer, Amos. (1997). In *The Emergence of Autocracy: Tragedy and Challenge* (p. 9). San Francisco: Institute of Contempory Studies.

Sawyer, Amos. (1997). In *The Emergence of Autocracy: Tragedy and Challenge* (p. 24). San Francisco: Institute of Contemporary Studies.

Sawyer, Amos. (1997). In *The Emergence of Autocracy: Tragedy and Challenge* (p. 9). San Franscico: Institute of Contemporary Studies.

Sawyer, Amos. (1997). In *The Emergence of Autocracy: Tragedy and Challenge* (p. 24). San Franscico: Institute of Contemporary Studies.

Sawyer, Amos. (1997). In *The Emergence of Autocracy: Tragedy and Challenge* (p. 24). San Francisco: Institute of Contemporary Studies.

Sawyer, Amos. (1997). In *The Emergence of Autocracy in Liberia: Tragedy and Challenge* (p. 24). San Francisco: Institute for Contemporary Studies.

Sawyer, Amos. (1997). In *The Emergence of Autocracy in Liberia: Tragedy and Challenge* (p. 275). San Francisco, California:: Institute for Contemporary Studies.

Sawyer, Amos. (1997). *Emergence of autocracy in Liberia: Tragedy and Callenge.* San Francisco, California: Institute for Contemporary Studies.

Sawyer, Amos. (2005). *Beyond Plunder: Toward Democratic Governance in Liberia.* Boulder, London: Lynne Rienner Publishers.

Schroder, G. & Siebel, D. (1974). *Ethnographic Survey of Southwesten liberia: the Krahn and the Sapo.* Newark, NJ: Liberia Studies Association in America Monograph Series No.3.

Schumpeter, J.A. (1934). Business Cycle. In *The Theory of Economic Development.* London: Oxford University Press.

Sharife, Khadija. (Winter, 2010/2011). Flying a Questionable Flag: Liberia's Lucrative Shipping Industry. *World Policy Journal Vol.27, No.4,* 111-118.

Southall, Aiden (ed.). (1961). *Social change in Modern Africa.* London: Oxford University Press for International African Institute.

Staundenraus, P.J. (1961). In *The American Colonization Movement, 1816-1865* (p. 22). New York: Columbia University Press.

Steady, Filomina C. (2011). *Women and Leadership in Africa: Mothering the Nation and Humanizing the State.* New York: Palgrave Macmillan.

Sundiata, Ibrahim K. (1980). *Black Scandal: American and the Liberian Labor Crises, 1929-1936.* Philadelphia: Institute for the studies of Human issues.

The Bible: Revised Standard Version. (1970). New York: American Bible Society.

The Bible: The Revised Standard Version. (1980). New York: American Bible Society.

Tsimpo, Clarence & Wodon, Quentin. (2012). *Education in Liberia: Basic Diagnostic Using the 2007 CWIQ Survey.* MPRA: The World Bank.

UNESCO Institute of Statistics. (2020, December). *Sustainable Development Goals.* Retrieved February 3, 2021, from Liberia: Education and literacy: http://uis.unesco.org/en/country/lr

van der Kraaij, F.P.M. (1983). *The Open Door Policy of Liberia: An Economic History of Modern Liberia.* Bremer: Bremer Afrika Archive.

van der Kraaiji, F.M.P. (1983). *The Open Door Policy of Liberia: an Economy History of Modern Liberia.* Bremen: Bremer Afrika Archive.

Walter, Rodney. (1972). *How Europe Underdeveloped Africa.* London: Bogle L'ouverture.

Wilson, Charles Morrow. (1947). In *Liberia* (pp. 205-206). New York: William Sloane Associates Inc.

Wilson, Charles Morrow. (1947). In *Liberia* (p. 76). New York: William Sloane Associates Inc.

(1962). In C. &. Woodson, *The Negro in our History 10th ed.* (p. 177). Washington DC: Associated Publishers.

Woodson, Carter & Wesley, Charles H. (1962). In *The Negro in our History 10th ed.* (p. 177). Washington DC: Associated Publushers.

Zimmermann, Kim Ann. (2016). *Definition of Culture*. Retrieved December 29, 2016, from Live Science: http://www.livescience. com/21478-what-is-culture-definition-of-culture.html

Printed in the USA
CPSIA information can be obtained
at www.ICGtesting.com
LVHW020800290923
759457LV00019B/945